TIMEPIECE

ANDREW BORTS

Thanks for reading :)

Andrew
AB

CONTENTS

DEDICATION

This book is dedicated to my lovely and patient wife, who nearly went mad for three years when her husband would shout "oh cool, did you know that when..." thousands of times.

Formatted with Vellum

1

AUGUST 22ND, 1920 - PROLOG

Leonard's steel-gray eyes stared through the maternity window as he marveled at his newborn son in the bassinet. He whispered to himself, "That's MY son, my baby boy." He stared transfixed and oblivious to the fogging of glass by his breath. Watching in wonder at this magnificent tiny person, his heart filled with pure joy. He saw both his and his wife's faces merged into the features of his son, who was all wrapped up in a blanket and absorbing his surroundings, not crying. A few years later, people would take him aside and correct him and say, "Look, Lenny, don't take this wrong, but your son... really looks like your wife, thank goodness." For now, this little boy was laying on his back, taking in his new surroundings. The hospital ward's theme featured the monarch butterfly. Monarch butterflies everywhere. Butterflies are the symbol of life. They must have gotten a deal on this annoying damn butterfly, because they stamped, painted, and placed it on every surface around him.

The other babies in this ward seem to be designed to sleep or cry. His child was quietly looking around like a tiny, focused sponge, trying to absorb everything in this new environment. Leonard thought everything must seem alien to his newborn baby. He was seeing it for the first time, as if he was from another world. Leonard amused himself, wondering how the glass between them looked at his new boy. Would he see his father? Or the reflection of the room? Or just the ceiling? Leonard imagined his son calmly placing new sensations into specific mental filing cabinets and then chuckled to himself. This child couldn't fathom how deeply he just changed his parents' future.

The nursery window bore a banner that read "Happy Birthday Newborns! Today is August 22, 1920." Leonard whispered, "Happy Birthday, son."

Leonard worked as a linesman for the Waukegan Illinois, Power and Telephone Company. He climbed utility poles and ran or repaired power and phone lines. His job site was so remote that it took two hours to find him, and another hour to get him to the hospital where his wife had gone to have their child. He recalled how ordinary the day had started. Their baby wasn't due for another week. She had gone into labor in the early afternoon. This fantastic gift made him change his perspective on everything.

Leonard's thoughts turned to his wife sleeping in her hospital room. She was exhausted after enduring nine hours of labor. Holy cow. How did she do that? In the waiting room, he listened to her blood-curdling cries as the doctor coached her to "PUSH!" He shrank in his seat as her shouts grew impossibly louder. Holy heck, that sounded rough. And his wife hated pain. Why she agreed to have more kids after giving birth to their twins four years earlier baffled him.

He stared for a while in awe. Then a tsunami of tears welled in his eyes, invading his happiness and turning it into intense sadness. His memories flooded back from two years earlier when he placed his son's favorite toy into the casket to share eternity with the child. Leonard's fingers could still sense the velvet of the stuffed bear in his hand. When he touched Samuel's cold, lifeless skin, it sent a permanent chill down his spine. Leonard had to stop himself from shaking his boy to wake him up. Forever after that, he could recall that feeling returning him back to that moment. His fingers had more memory than his mind.

Leonard and his wife had their twin boys in 1916 and poured love over them like syrup. Every moment was a lesson in "how can I love them more?" Learning to change diapers, figuring out feeding schedules, bathing, and play schedules was overwhelming. The endless tasks made them crazy at first, but once Samuel and Leonard Jr. were on a better sleep schedule, and their needs became routine, the kids were tremendously fun. Finish playing with one and a second copy sat charged and ready for playtime. He and his wife had their hands full. He'd come home from an exhausting day and still looked forward to the two faces that made him so damn happy. Even the constant fatigue made Leonard feel a sense of accomplishment. But once little Samuel became sick and passed away, it was like a horrible betrayal. Leonard resented his son's death. He had let this little extension of himself and his wife deep into his heart, only to have it horribly broken. Their hearts felt like they would never heal. Leonard Jr. was a mirror image of Samuel and a constant reminder of what they had lost. Wounds would constantly reopen when Leonard Jr. walked into the room, causing a torrent of tears to flow from him and his wife. The poor little guy must have thought he did something wrong when he watched his parents burst into tears. However, it upset them more when the boy looked for his brother, walking around saying, "Sammy? Sammy?" It was a year before they considered having another child.

Now, staring into the window where his new son was lying, wave after wave of sorrow flowed over him. Giving more attention to this new child he had yet to hold made Leonard sob with guilt. Heck, he hadn't even touched him yet. But this baby was just a few feet away, and his heart was open, raw. Leonard was mentally and physically exhausted.

He took a deep breath and said to himself, "Men don't cry." Leonard wiped his soaked eyes and took another deep breath. Once he returned his attention to his newborn, who was so close to him, his eyes dried, anticipating that *new baby smell,* and his profound joy returned.

Now what? He stared and wondered. What would his boy become? What was ahead for his new son? College? Yes. Leonard will send him to college. "That's my boy in there. He can do whatever he wants. ANYTHING," he thought. He'd fight to the death to make sure both his boys would lead happy lives. He stared slack-jawed, thinking of the incredible things this tiny miracle would accomplish.

Leonard's dad, Samuel, approached the nursery window and asked, "How's my new grandson? Is he good and spoiled yet?" Sam put his arm around his son, startling him.

"Oh Dad, he's a doll. He doesn't complain, he's quiet as can be."

"So... will you call him *son* or *grandson*?"

"This is hard. I'm thinking about it more, and well, Leonard Jr. is named after me. We really can't have a third Leonard. Samuel's death is still looming over us. He needs a... fresh name," Leonard replied. He tried his best to emphasize the words FRESH NAME. "Dad, we need a name that will help us heal."

"Little Samuel's passing was a shock to us. We were so

sad we couldn't fathom you and Esther's misery. Son, I don't envy your position. Your mother and I are thrilled for you both and our new grandson."

They both sat in silence for a few minutes while they beamed at the bundle wrapped in blue.

Sam continued, "We enjoy keeping the names in the family, but... there has to be a time to honor more than just family members, living or passed. No, the names in this family are too... samey-samey." Samuel was referring to the four previous generations of men in their family, all named Samuel.

"Dad. I'm really stumped. This family needs a new name for our baby boy. I can't emphasize enough how much this will help us heal."

"Got any ideas, son?"

"Esther likes the actor Douglas Fairbanks, but... I'm not naming him after a damn movie star. We're not... strange like that."

"No, son. That may not be right for his first name. You know... there is... well, no. Maybe I shouldn't suggest it."

"What? Look, if you have any ideas, I'd like to hear them." Leonard looked into his dad's eyes. He was serious.

"Well, there is a story from our family's history that I think it's time I told you. It wasn't written. It's passed down verbally... generation to generation, so to speak. After such a long time, it seems silly, but it remains a tradition to keep it spoken, not written. Our family arrived in the US over two hundred years ago. Matter of fact, our family comes from the Massachusetts area. Many generations, six or seven, I can't remember.

"This story dates back over 200 years. Your great-great-great-great grandmother was in serious trouble. Everyone loved her. She was a wonderful woman. Mary Perkins was her birth name. Anyway, it was crazy they accused her at all. She went on trial in Salem and a jury convicted her of witchcraft. To gain her freedom, her husband got 118 signatures on a petition. At that point in her life, she had eleven children and four grandchildren. Nobody believed they could convict an INNOCENT 77-year-old woman."

"Dad. My boy isn't being called Mary!"

"No, no, no. Let me finish. This story isn't about Mary. Well, it is, but not to the extent you may realize. No, Mary was only part of it. Someone was brave enough to help her. This is a period people are damn ashamed of. They told the future generations rather than write down the stories. There were unthinkable miscarriages of justice. Society seemed like it was breaking down. Neighbor was against neighbor. Everyone was on edge. They believed that the supernatural was the cause of their problems. This was... spine-chilling stuff. Mary was starving in jail and had been sentenced to death... and another prisoner helped her and another prisoner escape the gallows. It was only after she was freed that he introduced himself to her."

Leonard stood transfixed listening to his father's story...

2

SWEAT EQUITY

John walked into his shed and became overwhelmed by acrid smoke and spotted a fire near the floor. He grabbed the extinguisher and pointed it at the base of the bright orange flames until they were replaced by a black cloud.

After a moment, he pondered the mental image of a set of keys a professor entrusted to him and thought, "No!" - he would continue working in this smoke filled shed. It was his penance for causing the fire.

He continued panting and sweating in the doorway, holding the heavy extinguisher and gathered his thoughts. When he walked out moments earlier, his leg must have pulled the electric cord of the soldering iron, pulling it off the table. Like an intelligent multi-million-dollar smart missile, it found the pile of papers he had moved off his cluttered workspace onto the floor. The fire melted one of the most important experiments of his life, causing a painful feeling in his gut. The ashes on the floor mocked him, highlighting his stupidity. He yelled at the smoking carnage, "YOU ARE AN ASSHOLE!!"

John heard Reynold's ringtone and winced. He didn't want company now. John felt a colossal shame for avoiding Reynold.

The ring tone crescendoed again and John reluctantly answered.

"Hey Buddy!" boomed Reynold's cheerful voice.

"Hey Reynold!" John replied, trying not to sound like he almost burned down his shed moments earlier.

He held the phone in one hand and aimed the empty extinguisher at the smoldering ashes, daring the fire to resume. Nothing would test his resolve. John would beat the fire with harsh language and angry glares if necessary. He was too angry to let a single spark survive.

Reynold said, "We haven't seen each other all semester! Dude, you've turned into a hermit. You keep calling me with the craziest mathematical puzzles. You don't even offer me a cheeseburger or a festive spinach lasagne as payment. What gives? Wanna meet now?"

John shouted, "NO!!" then he slowed his heartbeat and continued, "I mean... yeah, no time. Later this week, for sure. I've been working on a thing... and I'll share my results with you, I promise."

He said farewell and disconnected. John felt guilty. He took a deep breath and continued assessing the damage to his lab.

The smoky interior of his lab at home needed serious airing out, so he left the door open and avoided inhaling the poisonous contents. He looked at the dark cloud floating near the ceiling. To make himself feel better, he yelled, "YOU ARE AN ASSHOLE TOO!!" But the gray mist didn't care.

John saw his right hand's hair was burnt to the skin and yelled, "Aw shit!"

After a moment of internal cursing, he closed his eyes and looked at the sizzling solid mass on the table, imagining his parents saying, "Oh, here's our boy with over 180 IQ standing next to the melted mess he created. Perhaps he wants to be an impressionist artist?" He sat down and rubbed his stinging eyes with his singed right hand.

John reached into his pocket and pulled out the keys he contemplated moments earlier and thought, "I'm pulling the trigger. I gotta get out of here." Professor Wilson's keys opened a clean, uncluttered, non-smokey office and would be perfect for finishing this experiment. Plus, it's walking distance from a lot of restaurants. Since nobody would know he was there, he could work uninterrupted. Rick Wilson would be happy he was using it. It's why he gave John the keys, saying, "Hey, can you pick up my mail while I'm away on sabbatical?" In actuality, he invited him to use this office for this project. Yeah, he did. John convinced himself.

He hated abandoning his little makeshift lab, since everything was within reach. Reynold would walk directly into John's backyard, since he was always working on projects in this 200-year-old smelly, disorganized shed.

He took a picture of the whiteboard containing the plans. John would operate paperless from now on.

He took two more minutes to assess the damage. This project would change the world. John needed to stop screwing up and complete it.

He packed up the car and mountain of work ahead. John drove west, and saw Venus as it disappeared on the horizon just before sunset. Venus preceded the sun, leading it to its hiding place behind the curvature of the earth. This was the orbit Venus followed at the end of April. He drove toward the little gray building. The new structure stood out from the historic buildings. This office has modern everything. He pulled into the empty parking lot and grew excited. It's past 7:22 PM, and this place is empty.

His plan was to grab Rick's mail and keep plugging away. He knew he had to be super damn careful. He couldn't afford any more accidents. John worried that he would sweat bullets doing the tedious bits, so he turned the A/C to freeze. He would pay Professor Wilson's electric bill. John would borrow the money from Reynold if necessary. Reynold had loads of extra cash for his quirky technology projects. His house was smart enough to start arguments. Reynold was equally responsible for the work John was completing. He needed to share the costs. Reynold was bound to help once John confessed.

John took a deep breath, grabbed his box filled with the materials and the new soldering gun from Dunne Electronics, Inc. and walked into the building.

This is a fantastic work environment. He could now perform the remaining portion of the build and test one device. Without propulsion, it shouldn't have adverse effects on the surrounding offices. John need only protect himself from his own stupidity. He thought, "There may be some fields generated that could..." He stopped himself. He'd address that possibility when it's proven to work.

John organized himself by creating an assembly line to complete the remaining units. He aligned the chips on the four remaining motherboards, making sure they had adequate space. After that, he had to laser-etch the chip locations on the boards using the 3D printer and etching device he had snuck out of the University. Once John completed that, he needed to cut holes in the mounting box for two buttons and an LED indicator. The pièce de résistance was setting up the capacitors to power everything.

Finally, he would close the boxes and watch an LED go through a panoply of status colors he programmed. He smiled. Panoply was an exaggeration. Out of 4,096 colors, he needed three.

John pre-fired the ceramic capacitors in the University's kiln to save time. Those were the key to the plan. His invention needed to deliver all the stored power at once using super capacitors. By adding graphene flakes, these supercapacitors were best at room temperature instead of needing to be super-cooled using liquid nitrogen.

The new method of charging was a game-changer. It was so simple it baffled him that it wasn't invented earlier. Slow charging was the sole problem. It would take between three and four days to replenish the capacitors. Version two would be better. For version two, he would add a colorful digital touch screen, instant recharge, the works! Walk first, John. Just get it done.

The finished project would be the thickness of two cell phones sandwiched together. What it did was unfathomable.

He calculated the time to complete everything. Three hours of work on the motherboard layout, one hour to make the connections, another twenty minutes for precise hole cutting, and one hour connecting the capacitors. Five hours, twenty minutes to complete the four remaining units.

It was time for food, and the nearest restaurant was Chinese food. His main cuisine for over a year had been Chinese food. John even slept wrapped like a steamed dumpling. He ordered his food and returned to the office. No more delays. He would finish by 1:00am. In three and a half days, the units will be charged and ready to test. This would be a fantastic parting gift.

John needed to tell Reynold. He couldn't keep being

cagey about their regular plans. Their conversations replayed in his mind like a digital recorder. Rey would ask, "Hey, wanna go to see the animated *Dark Knight Returns* with Peter Weller as the voice of Batman?" and John would respond, "No, I have, uh... family coming over." "Oh, okay," Reynold would respond. Reynold sounded so disappointed when John declined plans. He remembered that Reynold had a crush on the woman he commutes with. Are they dating by now? Are they married? Do they have kids? Hold on... this *is* Reynold. Male icebergs approach female icebergs faster. Male sloths approach female sloths faster. John stopped silently abusing Reynold. His best friend didn't deserve to be mocked. He had to talk to Reynold about their experiment. He also had to give him copious relationship advice. Maybe even the birds and the bees. It was time for all conversations.

Reynold finished teaching on Thursday. They would have an in-depth heart-to-heart over their end-of-semester dinner.

He had been working on this project with Reynold all along. Reynold will be pissed. A few days ago, John called Reynold and said, "Oh, hey Buddy. Can you... double-check the formula I emailed you? Are you sure it's not a big deal? Awesome, thanks."

Two nights later, Reynold called, saying, "Hey, those calculations were a PAIN IN THE BUTT. After buying a second whiteboard, I still had to write on my windows with a pen to complete it. What is it *for*?"

John replied, "oh... it's nothing... a curiosity... a pet peeve I'm... thinking about. Yeah, *that's* it," and hung up the phone. Reynold had yet to connect the dots... and John would soon help him do exactly that. He knew Reynold would figure it out if John asked him to complete one more hard equation, but John had completed that phase of the project. He needed to give Reynold a lot of credit for this invention. He was essential from the beginning. Damn Reynold for being better at these hard formulas than he was. Reynold wasn't a "theoretical" physicist. John thought, "I'm... outside-of-the-box, and Reynold is firmly within it. His calculations are *brilliant*. I mean, Reynold is collaborating on something *huge*, and doesn't even *know* it. Good thing we're friends, or else someone would have screwed him over with his naïveté years ago." John was there to prevent people from taking advantage of Reynold... the way he did.

John assembled the components and got back to building the four devices. Sweat built up on his forehead as he held the new soldering iron. "I can't have any more accidents," he thought. "I'm running out of soldering irons and places to work."

He hunched over the table, beamed with pride at his nearly completed project. John was elated. He interrupted his self-congratulations and reminded himself, "No! Stop jumping ahead. Keep focusing on finishing the damn things."

To document the experiment, he set up 5 cell phones on tripods and record the trials. Each phone could record an immersive 360 degree image or video. Using the same phones for all the recordings was easy, since they were inexpensive and available. The phones had highly accurate sensors for humidity, temperature, and 3-axis motion. They could even measure micro-vibrations. Professor Wilson's office had a large TV on the wall to review the recordings.

He only needed to keep the secret from Reynold a little while longer until he proved the results.

John mused that this small city was home to some incredible inventions and ideas. Alexander Graham Bell invented the telephone, George Parker partnered with his brother Charles, and formed Parker Brothers. Now he needed a name for this invention.

"Who knew it would be this easy?" John thought. "Once I publish the results, it could be dangerous in the wrong hands." He had to prove it right before revealing anything, even to Reynold. He had to test, test, test, and then test again. Afterward, If he wanted grants, John would just need to ask. He would reap the rewards of endless funding. Corporate sponsors, instructional sponsors, educational sponsors... Once this project had a bow on it, he would never need to write grant proposals again. I want money. Boom. Like magic. Reynold deserves significant recognition. Probably more. Wait. He shouldn't tell him that.

John knew Reynold loved to teach. Reynold was voted the Best Professor at Harvard by his students many times. Reynold's secret was keeping the material light and making sure everyone absorbs it. He sees into their eyes when they don't get it, then gives them a life preserver. If he sees anyone flounder, he changes his approach, so the person understands the material. He has this endless cache of quotes he tosses at them and an uncanny ability to use the perfect one every time. He applies this method to a room of two to three hundred kids four times a day. How does he read so many people? It's one of his many inherent abilities. John envied Reynold's playtime with puppies while he was stuck in the lab. Reynold's GOT to get out more. He needs to air out. Maybe he would make a move on that girl he keeps talking about. Reynold mentioned she was going out with a cement-head jock. Those guys don't wear enough headgear.

Soon Reynold will be so successful he can do anything

he wants. he's going to be pissed. Such a nerd. Damn, I hope I didn't miss him asking that girl out... uh... Rona? Nora? Oh man, I suck as a friend.

At 1:18am, he looked at the four finished gleaming units and was proud. Looking at the back of his hands, he rewarded himself by yelling "SHIT" one last time.

3

GIRL PLUS NERD EQUALS DESTINY

Reynold stared at the foggy reflection of himself in the steamed-up bathroom mirror. He had just exited his newly installed smart-shower after enjoying a relaxing massage, but the one thing it couldn't scrub away were his disorganized thoughts. They were still scrambled. Today he needed to have a conversation with his carpool partner, Nora, about something more than the university, the weather, or recent episodes from shows they both followed. Conversations he longed for. Today was the day he would move his peg further forward on the game of life. Today, he would ask Nora out for breakfast. Reynold annotated the formula and needed to balance the equation: What does Reynold plus Nora equal?

Nora signed up on the ride-share list to commute the 44 minutes and 29 second ride to the Harvard Campus, and the university software chose Reynold because he lived the closest to her. Reynold signed up because he hated driving alone and became dazzled by Nora.

Reynold calculated that today is the day to follow his feelings. From conversations they had, he noted that she was single for a full month, equaling one half of the time she was dating her latest "uneducated slab of granite." She realized he wasn't a good partner for her when she discovered that the "jerk face" kept a list of her faults in a note on his phone. Reynold realized she was angry about the list, not its organization. The "jerk face" tried defending himself profusely when he explained that he also made copious notes of her assets.

Once Nora had broken up with the "rock with legs," Reynold planned his approach to asking her out. A single idea formed. Ask her out for breakfast. Everyone eats. Problem solved. He needed to act.

During those car rides to work, he traveled in absolute bliss next to someone whose presence made his mind go numb. He listened and stared at her in short intervals to avoid getting arrested for distracted driving. Since the car made plenty of beeps and boops when he drove less than precisely, he didn't want to concern Nora lest she choose a less worthy carpool partner. He bisected the lanes with precision. Reynold would accelerate easily to avoid jarring their necks back. He'd signal for every turn. His hands never moved from nine o'clock and three o'clock on his steering wheel.

Nora's intelligence and charm distorted time. She was intoxicating.

Reynold practiced making listening noises to advance their conversations, encouraging her to talk more. "Umm hmm." "You're kidding." "I can't believe he'd do that." "You don't say." "He IS a jerk face!" Reynold didn't know what a jerk face meant, but he didn't want to become one.

Reynold was too shy to respond, so he let Nora monopolize their conversations. Reynold chided himself for not being honest about how he felt. "Why is she SO damn attractive? It's like talking to the sun," Reynold said aloud. Should he shield his brown eyes while talking with her for safety? Reynold realized it would look funny. "Sure, uh-huh. What am I doing? I'm averting my eyes." He couldn't say that. He imagined "BAM SMASH" and visions of his dented smart car being towed away, and her finding another carpool partner.

A photo of this strange gravestone popped up on his phone this morning, which threw his normal routine off. Reynold had spotted it in the city's oldest cemetery while attending a funeral. Unlike the other gravestones, this inscription was written in Hebrew. Upon closer examination, he saw it bore his name and his birthday, but the year was in the 1600s, and Nora's first name was on it but with his last name. The couple died on the same day. This was crazy-nuts-weird information for Reynold. This stone's existence meant something. He had never seen his name on a gravestone. This gave him the chills. So he took pictures for future analysis. After careful consideration, he emailed the photos to a friend who taught Hebrew at the university. She would translate the Hebrew on the stone and let him know the meaning. Since he helped set up her wifi, she owed him.

Reynold found the gravestone photos on the final day of the semester and knew he had to act boldly. Today he would stop procrastinating and cure his *lack-of-girlfrienditis.* Not just any girlfriend, but Nora. This would remedy the emptiness he felt after dropping her off.

After preparing himself for his lecture, he decided to change his life by asking Nora out to consume nourishments. Everyone needs to eat, right?

Nora wanted to complete grading her final papers for the semester. One student's paper contained an overuse of a relative pronoun. Liberal-arts colleges required their papers to be factually and grammatically correct. Hunting down every misuse of the word in their paper, she got a case of the giggles and didn't understand the source.

After completing her classwork, she showered, dressed, and contemplated her knitting project, which was crying for attention. Maybe clearing her mind would help locate the source of her amusement.

Carpooling with Reynold Woodbury was therapeutic for her. His shyness made him a fantastic listener. At first, she felt a need to fill the silence between them using her nervous energy. She might have taken advantage of his quietness/listening skills a little. He was very patient with her and absorbed her energy, returning calmness and serenity. She thought she sounded manic at times. He was so different in front of his students. When Reynold stood in front of a class of students, they would hang on his every word, and he blossomed while talking with them. She even learned something about physics from sitting in on his lectures. And Reynold was the perfect gentleman. Maybe he wasn't interested in dating her? Was it because they worked at Harvard? "Hey wait," she thought, "we don't work in the same department! Why didn't I use that rule with that jerk face? Am I using it as an excuse? Am I afraid of intelligent men? Am I asking too many questions? Is my real problem trying to get to a subterranean level of detail rather than trusting the helicopter level? Am I trusting only the helicopter level? Oh jeez, I'm *still* asking too many questions!" Nora took a deep breath to calm herself down once again.

She picked up her yarn and needles and knitted. Knitting took her mind off things and helped her expel nervous energy and relax. It allowed her to stop worrying about the meaningless details of life and focus on her craft. The patterns were easy to remember and replicate. Although, the devil is in the details.

She recalled the first sweater she knitted a few months earlier. She could almost hear her friends saying, "Start with something easy, like a scarf." No, no, no. She dove head first into a cable-knit sweater. She spent so much time on the intricate details. The perfect pattern for the sweater was identified and acquired documentation. She spent over two weeks planning the design, then laying it out. She would knit an incredible pattern into the whole garment. She chose an amazing texture and color. Finding the perfect off-white wool took another two weeks. She couldn't wait to see her boyfriend's reaction to a handmade bundle of "here's how I feel about you" all in one spot, one moment in time, keeping him both stylish and warm. They hadn't exchanged the awful "L" word yet, but she was close to saying it. She liked him. That's an important L word too.

Then she set upon honing her knitting skills. Start the first line of the project; a full two hours of intense, mind-numbing concentration, three stabs of her hands without drawing blood. Had she bled, she would have stained the wool, which would have ruined it. Nora needed to speed up. "Damn, those needles smarted," she thought.

After much analysis, she realized her hands didn't need to clutch the yarn and knitting needles so hard. "Did I crush those needles?" she thought. No, she didn't have super-human strength. Also, the pattern wasn't holding her back, she had that down pat. The action of holding the needles and making the intricate stitches that held everything together took loads of time. Nora knew she was clutching the needles too tightly. She had to fix that before she developed medical issues. She realized she was holding the needles too HIGH. "Ease up, Nora," she had thought. Maybe she could hire a coach? Perhaps she could watch a knitting sports channel to view competitions. She imagined their colorful commentary. "Look at the beautiful wool, Bob. It looks like Lisa *Da Pearl* is doing extraordinary this round." She turned on her TV scouring the channel guide and found no such broadcasting network, then returned to her work.

Refining the way she held the needles and coaching herself, it took only thirty minutes to sew the second line. "Now I need to stop licking my damn lips and getting that super-concentration face. I wonder what the heck I look like while doing this? I should knit in front of a mirror. No, no, no." She thought. Her face hurt after holding an *I can do this better* pose. "OMG if I had a video camera watching me. I must have made thousands of faces while pouring all my energy on the one stitch. Another mistake. Pay attention to the line, not the stitch," she chided herself. Nora wondered if she remembered to breathe? "Oh no," she exclaimed. Nora imagined herself being found dead after creating the third line, after forgetting to breathe for twenty minutes. She concluded that she was still alive, so she was, in fact, breathing. Nora got up and casually closed the shades just in case her neighbors uploaded videos of her as "The Crazy Knitting Lady," receiving millions of views and trolling comments.

Five weeks later, she was running behind schedule, and she began knitting while commuting with Reynold to Harvard. He was so kind to drive those weeks while she knitted for the entire trip. At stop lights, he'd stare at her in fascination, watching her worry about the details. "Is that correct?" he'd ask.

She quickly responded, "Sure. It's supposed to look like that." Then she would check the line he pointed out, and he was right. She face-palmed herself. Did he know how to knit? Reynold knew a lot of stuff.

She broke up with her boyfriend when he complained that he couldn't exchange the sweater she made at the department store.

Reynold watched her knit at red lights. "Wait a moment, was he watching me knit? Or was he watching me?" she thought. Reynold was the definition of stability. His hands never strayed from proper positions on a steering wheel. He wasn't attracting her attention by showboating and making a lot of noise. Was she suddenly curious about shy, nerdy, and nice guys? She thought, "He's been so patient with me. He listens, listens, and listens. Reynold was actively listening. He was reflecting about what I was saying." She understood that. Nora dwelled on the thought she had been an awful friend to him. She had sat there and talked, filling in the dead air between them. Was she being a flibbertigibbet? Correcting herself, she knew it wasn't dead air. Reynold cared. He asked terrific questions about things she was interested in. Taking a deep breath, she thought, "Still waters run deep." Maybe she should set him up with someone? "No. Stop solving other people's problems, Nora. He's ok, he'll find someone eventually," she said out loud to herself. She ended the thought with, "But was he staring at me? And would he stare today? With no knitting?" She planned out her experiment to be sure.

Reynold pulled up silently, cursing himself for being late, and texted Nora that he was there. He stood beside her door, waiting for her to glide gracefully into the seat. He quickly snapped out of it and opened the car door for Nora.

Nora saw Reynold's reaction to her emerging from her house and thought, "He's staring at me. He's not looking, he's staring!"

Nora breezed by, smiled and touched his face saying, "Thanks for being on time as usual!" and sat in the passenger seat.

Reynold stood transfixed by her touch for a moment longer and said, “But I'm two minutes late...” as she entered the car.

Once Reynold entered the car, Nora burst out laughing, realizing why she was so amused this morning. He looked at her with confusion.

She explained, "Oh, sorry, I was grading a paper this morning where the student overused the word *which* in her paper about *The House of the Seven Gables*. Get it? I was performing a *which* hunt on her paper!"

Reynold didn't get it.

4

ON THE LAST DAY OF CLASS

Nora and Reynold pulled up to the employee parking lot and he took a deep breath. "Hey, let's go to breakfast tomorrow morning? Around nine?"

Reynold had ached over the question until he realized that he shouldn't ask. Like he was begging. No. He's going to open with, “Let's do this." You can't say no to someone that suggests doing something instead of asking permission. He didn't want to ask to move the chess piece. He was moving his piece to the right spot.

This surprised Nora, but she replied, "Sure." Reynold's a good guy. It's breakfast. She had never hung out with him. Maybe she'd learn more about him and he would talk more? And he was staring at her.

Reynold's mind went a little numb. Well, that was easy. Was something wrong? Should he stop worrying so much? He'd save money on hot water from his super shower.

They walked to the lecture hall in a silence that didn't seem uncomfortable. Something had changed. Nora's lecture was not for another forty-five minutes after his. She enjoyed teaching "Local History" to help others see the streets as they once were. Plenty of interesting things had happened in the past. Maybe he could sit in and watch her lecture after he finished his class?

As they approached his auditorium, his demeanor brightened even more. This was his audience, and he had their attention. His forte was physics equations, but his joy was sharing knowledge about the cosmos. This was his throne, these were his subjects, and he ruled.

He unfolded his laptop, took a tablet computer out of what seemed like thin air, and smiled. Reynold was confident in this space. This day had made his heart soar with delight. She said yes! He needed to rein in his joy. Total concentration was required to deliver his final lecture of the semester. The day for student evaluations. He took three deep breaths and focused on lowering his heart rate.

Reynold knew patterns. He liked patterns. His job was to examine them, develop formulas, then prove them. Today was the crowning achievement of noticing that happy students write happier evaluations of their professors. He read the crowd and led them to their conclusions. This lecture was more edutainment than education. He could either end it early, like the other professors, or give them something to say "WOW" about.

He knew what was next. He felt the precursor pressure in his lungs. The *give us a break dummy* feeling that could quickly blossom into an attack and coughing fit. Reaching into his jacket pocket, he grabbed his asthma inhaler as he had many times before. He squeezed it, took a deep ceremonial breath and let the drugs open the airways in his lungs. His sport jacket never showed a wrinkle of all the stuff hidden within it. He had one asthma attack in class because he was self-conscious about grabbing the inhaler in front of the students, and he regretted not recognizing the pattern before it happened. He would never repeat that moment.

"What do you call a person who keeps on talking when people are no longer interested?" he paused for dramatic effect, "... a Professor!" The students laughed. Time for the students to relax.

"On the first day of class I told you only 65% of you will complete this course. Just so you know, 68% of you made it so bravo. Now, imagine the pressure of a real job. At the end of today's lecture, I'll open the floor to questions so you can ask anything about your future in physics. Speak up now, 'cause next semester will be much harder. Use the time now to focus your attention on your future studies. No more finals, you're done with my tests and you all passed, some far more than others." He looked at his brightest student for a moment and nodded. He continued, "So let's allow ourselves some distractions.

"Our history at Harvard is amazing. Harlow Shapley himself stood in this room lecturing and was one of the first people to publish papers on what he called *Climatic Change*, in 1953. He was one of the significant voices of astronomy, and we still have a lot to learn from his published theories and hypotheses.

"You can't appreciate where you're going unless you see where you've been. That's what history tells us. My favorite quote is *True knowledge exists in knowing that you know nothing. I know that I am intelligent because I know nothing. I cannot teach anybody anything, I can only make them think*. That was said by Socrates himself.

"Our university is almost 400 years old. We are the oldest university in the United States. Founded before the idea of a democratic republic. Our country is now an amazing experiment in how to treat all people equally. Before that concept was cemented, the country was brand spanking new. Every step was new territory. If John Harvard hadn't willed 780 pounds in money, and over 400 books to our institution, our name would have remained *New College*, as it was chartered in 1636. The original idea was to have the highest discipline, and to recite both Old and New Testament in Latin continuously," he paused for effect and continued, "which stopped being a requirement about five weeks ago." He garnered more laughter from the students.

"But it's this growth that has forever shaped our graduates. We don't require Latin anymore yet still hear it at our graduation ceremonies. Our evolution should guide you. We are a liberal arts college that is not requiring you to become a liberal. So conservative club members, cool ya jets. You are being sent forth to change the world around you. It's one of the very fabrics woven into the college.

"What if in the 1590s Sir John Harrington, the inventor of what we may see as the modern toilet, donated money instead of John Harvard in the 1600s, would we be *Crapper* College?" The students laughed again. "You might stop laughing when you realize toilet paper wasn't mass produced until the late 1800s.

"When we were founded, our motto was *Veritas pro Christo et Ecclesia* or *Truth for Christ and Church*, but at our University's bicentennial in 1836, we changed our motto to simply *Veritas*. Truth. We are all bound to it. We're armed with drilling down and finding truth. At first, it was a spiritual truth, and now it's moral, legal, and scientific truth. Elie Wiesel said, *We must always take sides. Neutrality helps the oppressor, never the victim. Silence encourages the tormentor, never the tormented.* We can't stand by watching the persecution of innocent people. You must champion what is right. He said, *There are victories of the soul and spirit. Sometimes, even if you lose, you win*. Elie was speaking out against everything that could hold back society. We need to give ourselves the freedom to make mistakes. And in those failures, something good emerges. The truth.

“A legacy of people are standing behind you encouraging you into the future.

"There's no way to avoid it. You may not realize what you have right now because you're also given the blessing of youth. One day you'll be standing in front of someone, and all these gears will click right into place, the light will shine from your pupils with an amazing clarity of the moment, and your heart and soul will become involved. You will enter the thick of that moment, and everything we've told you from these podiums around the university will overtake and overwhelm you. You will have this desire to find and thank all of your professors when our lessons connect out there in the wild.”

His eyes brightened as he drove home the punch line. "In my case, you can do that today, filling out your evaluation forms." The students chuckled.

“Remember the past and where we came from. How did we get here? Did I get here alone? Am I moving forward alone? Do I have the help of my friends? Your path will become clearer and clearer with every step towards the future. That's my advice to you: Remember the past to improve the future.

"So... questions?"

One student raised his hand. "Sir, if we pursue physics as our major, what are the pitfalls?"

"Oh, so a field about the fabric of the universe, and you're asking an open-ended question... BRAVO. Physics never stops. Quantum Physics or Mechanics is the stuff that'll make your brain hurt. Calculating 10-dimensional equations that can melt down supercomputers. Richard Feynman once observed that *Nobody truly understands quantum mechanics*, and he's right. String theory is synonymous with quantum mechanics. Max Planck talked about this in the 1900s. Mixing it up with Einstein, and that gang. Quantum mechanics puts the sub-atomic level into focus, where physical properties are hard to define.

"More to the point, objects radiate heat and light, which focuses the energy as the wave patterns tighten up and get shorter and shorter, turning it into what my 8-year-old nephew calls *Ultra-violent light*. Planck saw that this light approached infinity. Since we can't... really observe infinity, we had to accept that there are maximums to our ranges.

"So that's the pitfall. Not being able to prove an absolute knowledge and understanding. Be brave and take those chances."

Another student asked, "Professor, do you think we'll ever go at the speed of light?"

"The speed of light is 299,792.498 kilometers per second or 186,292.397 miles per second. We covered this a few weeks ago, and it was on your final. For those of you calibrating the speedometer of your Toyota Corollas after class, when calculating for time dilation, should we ever achieve that speed, the results would always calculate to infinity, which physicists seem to use as a go to number. Experiments today accurately prove Einstein's formula on time dilation. Now Einstein slam DUNKED that bad boy without the ability to physically observe this until at least 50 years later when we created the first atomic and cesium clocks. Every GPS satellite contains one of these clocks, so they all use that same formula to compensate before transmitting the time and location signal so you can triangulate your position in your cars or while hiking to your next class.

"So the bad news is, the acceleration would kill us, not the speed. When you're within a vessel, what you feel isn't the speed you're traveling. It's the acceleration to get there. Newton observed this while watching a ship at sea. That is the killer part, and I mean that as in literally KILLER. To accelerate to the speed of light, the craft would need to use the gravitational forces around planets to slingshot their way faster and faster in the vacuum of space. Using this, you accelerate until you eventually get as close to light speed as possible. This will take six to ten years, then we need to decelerate for another six to ten years. That is without jarring the passengers, so when they arrive, they don't look like a lot of chunky cranberry sauce. We still have lofty places to go. The nearest inhabitable planet is about fourteen light years away; our own galaxy is one-hundred thousand light-years across. Don't be too impressed. The next one over is two-hundred thousand light years across, so if anyone believes global warming is a myth, the nearest backup planet ain't even close. You can get to that planet in about twenty to thirty years, but our planet's relative age will be completely different. So TURN OFF YOUR DAMN LIGHTS WHEN YOU LEAVE THE ROOM." More laughter. The students were relaxing even more. Reynold thought, "Ok class. Take out a sheet of paper for a surprise quiz." That's too cruel. They'd kill him on the evals.

"So let's talk about time dilation. What will be back on earth? The closer you get to the speed of light, the more dilation your observers experience. For every year you travel at light speed is about sixteen-hundred years passing on earth. So we need to go fourteen years at the speed of light, but add seven years acceleration and seven years deceleration so we don't die from the g-forces our bodies can't take. Now that's twenty-eight years of going really, really fast for you and your shipmates. The earth will have aged about twenty-one thousand years during that journey. You'd experience dilation while approaching light speed, but I don't know how to guess the time and speed during the acceleration. Let's simplify this, focusing on the dilation experienced while traveling at light speed. So if we get to that planet, buy a sandwich and get a drink at a local fast food place, then jump back on ship and return, that would be about forty-two thousand years dilation back on earth. To date, the most realistic deep space travel movie that directly addressed this was the original *Planet of the Apes* from the 1960s." A lot of faces filled with realization.

"You would need food, a clean potty, a lot of board games, and people that don't get bored or mad when you kick their ass at Monopoly."

Another student asked, "Can we go back in time?"

Reynold took an audible breath. "Time is part of the 10-dimensional calculations we're still playing with within quantum mechanics. So you say to a friend, *Hey, let's go to get coffee.* You need some data to ensure you all arrive at the same place, at the correct time. This way you aren't waiting years before anyone shows up. You need the *when.*

"The only way to go back in time is to find, or build, a bridge. A scientist noticed a worm coming out of his apple. I think scientists love apples. Do you remember when I talked about how Richard Feynman speculated that the size of an atom compared to an apple is the same as the size of an apple to the size of the Earth. Anyway, John Wheeler speculated that if that apple's surface represented space, the worm digging in it could figure a way from one side through to the other in a much shorter period, eliminating the mucking about in all the big stuff we call space. This is our concept of a wormhole. This would save a lot of time.

Einstein came up with a similar idea known as an Einstein-Rosen bridge fifteen years earlier. This has never been observed in nature. Anyway, once you have that bridge, you need to keep the revolving door open; that is, if it *is* a revolving door. You would need something known as *exotic matter* or matter that has negative mass, which is kinda hard to find. If you can pick it up at a store, then it has mass. Get it? Pick it up?" Blank stares. Moving on. He continued, "That matter makes the wormhole traversable before it collapses, turning the contents inside into the tiny part of the toothpaste tube squeezing its remaining contents. Could they go to another place? Maybe? Could you go to another time? Maybe? This is 100% theory. These are the seeds of desire. This phenomenon may not be observable for a long, long time. This would require AMAZING forces. Generating and programming the wormhole to go where we want would be nothing less than... extraordinary. What language would it speak? Would it do the calculations, or would we need to supply the results? Egyptians gave us numbers. Would the wormhole understand that? How do you program a wormhole using human-created coordinates? The device would need so much power and size, it makes little sense to build it right now. The computing power to predict where you will emerge from the wormhole is overwhelming. The universe is expanding at sixty-eight kilometers a second. We would need to add that factor to the complicated mish-mash of the results. Those results would only be good for a fraction of a second. If your calculation is off by a fraction of a fraction of a fraction of a fraction, then the exit to your wormhole is close to Mars and you need to travel for another nine months at regular propulsion to get to Earth.

"What about the forces through the wormhole? Would these forces rip you apart? Squish you like that toothpaste tube I mentioned? If the wormhole collapses before you emerge on the other side, how would you complete the equation and return through it? The universe LOVES balance. Both sides of that equal sign need to balance out.

"Once you do all that... bully for you. BRAVO. People have been theorizing about the complications of wormholes forever. If you shorten the time to travel great distances using a wormhole, you would contribute a ton to space travel. The other potential use? Possibly time-travel? And with time travel, you truly test the limits of causality. Which came first? Those calculations are part of quantum mechanics.

"Let's think about the dangers. Can you kill your own grandparent? Or the famed butterfly effect? Where the smallest change in the beating of a butterfly's wings back in time can trigger changes in that time that cause a catastrophe in the future when you return. Can you prevent your distant relatives from meeting? You could cause yourself to not exist back in the originating timeline. But isn't that a Joseph Heller-sized catch-22? How did you exist in that timeline to go back in time?

"Should you invest in a stock to become rich when time traveling? I say YES. Could you prevent a terrible mistake? Make plenty more mistakes? People who focus on doing this are wasting their time. You can drive yourself mad, creating or hiding from that mistake. Don't worry yourself about it. You *can't* go back in time. Creating the wormhole on your own is impossible if it hasn't been observed in nature yet. We would need to observe many wormholes to understand them.

"We are more fragile than we realize. Our bodies are both giving off germs and bacteria and absorbing them all at the same time. Could you make people sick? Would you cure them? Then there are the complications of telling people about the experience. Would they consider you mad? If you change the past, how would you be able to tell? If you have no effect, would you be able to see that? By the time you return, would it turn out to have been a horrible mistake?"

"We're all just speculating until someone actually does it, and it's not even on anyone's radar as a potential project. We're too busy figuring out what's happening right here and now. For the moment I get to watch movies and think, *Oh no, if he doesn't kiss the girl, will he exist?* just like you. But I know he'll kiss the girl. He's got to kiss the girl. He always kisses the girl." He banged the desk for effect.

"We're both cursed and blessed with these limited lifespans, so don't procrastinate. We need to put our collective noses to the grindstones. Or else we don't get the girl, we don't finish the groundbreaking manuscript, and we don't feel complete. Nature always wants a balanced equation. This balance needs to translate into your lives. You have Diem to Carpe.

"These are good questions, class. I want to leave you with one last thought: Make a wish and toss a coin in a fountain. Will fate bless the coin, or you? The coin you bless has a better chance of survival, but you have to mean it. Put your heart and soul behind that coin because that's the only way to gamble away money you may need. You don't want to frivolously throw away money, but wisely think about that decision, search deep in your soul, then let that coin fly. You guide the trajectory. Your help lets the coin flourish. That makes the coin unique in that enormous fountain."

Reynold paused in silence to let it all sink in.

"NOW GO FORTH AND MULTIPLY. Fill out the teacher-evaluation forms while you still like me, and before you receive your final grades. Remember, they will beat me severely for harsh reviews."

Reynold's phone vibrated in its appropriate pocket in his jacket. He answered it and listened to the most fantastic thing he had ever heard in his life.

5

IS THIS A DATE?

Reynold was nervous as he drove to Nora's house. He had another errand he had to accomplish after breakfast with her. He HAD to. Somehow, this involved her. He couldn't sound maniacal at his request for her to come along. Matter of fact. Just... matter of fact. He took a deep breath. Oh no, I'm not forcing you to drive around and solve personal creepy mysteries, no sir, not this guy.

His nerves continued to bubble. It's so strange. He stank at keeping secrets, but if he blurted out what he knew, what would she think? Would she say, "Oh sure... yeah, makes sense," or would she stay home? He didn't want to pressure her.

This is just a... little errand. Yeah... Picking up... something, sure. Aw nuts. Without saying the thing he needed, he might sound a bit crazy. OK, ok. Calm down.

He dressed in what he normally wore to class. The explanation is when you don't have to choose your outfits, they all fit together. Without complex choices, your mind is free to make discoveries. One of which isn't "hey these socks don't match." His socks were the same brand and size. His undershirts were always black. They protected the shirt and acted as an accessory. They matched every shirt he owned. How about his outer shirt? Untucked and some shade of blue. Today he panicked and wore white and forgot his undershirt.

He only wore black jeans. Why? They could dress up or down.

Finally, he always wore his custom made sport jacket. He had found a local company to help him design his super pocket jacket. Each pocket tailored for its specific function. Oh sure, it took time to develop it, but he no longer needed to have a colossal briefcase nor a backpack. He always had everything he needed in pockets spread around his jacket. He considered patenting his and his tailor's invention, but why? Then... why EVERYONE would have one. And he loved his jacket. He enjoyed finding the newest gadgets. When they seemed impressive enough and jacket worthy, he'd go to his tailor and figure out a new place for the new gizmo, or in this case gizmos. Tucked into the jacket were his phone, tablet, inhalers, batteries, eyedrops for his contacts, and snacks when he needed them. Before flying anywhere, he had to take it off, and they had to X-ray it to death.

His tablet computer was his most prized possession and was always handy. If he wanted to take notes, he could just whip it out, and type or write like it was paper. If he needed to type more, he could take out a small keyboard hidden in its own pocket. His tablet saved his life on so many occasions.

The jacket didn't reveal bulges. Solid black denim

couldn't show wrinkles. From a distance, it looked like a wool sport jacket. If he put something in, he removed a corresponding amount of liner to have a net-zero effect on the overall size. Although the denim material seemed thick, it breathed, making it usable in all weather. He had two days of inhalers built into the liner so he could run off and party for a few days randomly and remain one hundred percent healthy. So he looked like he had a HUGE chest. Fine. Small price to pay.

He carried a super-duper extra fancy charger that doubled as a two-way radio for his phone. Reynold was rarely more than a mile away from a cell tower. He had purchased these items solely on a hunch. It kept his phone charged. At least he used it for something.

As he arrived at Nora's apartment, he had to brace himself for a potential grilling. But she had already walked out, probably having seen him pull up. Wow! Was she... looking forward to this?

She met him by the curb and he exited his car to greet her. "Hey. You're... stunning," he said, and immediately blushed. His eyes locked onto her, and he was a little ashamed for staring. She wore a blue peasant dress, with a loose fitting top. She looked radiant.

Nora blushed and smiled. "Thanks. You look so... formal wearing that jacket."

"Oh, this thing... it's... well, my security blanket. I have everything I need to survive in it. I guess I wear it out of habit. I have to stop someplace on an errand after breakfast. Is that OK?"

Nora replied, "Sure. I'm off today and don't have plans."

That was way too easy. Now what? Reynold regretted all the wasted time figuring out contingency plans.

"Want to go to a diner? A Restaurant?" he asked, trying to get ideas.

"Anyplace you'd like to go is fine," she responded.

Oh no. Choose the wrong place, and they're eating sawdust for breakfast. Choose a pricey restaurant, and he might not be able to afford it. DANG THAT EXPENSIVE SHOWER. Or... shoot from the hip and stop worrying. Maybe the outcome will be fine if he doesn't tense up over every word he says or thinks. Was that easier?

"I heard about a nice place on Essex Street." Oh nuts, he gave an opinion. What if it was the wrong opinion? What if she hates it? Shields down, this isn't a battle zone. Roger that.

"That sounds fine. I'm an omnivore," she happily responded. She added, “Look, if we were stuck in the woods, I’d eat you if necessary.”

Ok, she's not a vegan. What do *they* eat? Don't distract yourself, Reynold. Stay on target.

Driving around town was a lesson in "how to drive on 400-year-old streets." Sometimes you had to maneuver your car onto the tightest roads. But when you're from Massachusetts, you get used to driving around historic areas that weren't designed for cars. Some streets were only for walking.

After committing to a place, he parked, and they walked into the restaurant. Her doctorate in history seemed intimidating, but he was also a history buff. They had never brought it up in conversation when they drove to work together. Reynold said in his smoothest tone, "they originally called this street *Ye Main Street*."

She pretended to glare at him and said, "Hey! Are you telling me my business, mister? Actually, to save room for printers, sign makers, and engravers, they shortened it to Ye from *The* and pronounced it *The*. I have thousands of years of history around the world to choose for my speciality and I chose local history for my thesis. This city is tiny. Nearly everything is walking distance. Many of the houses in this area are hundreds of years old. History surrounds us. And *come on* - I'm just joshing you."

He smiled and asked, "Where did you grow up?" How was he conversing so easily? Small butterflies in his stomach were fluttering. Was he nervous? Hungry? The sensations flooding in were oddly comfortable. Strange.

"Rhode Island, in the Providence area. I've always lived in New England. I completed my undergraduate degree at Rhode Island College. It was originally the *Normal School* as it was a teachers college as many of them were named. I loved the intimacy of the campus. You could get to know the professors. It wasn't this enormous place designed to churn out teachers, but a diverse liberal arts school. I wanted to be in a big enough environment where I could compete, but not disappear as a number amongst the professors."

"Did you always want to be a historian?" he asked.

"No. I was an English major until I caught the history bug. The things I longed for had already happened. It wasn't in the here and now. I think the adventure is in the lessons we learn from our past. It's all sitting there for us to look at, and wonder why?"

He stared at her, drinking in the moment.

She interrupted his thought. "Do... I have something on my face?"

"Oh. Sorry. I was just admiring your passion. The stuff we find amazing fuels us. It gives us a spark that's important. How much time did you spend on your doctorate?"

"Hey WHOA... now you sound like my dad," she teased...

then had to explain, "I'm kidding! I received my master's right before I took the research position at Harvard and completed my doctorate a few years later. I really enjoy teaching because I can't exactly quit and open a store and sell *history*. *Hey Kid, wanna learn about where you came from?* I was unsure what sort of paycheck that would deliver." He chuckled at that. "No, I love doing this. It's my wheelhouse. I've always admired people with deep passion. They drive and drive to finish things. It's why I love studying where we came from. Although, I got a little sick of *House of the Seven Gables* papers I graded this semester. I'll never know how I read that many papers about it without going mad."

She was feeling at ease... and... not worried. Reynold had this comforting aura. Weird. Her inner instinct to always fill the silence dissipated. Here she sat, and felt the calmness come over her, and allowed it. Maybe Reynold was a warlock to her psyche?

He ate a few bites of his waffles, so she took advantage of the opening to ask a personal question about him. "When did you decide to go into physics? Or whatever you do?"

"That's fair." He sipped his coffee and replied. "I was always analyzing things. It was tough to bring me to a movie with any special effects. I wanted to see how they made the magic happen. Peek behind the curtain, so to speak. So I was no fun. Imagine my friends wondering what amused me? Leave a science fiction movie with my friends elated, and me saying, *oh they filmed that with timed photography controlled by a computer that made a certain amount of frames per second to fool the eye into thinking it's moving, but only the camera was moving.* It annoyed my nerdy friends. But I was always curious about how things are made. My uncle gave me a calculator when I was younger. After some time it started acting wonky. I took it apart and looked at all the pieces, which stunned my parents. *How Could you do that? It was a gift*! Well, it wasn't working. So I analyzed all the pieces and noticed that the contacts inside the buttons were slightly askew. I blew out the dust behind the rubber buttons, shifted them a little, re-centered everything, and put it back together within the yellow plastic case. I marched downstairs with a functional calculator that wasn't doubling the number you pressed, nor looking like the screen got all jumbled up. It worked perfectly for years until I needed a powerful scientific calculator. Man, I miss that old thing."

"My moment of truth happened when Uncle George visited me a few years later, and he looked at me and said, *You need to figure out how the universe works. It will help all of us*. He then took this off his neck, and says, *You have the key.*" Reynold took out an old-fashioned but shiny key he wore on a leather necklace around his neck. "I could never find a desk, door or anything that fit this key. It was more of a symbol I guess, which he wore around his neck, perhaps for a long time? He never told me the history of this key. I always wear it as a sort of... a talisman. I never was into wearing jewelry, but this key has always meant something to me. It has always helped me focus.

"I've always been good at math behind physics problems. I have to slow down and write out the formulas properly. One calculus teacher got mad at me because I kept doing the work in my head. So I had to learn to play with others.

"My dad would say, *See this bird, it's an Eagle. In French, its name is Aigle, in German, its name is Adler. In Swedish it's an Orn. Now, what do you know about it? Nothing. Absolutely nothing. No matter what the bird, if you only learn the name, you still know nothing about it. Look at what it's doing and concentrate on that.* So I learned the difference between knowing the name of something and knowing the something I was concentrating on. Years later, someone walks over to me and blabbed on about a *so and so* theory, and I looked at them and had to ask, *What the heck theory is that?* and he described it. It turns out I published the damn thing two years earlier and had named it. So I learned, you also *need* to know the names of things if you will interact with people."

Nora laughed and said, "I see how you teach your students. I really understand why they like what you're doing. You grab their attention and hold on to it. Did you always want to be a professor?"

He answered slowly, "No, but I was always good at talking to crowds of people and was always a good debater. I enjoy arguing a point. More so when I've got a fire in my belly about it. Almost to a fault. It's one of my *mutant powers,* I guess."

Nora cocked an eyebrow at Reynold and queried, "Mutant... powers?"

"Yeah, like in the comic books? We all have something we're unusually extraordinary at doing. They're just mundane things. Such as seeing patterns. I'm great at that. But I'm especially good at convincing others that those patterns are important and why. Even the tedious hard to find ones."

"Ok, so you don't shoot webs from your wrists as if a radioactive spider bit you?" she said, smirking a little.

"Ah ha! so you understand mutant powers!" he exclaimed.

"That's Mutated. I go to the movies and see things about the present! It's not all about the past," she replied in the best matter-of-fact tone she could deliver.

Breakfast seemed like a resounding success. They had consumed meals, and nobody felt uncomfortable. What an awesome foundation. Reynold had ventured further into the unknown than he had dared in the past. Something gave him the confidence to acknowledge the amazing seeds being planted.

He had almost forgotten what had given him chills up his spine only twenty-four hours ago.

6

LET'S CALL IT ELMER

They returned to the car and Reynold drove to the address he had received only a day earlier. This was more than a little exciting. What or who would be there? The time is 9:55am. In five minutes, this mystery will reveal itself. What was this? A hunch? A guess? A coincidence of epic proportions? He couldn't explain. He needed to understand.

"I have to ask one thing, Nora. Is your birthday July 1st?" Reynold asked. Fair question. He had to know.

"Yeah, how did you find out? I never tell anyone my birthdate. All that celebration just because I aged a year. I age every day," she replied. Reynold stared in silence. Noticing a hesitation, Nora asked, "Is something wrong?"

"I don't know, but we'll know more in five minutes," he replied.

"Oh yeah, she will think you're a nutcase now," he thought.

Reynold said, "I'm not sure how long this may take. You may not want to wait in the car." Did he push the issue this time? This definitely involved her. He didn't sense danger, but it was getting weirder by the moment.

"Oh Ok. No problem. The sun is strong. I really don't want to overheat in the car," she replied.

Wait, how could this be working? I could be an axe murderer! She shouldn't trust me. Do I own an axe? Should I warn her?"

He breathed an inaudible sigh of relief. Level achieved. He walked in feeling like he was part of a strange game being played out with human pieces. Was this an elaborate hoax? Were his friends and colleagues playing a cruel trick on him?

They walked into the front of the building. Reynold was holding the printout of the gravestone as he knocked on the office door. The familiar Harvard watermark distorted the printout since Reynold used a campus print-station. Earlier that year, the acquisitions manager noticed that professors grotesquely overused paper. To combat this, she contacted a supplier and added a unique watermark on all campus paper. This stopped the professors from printing papers for their students. Within a month, the college had saved a hefty sum of money.

John Milners opened the door and said, "Hey buddy. How did you find me here?"

Reynold stood and stared for a few seconds. His forehead filled with sweat, lowering his temperature and giving him goosebumps. He exclaimed, "What are you doing here? I KNEW this was a hoax! This is worse than when you made me put my tongue on the nine volt battery in 7th grade. That battery wasn't dead!" This was a prank, and a damn mean one. Was Nora in on the joke? He couldn't yell at her. It took all of his energy to ask her to breakfast. It really felt that way.

"You... uh... got me, buddy... sure... now, what are you talking about, and how... and why are you here?" John responded slowly. His face registered his confusion.

Reynold was furious. An elaborate scheme was afoot, and he was on the wrong end of the joke. The puzzle pieces fit too well together. It was a shock to his system. He was a scientist. Too many coincidences were happening at once. Coincidences that seemed supernatural didn't exist in his world. Everything has a logical explanation. He's confronted with an ancient gravestone with his and Nora's name on it, and in Hebrew? Did John know Hebrew? After the language lab translated the message, he was both confused and chilled by the content. It seemed like an elaborate hoax was being played on him. Reynold's grasped at the chance it was a mystery rather than being a stunt. Was John and Nora in on it? It is a cryptic message, but correct address, and precise date and time. He looked at his friend of over thirty years, who wasn't laughing or pointing and jumping up and down at his foolishness. Could John also be a victim of this hoax?

Reynold shoved the printout of the gravestone at John for him to examine.

John read the engraving that said, "Here Lyeth," with the T and H combined into a single letter. The eroded letters, gray and smooth, read "Reynold Woodbury, 13 Oct 1666 - 22 Sept 22 1692, Nora Woodbury 1 July 1667, 22 Sept 1692." Then there was a separator line and Hebrew letters that read;

~

לך לפינת רחוב פדרל וושינגטון ב-28 לאפריל ב 10:00 בבוקר חדר 102

~

REYNOLD'S distinctive southpaw scrawl was in the margin where he wrote *translates to go to the corner of Federal and Washington Street on April 28th at 10:00am Suite 102.*

If a picture was worth a thousand words, John's face spoke five thousand confusing ones. He handed the paper to Nora and said, "If you're Nora, read this." A person down the hall opened their door. “Hey, let’s go into the office, and we can talk like normal people,” John said in a calming voice. Seeing his friend this agitated was so out of character. He had rarely seen Reynold so upset. Last time Reynold was this agitated, John had kidnapped him to go to the movies. Actually, John said, "Reynold, get in," and they sped off to see *Big Trouble in Little China.* Since John didn't even have enough money for a ticket, Reynold even had to contribute to his own kidnapping. John wondered if *Stockholm syndrome* defined their friendship.

Nora looked at the printout and said, “This has got to be bullshit... The Hebrew does match the English you wrote down. Who would put that on a gravestone?”

Once inside the office, John took a breath and said, "There must be a logical explanation. I didn't make this gravestone. You have to believe me."

Reynold saw the truth in his friend's eyes. Oh nuts. He realized his conclusions were wrong and regretted losing his temper in front of John *and* Nora. She must think I'm crazy, but she was looking at the printout.

“Why didn't you show this to me sooner? I’m fluent in Hebrew,” Nora asked.

John asked, "Couldn't this be a wild coincidence? Granted, it's interesting to see both of your names on a gravestone, with this message from the Hebrew translated... There has got to be a logical explanation other than an elaborate hoax is being played on all of us."

The three of them stared at the paper. Reynold began, "Look, I am sorry about this. But the person I sent this to in the language department thought I had made the stone on a website that makes fake gravestones and signs."

Nora offered her hand to John and said, "Hi, I'm Dr. Nora Foster. We met once about three years ago when you came to work with Reynold and me while your car was being fixed."

John reached out his hand and asked, "What's Nora short for?"

She glared at him, furrowing her eyebrows and said, "I don't know... I have a small torso and legs? Why did you wax the back of your right hand without waxing your left hand?"

John looked away saying, "I don't wanna talk about it," feeling suddenly embarrassed.

Reynold interrupted, "NUTS! I'm sorry, you two. Nora, this is John Milners, another physicist, like me, but on what we call the *dark side*. He's a theoretical physicist. Nora, use small words with him. He only has a master's degree. This has got to be a prank."

John glared at the comment about his master's degree and returned to his blank look. "No. I'm pretty confused myself. I got the keys to this place only two weeks ago and moved my experiment here only a few days ago. Professor Wilson is in India with his wife studying something. Indian culture I think? But this city is tiny. I mean, come on, you can walk it in thirty minutes? Forty? Where did you see this gravestone?"

"At the funeral I attended in February. I walked to the site where the interment was taking place and passed the only gravestone in Hebrew. That's when I noticed it had my name and birthday except the year was in the 1600s. And I found out that's Nora's birthday before walking into the building." This was weird.

Nora scratched her head and said, "That is my birthday, but it must be a coincidence. The same names and birthdays," she pondered for a moment and continued, "This is weird, YES. Do I have the desire to play lotto? Absolutely. But I need to add, we aren't married. Do I have an impulse to ignore your texts for the next two weeks and let your calls go to voice-mail? Sure." She said this using as much sarcasm in her tone as possible. Sarcasm was impossible with people who take things literally.

Reynold feigned his best hurt expression, and slowly replied, "Hey... well, this was just breakfast, you know," he tried to defend himself. His face flushed with embarrassment. It had taken all his courage to ask her out, and now it could go up in smoke. Shields up, captain.

Nora saw her literal minded friend's eyes widening, and said, "I'm KIDDING! This isn't the weirdest meal I've ever had. It's the second weirdest." In her mind, she filed this under *kinda weird.*

After a silence for fifteen seconds, John said, "Oh, that is crap. That French prophet Nostradamus writing poems in the 1500s had all of them interpreted weirdly and predicting crazy modern stuff. It's all interpreted. There are a lot of coincidences here. Two people had your names and birthdays, and someone had a terrible command of Hebrew in the 1600s. You are freaking yourself out for absolutely no reason."

Reynold took a deep breath. Was it all coincidence? It was weird. Could the Hebrew just be bad Hebrew? Was this an unspoken dialect no one had heard or seen for three hundred years? No, that's crazy. Hebrew is a consistent five thousand year old language. Reynold looked at him and said, "John, that's just not possible. Hebrew is over five thousand years old. I don't think they changed how they pronounced things."

John said, "Here, check this out." Within four seconds, John produced a picture of a Hebrew tattoo on his computer that said in a caption, *This is just a dumb tattoo.* John continued, "See? This is like someone getting *beef-with-broccoli* in Chinese tattooed on their arm, saying it means *strength and wisdom* when it literally means *BEEF WITH BROCCOLI.* Now look at this." John was convincing. He showed Reynold a picture of a cake with an image of a computer thumb drive on it.

Reynold stares at the screen it blankly. "What am I looking at?"

"Do you think the people wanted a picture of the thumb drive? It should have been the files *in* the thumb drive. This is a colossal mistake. That's the only Hebrew gravestone in that cemetery. So I'm sure they thrilled the gravestone guy, working his butt off after apprenticing for years that he had to carve this crap. This is over three hundred years ago. Who could that guy ask? There was no internet. Weren't there only Pilgrims or Quakers living here? Not a lot of the *chosen people* walking around for reference. *Hey Moishe, when you have a moment, can you check my work?* You're looking at a string of coincidences of epic proportions. I will say this much. I wanted to see you today for a reason of my own, but you said you had this date thing."

Nora's ears perked up. "He told you this is... a... date?" She said.

Reynold's eyes went wider, and he stammered, "No... I... well," his complexion hid that he was blushing.

Reynold took another breath and considered John's statement. Could he be making too much of this? He had a glorious breakfast with Nora and didn't want the day to end so poorly. "What are you doing here anyway?" he asked John.

John replied, "With these pleasantries out of the way. I have been working in my woodshed for months on a project. It's why we haven't been playing pool on Thursdays. I figured out... something that should take your breath away. You have been helping me with the project... without getting suspicious. I'm so glad you're gullible and naïve, buddy."

Reynold stared, then smacked him in the arm. "WHAT? You mean all those formulas I was calculating for you?"

"OW, and yes. It's our first collaboration." John replied.

"Some of those formulas took me a few days, like five white boards. And you kept rushing me too. *Oh hey, where are those formula results?* Dude, some of us teach classes and don't lazily work in labs? It takes a lot of work to... manage teachers assistants that grade tests for me."

John decided to give him a few hints. He said, "Well, the one formula you worked out for me was for a storage device that absorbs electromagnetic waves generated naturally by the earth. I've created an awesome super-capacitor that translates electromagnetic waves into electricity. Screw this inefficient solar crap. I'm absorbing what's coming out of the Earth, baby! I've created another storage device that absorbs the waves directly *au natural,*" John said with air quotes and a faux French accent. "I've increased its efficiency, so I can absorb what I get, then blow it all out in exactly a minute. Think of taking a picture with an old camera flash. It takes a few moments to charge that capacitor so it can output the electricity to pop the flash. That's the whining noise it makes while charging. Same idea here, it needs time to charge. I made a ceramic super conductor without freezing it to be more efficient. Complete with little flakes of other alloys like graphene in the slushy mixture before it hardened. This makes them many times more efficient compared to frozen super conductors. It's also a fraction of the size, working its butt off at room temperature. One day I'll mess around and freeze one for the heck of it. The imperfections of handmade product concern me, but they help generate and store the electromagnetic field more efficiently. I poked holes in the graphene to make it faster at charging. This came in handy while converting those waves to electricity. The imperfections make it work better. Creating graphene in a lab is easy, but cumbersome. Mass producing it is a pain in the butt."

"*What*?" Now Reynold's mind was reeling. John had fed him a bunch of these formulas over the past six months. They weren't easy, but they were fun to work out. Oh nuts. Were they accurate? Sure, he always double-checked his work. "How long does it take to charge? I think one of my results was about three and a half days?"

"Spot on," John replied. "Three and a half days from red to green colored LED."

Nora used as much sarcasm as she could muster to say, "Wow, you guys, this is loads of fun. You know how to show a girl a whopper of a good time. What the heck are you two talking about?" Nora was staring at them both. How could they ignore that weird gravestone and move so quickly to another topic? Do *all* boys have attention deficit disorder? How can they miss the tiny little details surrounding them? Are they messing with GIRLS?

Reynold explained. "The Earth is generating a LOT of electromagnetic waves using its liquid iron core. It protects us from radiation from the whole galaxy. The gravity of the moon and the earth, plus the spin of the magnetic iron core at the center of the earth, also helps keep the moon tidally locked. We see the same face of the moon all the time. That relationship helped slow down the earth's spin at the dawn of our existence four billion years ago by causing friction from the gravity, and the tidal locking. You can thank the moon for our 24 hour time clock too because it helped slow the Earth down from its initial spin. Thank BOTH sets of waves for keeping everything shielded. It deflects radiation, even the orbits of the meteors that nearly hit us. The core of the planet does that naturally with its large mass. John figured out how to harness this as energy, but you're capturing the field directly as well... why?"

John gave his best Cheshire Cat grin and said, "Ah, well, that's the other part. When you pick up a flashlight and turn it on, what speed is the light coming out of it?" John wanted his friend to see what was ahead.

Reynold answered, "The speed of light." The answer seemed too simple. Was it a trick question? Reynold's mind wanted to move ahead, but couldn't. What was the next part of this?

"THE SPEED OF LIGHT! So did the flashlight give a kick back? I mean, your arms are as flabby and formless as mine. Picking up a laptop computer is our idea of a workout. Maybe picking up an occasional check at a restaurant would be nice of you."

Reynold feigned a hurt look. He had spent all his money installing his new smart-shower and was a little short on cash. He wasn't revealing that now. What's missing with this puzzle in front of him? "I feel nothing... so what's your point?" Reynold replied.

"When you walk outside, you are feeling the MOST INTENSE force in our solar system from the Sun. Is it pushing you against the pavement, rendering you unable to move? In a single hour the sun gives us more energy than the earth filled with TVs, smart phones and video games you can use in a year. Why aren't we all crippled and crushed against the ground when we walk outside? What's missing?" John was about to leap out of his skin with excitement. He needed him to say it.

Nora said, "Hello you two. Our names... are on... a gravestone!" Two boys geeking out over science things. Not spending enough time on the weird stuff.

Reynold was astonished. Reynold said, "John, there's no mass... or perceivable mass."

John was prying the words out of Reynold's mouth and said: "and therefore?"

Reynold's eyes widened. He said, "No acceleration!"

John said, "No acceleration!" John bounced with excitement. If he had a dog's tail, it would beat against anything, ignoring the pain to transmit pure joy. "Light doesn't accelerate! It goes the speed of light. Now wrap a protective electromagnetic shell around stuff you want to travel with, making it a compressed package turning it into an enclosed vehicle. That EM package is going the speed of light, making that shell and everything inside the fastest thing on the planet!"

Nora looked at the two grown men geeking out over jibber jabber. "Who cares? So what? A formula worked?"

Reynold said, "Nora, this is huge. If going the speed of light requires no acceleration, instead of turning a human into a lot of chunky red goo by the end of a trip to the outer planets, you'd get there in one piece, and quickly. Well, at light speed, a few hours, but this is still huge. Like Einstein may be looking for a job. E no longer equals m-c squared. What would that formula look like? OK, ok, ok. How does this all fit together? I mean, you have the electromagnetic field tamed, and power. What next? John Clarke Maxwell came up with formulae in the 1800s for this. That man was BRILLIANT. He discovered that electromagnetic waves traveled at the speed of light."

"That's where the harder formulas worked. Actually, we will address how his formulas acted upon those molecules as soon as this experiment is over. I think that's where we will get the acceleration from," John started... but he noticed something out of the corner of his eye. "Wait, what time is it?"

Reynold looked at his smartwatch. He marveled its ability to be 100% accurate time. "10:21am."

John directed them to an empty table surrounded by tripods holding cell phones in four locations. The phones were recording nothing?

John began. "So I made five devices. One had an... unfortunate... accident," Reynold made a *huh* face and John continued, "I don't want to talk about it... but after creating the other four, I charged the batteries, expecting more tests... well, what would have been an experiment. The device first generates the electromagnetic field, which surrounds it and the user like a bubble. The earth has such a powerful electromagnetic field, it stretches out and blasts the moon with it when the moon is full. It's why seeing the moon helps charge the devices. Our electromagnetic field gets stretched by the solar winds while still protecting the earth. I borrow that electromagnetic field. I used the cell phones to video what it was experiencing, plus to take readings of surrounding environment and showing vibrations, and fixed the timers in the devices for two minutes as an initial speed test. I'll make fancy digital displays and adjustments later. The field takes exactly a minute to output and surrounds the device, and whatever is in contact with it. One minute is excruciatingly long. I'll fix that during phase two of this project. But once there, the device detects the field and empties the capacitor immediately, so the device and anything within the field instantaneously goes the speed of light. The crazy thing is, once I hit the button and the EM field formed, a minute later it... Disappeared. We can't see it. I'll review all the recordings when we complete this experiment. Since the electromagnetic field is the same natural field surrounding the planet, it envelopes the device and the phone with a comfortable margin. It's slightly more powerful than the field surrounding the earth because it's only surrounding whatever or whoever is holding the device. It did all that with no need to know its surroundings. It just did it. I'll analyze more when I get more data, but for the first experiment, it seems to be working great."

Nora interrupted, "Wait, two minutes? Well... where is it? When did you start this? We've been here longer than two minutes."

"I started it at exactly 9:54am," and as if on cue, the table lit up briefly with a light that wasn't any more dramatic than a bulb getting brighter, then dimmed. The time was now 10:22am, and a rectangular object appeared as if by magic with a phone sitting on top, like the letter T upside down. It dropped a little onto a pair of small square wood dowels waiting for its return and rocked a little, but no more than if someone had held it about a half centimeter too high and let go rather than placing it on the table. The LED on the side glowed red, but blinked yellow within a few seconds. It was now charging.

They stared amazed at the unimpressive entrance of a box no larger than a thin book, with the cell phone sitting vertically on top of a stand that held the phone upright, recording the experience. John and Reynold were kids in a toy shop and couldn't contain themselves. Both stared at it, wondering if they could safely touch it.

After some loud whooping and hollering, Reynold broke the excitement and reached for the box to touch it. "It doesn't feel out of the ordinary. In fact... it's not even as warm as my laptop gets when I'm using it. For the effort that was just exerted, I was expecting some physical reaction." It felt completely normal. Some crazy things were happening. There was data to look at. "What is the cell phone recording?"

John was soaking it all in. Holy shit. It worked. He hesitated, then responded, "Environment, G forces, vibration, temperature, but most important is the time to five digits accuracy. Plus perfectly recording 360 degrees around it. There are 180 degree lenses on both sides of the phone."

Reynold said, "Let's see it." He picked up the phone and asked, "Can we play it on the TV over there?" John had the display ready. Hitting play from the phone, the screen counted a long time for the first minute, but after that... sheer excitement. Everything outside the periphery of the camera was going super fast. The video frames were blurring along at breakneck speed. The world around the phone had taken uppers while the phone rested peacefully. Nothing even jarred it. The temperature didn't change for the entire video when people rushed into the view of the lens as if rocketed there.

Reynold thought out loud, "Since the EM field is encapsulating the contents, couldn't we also use this so we can transmit... US, using modern communications? Like a transporter?"

John responded, "Uh... well, yes. However, using the fastest communication, the electromagnetic bubble, and its contents, assuming one megabyte per cell of your body, taking into consideration the complexities of DNA, and all that makes it hold together, assuming about thirty-seven trillion cells in your body, ignoring the clothing you are wearing at the moment, which calculates to three point eight to the nineteenth power of bytes or thirty-eight exabytes of information, it would take three billion days, thirteen minutes and twenty seconds to download. So plus or minus ten million years to beam yourself to China at a gigabit communications speed. Now you can't compare that to an eighteen hour flight in first class. Not to mention, that information would be going the speed of light."

Nora was unimpressed. "Ok, you made it a longer trip now. It may take years for the airline industry to stop laughing at you. There are only three minutes of video. You said it started at 9:54, but that was about twenty-eight minutes ago. Where're the other twenty minutes?"

Reynold looked at John, who was looking at him with his eyebrows raised as high as possible. Reynold's eyes widened, then he blurted out, "TIME DILATION!"

In his best English accent, John said, “By jove, Watson, you're RIGHT! That was the final calculation. We're not going the speed of light exactly, but if twenty-seven to twenty-eight minutes is accurate, and I saw twenty-seven minutes, thirty-one seconds from the cameras here. That calculation would prove that the device was going 299,000.458 kilometers per second or 185,790.271 miles per second. Now we ARE seven-hundred-ninety-two kilometers per second slower than light speed, but the fastest rocket on earth can only go twenty-seven kilometers per second. Let's double it to say fifty-four kilometers per second. This speed is," he paused dramatically and took a deep breath, then finished, "... more!"

Reynold stared silently for five seconds then screamed "DAMN!" This was the closest Reynold came to cursing.

Nora said, "But it went... nowhere?"

"It really did. Right now our perception of it is skewed. That's the thing," John interjected for his now surprised friend. "We have the vessel, the electromagnetic field or shell is acting as our *boat*. For the sake of discussing things in human terms. What's missing is propulsion. This isn't a bad start. We're looking at a moment where we have a device that IS going the speed of light, more accurately DAMN close. It's a huge discovery. We may only need a flashlight to propel us since we don't have mass at light speed. We'll do piles of experiments before we talk about propulsion of any kind. The field is giving protection in our current environment on the ground here which keeps a chunk of the atmosphere also going the speed of light. I was hoping for that bit of information. I was curious thinking about how this would work, but the earth creates the electromagnetic barrier that envelopes us all naturally. It keeps us safe from radioactive solar winds. I'm borrowing a little of that since the earth is generating it constantly. I'm taking a tiny bit that it wasn't using, anyway. Reynold helped so much with these formulas, I'm giving him a lot of the credit. Your TV at home beams an image going the speed of light captured on a screen in front of you. It's contained. Think of the bubble containing your cells going the speed of light."

Nora watched the giddy scientists. "So what. You're the fastest nerds in history? Anyway, shouldn't you name the device?"

John looked at Reynold and Nora and said, "You both *need* to come for the second test. Nora, you can give an outsider's opinion. It's perfectly safe, as you can see. Barely a blip, and three minutes of your time. You know, Reynold... I like her. Now I see why you have a mad crush on her."

Nora looked at them and said, "Reynold has... a crush on me? What?"

Reynold glared at John hard enough to make his eyes ache.

Nora said, “Hey, was the name of the test dummy in the movie *Contact* Edger or Elmer?”

7

HUEY LEWIS WAS HERE

The three let the moment sink in and they continued to the next phase. Reviewing the video took another hour. The footage revealed the precise speed of the actual test, using time dilation to back solve. It may not have covered space, but it covered time.

John said, "Approaching the speed of light is fine. Except the closer we get to it, time-dilation intensifies approaching infinity. Once that's achieved, the surrounding relativity also increases, and you can't measure how much time will become dilated."

The recordings revealed that the atmosphere within the EM bubble didn't change during the experiment. There was no measurable vibration. They compared to the videos taken in the room where vibration registered nearby air-conditioning motors and passing cars. Internal temperature, pressure, and atmosphere were all normal. A human could breathe within that static bubble for about twenty-three minutes. For a two-minute trip, this wouldn't tax the quantity or quality of that atmosphere. The device didn't have enough power to function for longer than three minutes.

Further review of the video showed that anything happening outside the bubble looked like a mist. It would be impossible to capture details unless they had a camera capable recording of hundreds of thousands of frames per second. An outsider would perceive a light, no brighter than a 40-watt bulb getting brighter, then turning off. The excitement of a lightbulb turning on. They reviewed the video the phones captured in all directions. A red-dot showed you the orientation of the device while recording. They watched on the larger screen on the wall while one of them turned the phone in the direction they wanted to see captured.

They had three charged devices. The math worked out. It had all the markings of going no place FAST and living twenty-seven and a half fewer minutes in *real time*. A test would cost them three minutes of their lives, so they agreed to do it together. It seemed perfectly safe.

They took another half hour to set up the cameras and had lunch. After that, an exciting three minute journey to no place fast. They placed the cameras to record from four different points of view: one from the corner of the room, and one for each person.

John captured everything on the smartphones he bought. Apps existed to do ANYTHING. This app captured the temperature, air sensors, atmosphere pressure, and sensors from 3-axis motion sensor thousands of times a second. It could capture 400 frames a second in slow motion, synchronizing all the sensors, plus a time-track to see how much time had elapsed precisely per frame. One unique feature caught John's eye: the ability to start in slow-motion to review details for thirty minutes. After that hurdle, the program switched to sixty frames a second recording, then switched to time-lapsed recording, keeping only a few frames a second. Plugging in the phones gave almost unlimited recording ability. Even without power, the phone's built-in battery lasted over nine hours. So they became the perfect companion for experiments. They would hold three more phones to record within the EM bubbles.

Nora wanted to break some serious speed limits. She had taken driver's education using a seventies muscle car, and she missed the acceleration compared to her car. She wondered if this moment would become part of the next *Fast and Furious* franchise? Fast and Furious for NERDS. They wouldn't propel themselves through walls nor go through a window. No mass meant no propulsion yet.

Nora listened to an endless stream of excited vociferations from the two nerdy mad scientists. Were they even speaking ENGLISH? They kept repeating, "HOW COOL! blah blah blah blah WOW HOW COOL blah blah blah." One day she'd turn the tables on them, and it would be a joyous moment for her. "Do you know why the signing of the Magna Carter in the year 1215 is significant... HMMM?" She wanted to see and revel in their surprised blank stares at that moment.

The device had a single multi-color LED that blinked yellow when in "Charging" mode. Green meant go. It glowed red after the superconducting capacitor depleted itself. The device had only two buttons. One was to pre-synchronize with the other devices, which made the LED blink green twice in acknowledgment on the other devices. This way, one device controlled all three devices. Once they synchronized all three devices, one of them would hit the start button. At five seconds before the device hit light speed, the green LED would blink twice per second. At light speed, the green LED blinked once per second. Count the blinks to 115 until the last 5 seconds before the cycle completes, then the

LED blinks twice as fast, and there's your two minutes. Super plain, super simple. Either the timer would turn them off, or the power would run out, whichever came first. The device fit into pants or a jacket pocket, so Nora put hers in her pocket and held the recording phone in her hands, as had John and Reynold.

The moment of truth approached.

What would it be like? They would start the devices at noon. When the time came, John hit the synchronization button, and counted down, "5. 4. 3. 2. 1." and pressed the *go* button.

Silence. Like having a pair of the BEST noise canceling headphones over your ears. The world around the bubble seemed cut off. All three bubbles lifted their occupants off the floor by about an inch and then formed a single giant bubble surrounding them. They heard each other breathing, and John said aloud, "I think the bubbles merged." The fascinating sensations kept them from talking within the complete silence.

Seven years earlier, the anti-matter produced by a dark star turned into a black hole and escaped its gravity. That *space pollution* aimed with precision towards the earth. The gravitational pull from nine planets slingshot the anti-matter and corrected its trajectory. It lined up on a direct course to its final destination just above the atmosphere. Another dark star located three hundred twenty-four light years away produced a focused gamma radiation pulse. The gravitational field of thirty planets and stars corrected the course until it reached the exact same point above the earth's atmosphere. With similar ingredients and circumstances of the big bang, both of the energy waves collided, forming an Einstein-Rosen bridge wormhole 20 nanometers in circumference which hovered 400 miles above the surface of the earth. It was twenty times the size of a glucose molecule.

The EM bubble was almost formed at fifty seconds, and the wormhole raced towards them. With nothing going the speed of light and nothing large enough to enter the wormhole, it passed through a satellite, the international space station, and a jet airliner, and passed through the ceiling of their office on the ground floor the same way radio waves penetrate building walls and hovered directly above them within 2 thousandths of a second of its formation, and disappeared immediately after.

Just as the timer hit one minute, the bubble was moving at near the speed of light. Within nanoseconds, the wormhole increased in size and encompassed the combined EM bubble with the three occupants, and swallowed it. The EM bubble and its speed opened the wormhole.

Above the office building, the clouds formed a neat blanket. When the wormhole swallowed the bubble, a sky punch went through the clouds in the form of the circle above the roof. The noon sun shone through the hole in the clouds, spotlighting the exterior of the office building as if it had a solo in a play. Two people walking on Washington Street witnessed the strange hole in the clouds and emailed the photos to a local weatherman who brushed it off as a prank.

The Laser Interferometer Gravitational-Wave Observatory, known as LIGO observatory, was founded to study astrophysics through the direct detection of the waves predicted by Einstein's General Theory of Relativity. Reviewing the logs and readings, scientists noticed a spike closest to the Louisiana facility. The amount of energy readings were off the scale of ordinary. Since it came from just above the atmosphere, then shifted instantaneously six feet above sea level for a fraction of a second and not outer space, they circled the results and labeled it as an anomaly. Eighteen years later, an MIT student named Jocelyn Bell reviewing yards and yards of log printouts discovered the wormhole that existed for 2 thousandths of a second. It would take her another year to prove the results, and track exactly what happened, which would become the thesis for her doctorate in astrophysics. When she approached her professor about her findings, he burst out laughing, rudely yelled, "SHUT THE FRONT DOOR," which she did and sat down in the chair across from his desk. He then called someone, repeating, "It existed for only 2 thousandths of a second, WOW," over and over. When she accepted her Nobel Prize for this, she repeated this confusing story to the amusement of the audience watching world-wide.

The traversal through the wormhole was perceivable to John, Nora, and Reynold as a pressure change in their ears, as they suddenly felt a little congested. Around them, their vision picked up a blurring of the corners of their eyes with blue and red streaks coming toward them, contrary to the sensation that their bodies were perfectly still. Their feet seemed disconnected from the ground, and yet they weren't floating as if in zero gravity. They would need to review the video of their time in the bubble so they could see the differences with this trip compared to its initial journey. They were at the mercy of the wormhole.

Within the bubble, the imagery stayed unfocused. The rushing of the surrounding scene was like watching a video at an extremely high speed. There was no frame of reference. Two minutes seemed to last an eternity to them. Something different was happening. Because of the pressure change, John became concerned with the differences from the first inconsequential trip. Nobody talked for the entire two minutes, as life within the field seemed unreal and impossible to describe.

The EM field was about to collapse in a few seconds as the LEDs on the devices blinked in double time, indicating the last five seconds. Reynold and John didn't understand what had changed from the first experiment. Perhaps the mass from the three individuals, or the merging of the three bubbles, but something was different. Within the bubble, their mass was meaningless. The bubble counted as their *craft* satisfying Isaac Newton's laws. Objects at rest stayed at rest. When a force acts on mass, it accelerates. They had no mass, so no acceleration. For every action, there is an equal and opposite reaction. Here, the EM bubble was their vessel, so inside was their own set of relative behaviors. They traveled near light speed, and within the bubble, they were safe from the relativity outside. It couldn't do anything differently, but their instinct told them something had changed the outcome.

The EM bubble evaporated, and they fell seven inches. Like they were walking up stairs and thought they missed a huge extra step. The temperature seemed much cooler. All three sprouted an endless supply of goosebumps. They landed on their feet, except for Reynold, who landed with one of his feet on a higher root. This caused him to go down on one knee, making a distinctive dent in the mud. His knee squished into the thick wet goo. Something went wrong with Elmer, he thought.

They stood within a dense pack of mature trees, shielding them from their surroundings. It wasn't a forest, but enough to prevent them from seeing everything around them.

Mechanical noise was eerily absent the same way a loud noise was shocking to the system. They absorbed their situation, stunned that their office was gone. It was like a magic trick. They were undoubtedly in the wrong place. There would be considerable debris if an accident had destroyed the office. There shouldn't be an outcropping of thick trunk, unscathed trees around them. The trees didn't seem grown by any pattern, and they surrounded them in various sizes, from two feet in diameter, to older trees of nine feet circumference. The trio took turns looking around them beyond the trees. In one direction, they could see a dirt road, and in the opposite direction, they saw the back of a short, squat stone building. The thing that was stranger still was the complete absence of light around them. It was very dark. If they started the experiment at noon, how long did this trip take?

From the direction of the stone building, they could hear noise. It was bizarre. Their ears picked up the smallest sounds, like wearing the most detailed headphones. It was disorienting without mechanical noise. Everything they heard sounded familiar but isolated.

Out of the corner of their eye, they saw a dog... wait, not a dog. That was a wild dog. No. That was a wolf confidently walking around, keeping its distance. Had they been blasted deep into the countryside?

The temperature felt cooler than the office they were just standing in, and they rubbed their arms for warmth until they acclimated to the temperature. They stood silent for a moment longer in shock, trying to digest their current surroundings.

Nora whispered, "Ok you nerds. Where the hell are we?"

8

WHERE ARE WE?

"Where the hell are we?" Nora repeated. She was standing in wet mud that hadn't been there before they turned on the gizmos.

John stood rooted in place. "Oh shit, shit, shit," he whispered. "I... have a terrible, terrible feeling about this." In the coolness, his nervousness caused him to sweat profusely, giving him a chill.

Reynold looked at him and said in his most sarcastic tone, "Really? 100 points for being obvious."

John snapped back, "It's now dawn! We hit the button at noon. It should be 12:27 and 31 seconds, but it's fricking dawn!"

Reynold said, "I've known you for a long time. When did you become a time savant? How do you know it's dawn?"

John pointed at the sun rising. "There's the east toward that wood building, and that's the sun peeking over the horizon."

John spun Reynold around ninety degrees until he faced the North Star. "Polaris. That's Polaris... better known as the North Star. The Little Dipper spins around it, but it stays in our north." He turned Reynold ninety degrees back towards the sun. "That's the rising of the Sun. Venus is completely out of place. Last night the sun set in the west and Venus chased it. Look east and a little right, *there is Venus*!" he pointed. Reynold could make out the outline of a brightly lit planet. When had John become an astronomer?

John pondered that he had never seen such intense darkness. There are so many stars! So damn distracting. It was like someone had radically increased their luminescence.

Reynold asked, "How can a planet be out of place?"

"That's what I'm saying. Planets don't suddenly shift. Venus doesn't follow that path until the fall around early October. Nothing propelled us, so we're at least six months or more into the future. Perhaps someone cleaned Venus because it looks crystal clear. We must have approached the speed of light, which exponentially added to the time dilation." John continued, "So twenty-seven and a half minutes of dilation from the first experiment is nothing. We may have reappeared in the distant or distant, DISTANT future. The building we started in IS GONE! So, Nora, it's not where the hell are we, it's when!" John wiped sweat from his brow to emphasize his point. His stress levels messed his body's functions, and he sweat even more.

Nora looked towards the east at a building about eighty yards away and noticed a man standing guard. She also heard... moaning? "Guys, are you so sure? There's someone over there. Should we ask him?" The man stood at attention with a tall stick next to him. Strange that. "Also, what about that gravestone Reynold found? And I don't want to go all *tree huggy* on you, but these trees are enormous, mature, American chestnut trees, unaffected by blight."

John ignored her and blurted out, "Let's establish right

now it's impossible to travel in time. That gravestone is definitely an anomaly. The only direction we can go is forward, Ms. Tree Hugger," John tersely responded. He immediately regretted his choice of words after Nora icily stared at him, showing he wasn't making friends.

They stood in a solid group of trees, but they thinned out after thirty feet. Beyond the edge of the trees, Nora pointed to the person she had spotted who was standing in front of a solid, short building. Still too dark to understand what was happening, they gawked at him. The man had a lit lantern next to him, the only discernible detail. The lantern seemed to be burning something, and flickering, possibly oil? Is it a candle? So hard to tell in this darkness. Nora thought, "You don't see *that* every day."

They stood there and stared. It was jarring to be standing in wet mud in the woods without wanting to get out.

They waited for a few minutes as some light added to their confusion rather than taking it away.

"Could we have moved?" Reynold wasn't thrilled about asking that question. He didn't believe this, but everything around them seemed utterly foreign.

"To take an educated guess," John replied and considered each word of his response, "we stayed in the same place. I'm not sure what happened to the building. There is no evidence of the foundation. That's not an easy task. But everything that was around us four minutes ago is gone." John had few answers. "These trees around us are mature. Many years old. We moved into the future. FAR into the future. At least one hundred years or more." He let it sink in. Everyone they loved was dead. "I screwed up, guys. This totally sucks."

They were in shock and couldn't react.

Reynold said, "Do you guys notice how quiet it is? There are no sounds of machinery. No sounds of airplanes, no sounds of highways, no sounds of cars." His mind went into overdrive. What was happening? How did they get here? Were they propelled? The walls should have stopped them. Why weren't they harmed if the experiment destroyed the building? How did they end up within this crop of trees without destroying the branches above them? Any rush of nerves usually prompted him to just want to take a breath of his inhaler and calm himself down. He didn't feel he needed it at all. That was strange too.

Reynold thought the surrounding smells were more natural. It smelled like a bunch of cows and horses just took a crap nearby. Probably took a few turns doing it. Stinky, but... natural. Like low tide.

As the sun inched higher, the person standing in the distance in front of the wood and stone building became more defined. He seemed out of place in time. He stood there rigid next to a pile of stones.

Nora finally spoke. "This isn't right. Look at that guy over there. The outfit he's wearing looks quaint and out of place. It looks less modern, as strange as this sounds. That guy is standing guard next to what looks like a pile of rocks. What the heck is that about?" Nora was just as focused as John and Reynold on figuring out their mystery.

The sun wasn't helping. It was chilly. Since they were New Englanders, their blood thickened up. As children, they grew up knowing waiting five minutes changed the weather. All they needed was time. The weather gods were always temperamental. This felt... different. It felt like the fall. The air was devoid of humidity.

They stared at each other, trying not to draw attention to themselves, merely thinking. The shock kept them silent.

John took out his phone. No Signal? That's strange. He searched for wireless network signals. Zilch. He looked at his mapping software, and it couldn't find any GPS satellites. He thought they were in the future and maybe people weren't using these frequencies anymore? Houses looked like all wood structures. That building near them looked like a squat stone and wood structure. If society continued on the path it was following, the population would increase, not decrease. Did something wipe out everyone? A plague? Cataclysmic War? Were they sitting in some strange dystopian future, now in need of running for their lives? Would someone attack them for their appendixes? John imagined alien beings or zombies shouting, "Now we know what it's for, give us your appendix!" He got the chills thinking about it. Why didn't he pay attention during biology? John said, "Hey Reynold, do you still have your appendix?"

Reynold glared at John. He somehow knew what his friend was thinking.

It was so damn quiet. Wherever or whenever they were, this seemed like technology was missing, not overwhelming. The constant mechanical sounds he always had surrounding him were silenced. He was aware of his own breathing and belly gurgles and became self-conscious, wondering if Nora and John heard them too. He had lived between two highways when in college and the constant noise seemed like it was missing from his ears. The trees they stood in couldn't be blocking all the noise. They saw a few houses. The houses' color palate seemed to comprise dull gray and duller gray. Had people forgotten how to paint wood? Only a few had windows. Some looked boarded up. Actually, they looked like doors instead of windows. Were they boarded up for security, or an approaching storm?

What about protection from radiation or a cataclysmic problem they had experienced? Did they make advanced materials that looked like wood?

The smells bothered them. Not counting the endless cow poop smell, it smelled like ozone from after a thunderstorm. It seemed to linger rather than dissipate. The air was also... to describe with a word, heavier? What was that about? Everything is closer to nature, not further away. If a plague had wiped away the population of the planet, you'd think it would look like the houses had survived and nature was swallowing it up. This seemed different. The building they had been in when they started the experiment was completely gone, replaced by the small patch of trees that was giving them some refuge.

The sun kept rising, and they became increasingly braver. They approached the edge of the trees and saw roads. There were areas that vehicles could use if they dared and had fantastic shock absorbers. Rocks and mud were everywhere. The roads were unfinished, even for dirt roads. Where was the damn pavement? Cement?

People were waking up and starting their day, but it was a prolonged process. An occasional window-opening door thing would creak outwards. They were in a foreign place and wanted to remain concealed. They wordlessly understood to proceed with great caution. Stay out of where a bull's eye could be on them. Don't become a target.

People gathered near the person with the lantern and stick. He now looked like he wore a nostalgic uniform and held a tall rifle. Another soldier came and relieved him, then continued to stand guard next to the pile of rocks. The sun rose higher, and they watched. Finally, Nora said, "Whatever that man is guarding over there is important, but who the heck guards rocks? People are now gathering in that area. They're wearing such strange clothing. They sort of remind me of... pilgrim paintings. I know it sounds fantastic, but that's what these people look like."

John replied in a hushed tone. "I don't understand... I keep hearing people talk. I pick up a word occasionally, but it sounds like strong British accents. Could England re-acquire the United States?"

Reynold whispered his reply, "The road behind us is a dirt road. I'd swear it's like a thinner *rock and dirt* version of Washington Street. I can't put my finger on it. There are no cars, trucks, or motorcycles. Unless everything is electric now? I haven't seen vehicles of any kind.

"And don't laugh, but does the atmosphere smell sort of cleaner?" Reynold asked.

"What do you mean? It's really smelly... like how much livestock is close by?" Nora replied. Nora got an idea and walked away from them.

"Yes, it's quite strange. Other than the complete... stench, the air seems to be more... natural." Reynold considered this, but it seemed hard to put a word to it. There had to be more to this puzzle. He also thought, "hmm... where did Nora just go?"

Nora returned a few moments later. John asked, "What did you investigate?"

Nora replied, "Uh... nothing. I didn't... investigate."

John looked at her curiously. "Where did you go?"

"Uhm, I had a *need*," she said, opening her eyes widely.

Reynold looked at her. "You found a bathroom?"

She gawked at the two supposedly smart people in front of her. "Haven't either of you gone camping? I had to pee and didn't need a hall pass!"

John and Reynold looked at each other, simultaneously trying to block out the one time they had to share a hotel room for a conference, which was roughing it enough.

John looked at Reynold and said, "They must have cleaned the atmosphere. We may be a few hundred years in the future guys, maybe longer. I'm fixated on how large these trees are. They've been here a while. It makes no sense, but trees are trees and grow the same way no matter what. They didn't move them here. What's around us is crazy, but it's here. This is our reality." He let that sink in. His brain was trying to wrap around how screwed they were. What would they use for currency? Did they close their bank accounts? If they were still open, were they millionaires now from compound interest?

"My friends and family may be dead?" Nora said. She was in shock from this revelation. Nora would need to schedule a time to be really upset. Excitement and intense curiosity kept her emotions in check. "That's the last time I go out to breakfast with a damn physicist," she said under her breath.

John began. "For the moment, we don't know. Without propulsion, we traveled in time, not space. I'm certain of that. So time-dilation has rocketed us forward. How far, I just don't know. Without reviewing the cameras in the office, it's impossible to know."

Reynold said, "How could we have sped up beyond the speed of the first experiment?"

John looked at him wide-eyed and calmly said, "I don't know. I just don't know. That's the only thing that makes sense. We went forward in time. The calculations... well, mental calculations right now point to that."

Nora said, "You guys are smart. Can't we go back to where... sorry... when we started?"

John said, "Nothing can go back in time. The only direction we can travel in time is forward by living it, or dilating it. I created the experiment to go the ultimate speed limit, or at least close. Well, we did it. Now what?"

They were numb. Maybe they were years in the future. Time dragged onward. They kept quiet as life stirred around their outcropping of trees. More people were on the streets, and they were afraid of alerting them to their presence. Knowing they were in such an unfamiliar situation made them stay quiet.

Occasionally they mused about what animal made the dung smell that bombarded them.

Without the internet, nor activities, and functioning phones, they stared at their surroundings. Eventually, they decided that venturing out seemed more interesting than waiting to be discovered.

People walked by, wearing pilgrim outfits made of thick cloth. They were from another century altogether. Perhaps there was a costume party they were all attending? Some wore tan work slacks, and a few had out-of-place puffy white shirts, but that was the closest to the clothing they recognized as normal.

Nora said, "We need to investigate. Those rocks and that crowd are puzzling. Sitting here isn't solving our problems. We need to know what's happening."

John said, "Nora is right. Let's follow them and see why they're standing around those rocks. I'm curious as heck, and if we don't move soon, we may explode." They counted to five, stood up, then caught up with the next group walking past them, eavesdropping on their conversation and walking toward the field across the street from the squat building. Then they saw a man ride up on a horse and dismount gracefully. He put a walking cane under his arm and strode toward the rocks. Judging from the position of the sun, it looked like it was now noon.

Reynold discreetly looked at his watch. The digital readout read **6:55pm*. Without a frame of reference, nor the ability to set itself, his watch had stoically stayed in the last time zone it remembered. It added an *asterisk* next to the time indicating some problem with its accuracy. It said, "Hey, I'm not able to call my friends to figure out the real time. You're on your own, buddy."

As the trio approached the crowd, they saw that their reactions to the rocks varied from horror to amusement. Is this their entertainment? Why? Wouldn't they have 3D TV or whatever modern entertainment existed in the future? What is important about these stupid rocks in front of this building? Do these people worship stones?

"Giles Corey, what say you?" the horseman's voice boomed loudly. Nora, John, and Reynold stood close to the people they had followed. All of their outfits came out of another century. Nora was spot on. Were they in the place that produced every single pilgrim painting ever made? So strange. The outfits didn't seem comfortable; they looked stiff. There wore mostly dark-colored outfits. Nobody wore clean clothing except for the man speaking to the rocks, and his outfit seemed more aristocratic, and his voice sounded like lower class British. Almost cockney.

Now standing near the crowd, Reynold thought nobody around them ever bathed.

“Giles Corey, what say you?” the man boomed again, louder this time, and emphasizing each word.

John and Reynold thought, “Who is he speaking to?” Nora stared in shock at the pile of rocks as the truth dawned on her.

Reynold sensed the change and whispered, "You ok?"

Nora quickly responded, "Yes. I'll tell you when we're alone."

The aristocratic man looked down at the rocks. Upon closer inspection, a man's contorted face was barely visible under the stones crushing him. His face was horribly red and swollen, as if he had a terrible allergic reaction or as if someone pumped him with a lot of air. He looked ghastly, and yet they couldn't look away. His eyes bulged out of his head. The horror was real.

The crowd quieted to hear his answer. At first, the man with the loud voice yelled, "I don't hear you! Speak up, will ya! Speak up for all to 'ear! The court needs your plea! Ya can't keep it silent any longer! The court will rule that your last will and testament is null and void. You wrote it in prison and can't get it authenticated, so staying silent will not protect your family's land. Speak up!"

The man under the rocks seemed to move a little. He made only small amounts of noise. The man tried to talk but could only make raspy gurgling sounds. He couldn't catch his breath. When the man attempted to speak, his tongue popped out of his mouth, and he couldn't get it back in. The loud man walked over and shoved it back in with the point of his cane, making the man under the rocks angrier. Finally, a loud unearthly voice came out of him. It was like nothing Nora, Reynold, and John had heard before. Giles cried out, "MORE!! WEIGHT!!" with his remaining breath and then stopped breathing. The rocks didn't even collapse, but settled in place and stopped moving.

From his lack of movement, and a now frozen, contorted expression on his face, it was clear he had died. His mouth drooled thick black bile from it.

The three of them stood within the crowd, equally

dismayed. They had a new horrible drama to think about. The crowd murmured amongst themselves.

After a few minutes, the people in the crowd turned their attention to the three strangers standing behind them. Reynold was feeling eyes on him, as he had never felt before. He had never stuck out like this. He stood out because he was always smarter and excelled in his grades. That made him stick out. But this time, he could feel he didn't fit in at all, but he couldn't put his finger on it. The people around him spoke with thicker than usual English accents. They were dressed in these thick wool outfits which ignited his wool allergy, which made him mentally itch just thinking about it. Could it be their clothing? Could it be his clothing? Reynold thought the crowd wasn't focused on that. The people were staring directly at him. He knew it. The only people that weren't staring were the guard, and the man with the cane who had been screaming at the deceased guy named Giles under all the rocks. This was a strange sensation he hadn't felt in a long time.

"Why are they looking at me?" Reynold whispered to John and Nora.

It was Nora's turn to contribute answers to their situation. She knew the answers. "Damn!" she whispered, "... because you're black." She was pleased to see that John and Reynold had, in fact, practiced their surprised blank stares.

9

HOW DID WE GET HERE?

They watched the crowd disperse, hurried past their trees, and ducked into them, retreating to the safety of the woods. Nora took pride in knowing more about what was going on. They maintained their surprised looks and gave Nora the full floor of attention.

"Guys, now it's time for me to school you. You are right. We are still in Salem, Massachusetts, in the exact place where or when we left. But it is September 19th, 1692 at exactly noon. Also," Nora abruptly looked at John and made air quotes, "... Mister, it's impossible to travel in time owes me an ingratiating apology." Nora said with a tone of finality.

"What proof do you have of that? How can you give us a time and date? And what did you mean it's because I'm black? Are you telling me you have an objection to that?" Reynold talked with an annoyed whisper that sounded like a shout in the stillness of the woods.

Reynold's stressed brain rewound to the time when a police officer had pulled him over. His heart raced, and his palms and forehead became uncontrollably sweaty, and he was short of breath. He had instant recall of the headlines of black people being pulled over for minor things, only to result in them being shot or killed because of the officers irrational fear of the situation. Police officers know there are more guns than people in the country. The chance of a traffic violator carrying a gun is high. The officer that pulled Reynold over told him his blinker was still on from a turn he had made a mile earlier, and he calmed down a little. If the officer hadn't explained that, Reynold would have passed out from a panic attack.

Reynold ignored the sweat forming on his palms now. He took a deep breath and tried to show Nora he could hold it together and get them through this somehow.

Nora explained. "Giles Corey was the only person in the history of the United States tortured for not giving a response to a judge who asked *how do you plea*? as in guilty or not guilty. Someone accused Giles in the oyer and terminer court of being a witch. Right over there is the site of the original jail used during those trials. In our original *now*, that is the corner of *Federal Street* and *Saint Peter's Street*, but it's named *Prison Street* now. Reynold, we're in the late 1600s. Unless you're a sailor, black men don't have the rights you have in our *now*. Many people are indentured servants to companies that sponsor them to the New World. Oh and one more thing, almost all the American Chestnut trees taller than fifteen feet in North America died from blight brought in from Asia in the early 20th century. Oh and Reynold... I'm not going to eat you."

"How are you so sure that wasn't a reenactment? And don't you mean Warlock?" John asked.

Nora gave him an icy stare and drove her point home. A glare from a woman is as obvious a thing as removing one's vocal cords. Darth Vader used a hand gesture to silence people. Women use a glare. She continued, "This moment in history is embarrassing. Nobody reenacts it. Being a witch was worse than being a murderer. These people believe in witches as much as they believe in their church. Satan is something they hear about daily. I think eleven people have already hanged for being witches, two of them men. Five died in jails around Salem. This is the very place and time in the world that defined *witch hunt* because they would accuse you and then make up the evidence. They would claim that your mind could invade someone's dreams, or could spook animals by manifesting your *living ghost*, and the animals would jump. They hanged you for pleading innocent. You couldn't even say the proceedings weren't legal because they were for this time period. Each person accused could have witnesses. They saw the judges in the highest court in the colony, and a jury of their peers decided their fates. The courts documented their individual testimony, and how the *star witnesses* - the afflicted girls in the area helped convict the accused. The evidence could be as ridiculous as my cow's milk dried up because that woman bewitched it. A woman or servant couldn't convict a man of domestic abuse unless they used the context of witchcraft. Women didn't have rights. The girls accusing them couldn't convict them for scolding them or poor treatment, but they could come out and point and say his image as a witch yelled, beat, or abused me. The towns around Salem have a few hundred accused witches sitting in jails right now who are slowly dying from the horrible conditions. Giles Corey was the clue about when and where we are, but how did we get here... urm... now? John said nothing can go back in time?"

Reynold said, "Hey, I think Jonathan Swift is 29. He hasn't written about Gulliver's travels yet. We can meet him!

Or how about Jethro Tull? We should ask him why a flute player would adopt HIS name, and play Rock Flute. Who does that? Sir Isaac Newton isn't even a Sir yet. He's about 49 now. We should send him a note to tell him we are super big fans. Or just say a simple thanks. How about Benjamin Franklin's father? Josiah is in Boston someplace, making candles which we'll need for survival, anyway. Let's buy a bunch of candles so young Benjamin can get another year of schooling, so he becomes a school drop out at 12 instead of 11. Leibniz is someplace in Europe and alive. Maybe we can challenge his ideas about CALCULUS at this point since we know it BETTER THAN HE DOES?"

Nora looked at John and said, "Hello - these chestnut trees? Nobody in our lifetime has seen American Chestnut trees this big, ever. You should be happy and furious about that!"

John looked at Reynold and Nora and said through clenched teeth, "Will you two CALM DOWN! There has got to be a reason for this. Nora, do you know a lot about this specific point in history? Any survival tips will come in handy dandy."

John then had an epiphany and grabbed the phone from his pocket and reviewed the video from the experiment without saying a word. Two minutes later, he held out his hands and said, "Give me the phones we used for the recordings!" Nora and Reynold shoved the phones into John's hands. Until now, reviewing the video didn't seem necessary. They assumed they had gone forward in time.

John reviewed the video, holding it level. When he rotated it upwards, he saw a glass bubble, and when he looked down, he saw the muddy area. This was entirely different from the first trip in the original experiment.

Nine minutes later, John's face was ashen. "This will

sound fantastic. What I'm about to say will make Reynold a little giddy, so stay quiet until I finish. We definitely traveled through an Einstein-Rosen bridge that opened and swallowed our EM bubble. Now I don't understand if we formed it or... where the heck it came from. But above our head was a glass globe that matched our speed, and it seemed to blow up like a balloon which swallowed us up and we appeared here... uh... now... there. WHATEVER. All three of our videos confirm that it appeared, and we went through it. So congrats to everyone, we either created a wormhole or found one. Double congrats for not being killed to death and crushed by going through it. Good job everyone, stars on our report cards. We must thank it for not collapsing on us while we went through it. That was really neighborly of it."

Reynold looked at him with incredulity for a full ten seconds. He responded, “We need to leave a note someplace for Einstein. Not bad theoretical observations for a guy that made them 50 years before the Apollo missions. Bravo buddy. You know it's times like these when I wish I had listened to what J. K. Rowling said during our graduation at Harvard."

John looked at Reynold and asked, "Why? What did she say?"

"I don't know - I didn't listen!" Reynold looked at the video on his phone. Although outside the electromagnetic field, the world was murky. The unmistakable glass globe seemed to hover over their heads, then envelope them, going one frame at a time. After the electromagnetic field shut down, they were standing in the trees. So that's how they got to when. Reynold reviewed the video again and stopped it when they got into the woods and looked up. Since the playback of the video could show you your entire surroundings, you had to move the phone to shift the perspective of what you were watching. When he looked up with the electromagnetic field still around them, he saw the glass globe, and what he saw was a blurry view of the ceiling of the office they had stood in only hours earlier. Looking down, he saw the muddy ground. Now that's something.

John said, "The three units are re-charging now, which will take another three days. They borrow from the earth's natural electromagnetic field to charge so yay. We need to lie low and not interfere with history. I will speculate that we made it through the wormhole, and it may not have collapsed, so there's hope. This is all a guess guys. I'm gonna have to science the shi..."

Reynold interrupted, "Don't say that phrase! I really hate it when you say that phrase. It bugs the living HECK out of me. Guys, I'm positive I saw the wormhole above us after the field collapsed. If our EM bubble counts as a complex matter, or as a negative mass as the theories require, we may be holding the wormhole open until we complete and balance the equation to return through it. We can't see it, because we're not going at light speed. Since nature abhors an unbalanced equation, it's waiting for us. Man, I need a big boy computer to calculate this. Being hopeful will not solve this problem. Anyway, Einstein's speculations about this may be on our side so, yay Einstein." He held up two thumbs up, approving this. There was hope. "If we can get back through..." he paused dramatically, then completed his thought, "everything will be fine."

John was curious to know if there were ways they could get by until they could leave. Getting tenses right would drive him nuts.

Nora looked at them. "If we have to sit here in these woods for three days, we may die of hypothermia - or more likely, boredom. We may have to get someplace where we can stay a little... alive. We will need water and eventually food. The water here... uh... now... is not safe. They pee and poop in the same water we may need to drink from, not to mention all the lovely bacteria and mold we've never experienced in our water. We will need to capture rainwater. Thank goodness I studied this period during a course on the history of the original settlers of the United States. Giles Corey was easy to remember. Heck, you two live in Salem. Why don't you know the history *here*? You know science history but not... *history* history?" She wished she had her knitting needles and wool to keep herself busy and not talk to them until she got over being angry at John.

John stammered his response. "We're... physicists." Reynold glanced over in agreement and gave a few quick nods. John knew of people that drove by the Statue of Liberty daily without visiting it. Guess it was the same with these houses in Salem.

It frustrated Nora how calm they were. She resisted the urge to throttle them. "FINE!" She gritted her teeth. Using gritted teeth, the word *FINE* means that you should hide the poison and sharp objects. Nora said, "Water will become necessary soon. We can go weeks without food; we can go without water only a few days."

"Right now," she continued, "there may be a public house we can go to get food, maybe stay for a night or two, but we have no money, nor anything to barter for food. I think they are still using British currency. Maybe local bank notes. We're dressed strangely and speaking a dialect that people won't hear for at least a hundred years or more. Good news is, nobody has ever seen a science fiction movie yet, so hopefully nobody will be too curious about us. Our *New England* accents may not have appeared yet since these people arrived in this new country only seventy years ago, and not enough immigrants have come yet to muddy up the way they talk. Many of these people came from England. We're sitting in an area of the country that hanged people because someone else believed their *specter* invaded someone or something, or visited their dreams, even though that person may have been someplace else physically. And I know Reynold can magically produce his tablet computer like it was part of a Vegas act. You both have smartwatches you probably shouldn't show anyone."

"Specter? You said that a few moments ago." Reynold was curious enough to ignore Nora's comments.

Nora began, "Since there was no real evidence of witchcraft, they would claim to see you in their dreams, or that part of their livestock would jump funnily. You could sit and have a conversation with someone, but meanwhile your *specter* could leave you, and go haunting someone. That's serious stuff. So having a witness say they saw you at that same moment wasn't enough physical evidence to protect you. Your *specter* was off on its own bugging people."

"Why would anyone accept this?" Reynold asked. "You can't recite your dreams. Nobody fully remembers them unless they are vivid dreams. These people are making it up to pick on people. So someone accuses you of being a witch, they can't prove it, they walk free?"

Nora responded, "this isn't entirely like that. Being a witch is serious. Europe had this same problem only a few years earlier. They stopped the nonsense in the mid-1600s. They persecuted people that didn't practice a religion they acknowledged. That's not right, but at least there was some reason. Here, the problems aren't just the accusers. Being accused is one thing. If you say you're innocent, that's when your life is in true danger. As I recall, they questioned the people, and that would lead you to the conclusion you were a witch, so you needed to repent for your sins and accuse others. They asked questions like *So tell me why you are a witch*? You're guilty before proven innocent. Nobody is without sin in this society. Accusing someone else was how you remained in jail, but alive. If you felt lying was also a sin, they hanged you for pleading not-guilty, because the court and these girls said you lied. Since this is a society of people who read the Bible, women around now or... then... DAMN, MY TENSES ARE SCREWED UP. Anyway, women are literate to a high degree. You can't read the Bible if you can't read. When confronted with being a witch, many of them had to think, Well, I'm told I'm bad by the one place I go to seek solace. At some point, everything around you leads you to believe you're a bad person. The church is the central structure in town, and I don't mean the building but the institution. Your neighbors accepted you into the church. They expected you to be in the church and contribute. Many of these victims became hurt the most when the church abandoned them, accusing them of being a witch and excommunicating them. These people are Puritans and don't like the abomination of Saturnalia, what we call Christmas. They came here for religious freedom.

"A few girls became the star witnesses acting as witch detectors to determine if the people were telling the truth. They sometimes touched the accused and reacted in a variety of ways. Some would convulse on the ground, some would act like they were being choked. Many people speculate that they originally did it to gain attention, but then couldn't figure out a way to stop what they'd started. Think of the brutal beating they could receive if they got caught in a lie. Years later, a few of them repented and apologized for their horrible behavior. One girl named Abigail Williams started the whole thing with her cousin, Betty Parris. Rumor had it, Abigail continued having seizures well after the end of the crisis, which wasn't perceived well. Abigail's testimony stopped appearing in the written documents, and she passed away at age 17, buried in an unmarked grave. A lot of the history around this period just seems to have vanished, leading to more mystery about it. For years, I imagined the moment we just witnessed with Giles Corey. We only know about it in our *now* because witnesses told their descendants for generations until finally someone wrote it down without fear of censure.

"During this horrible period, a few people never made it to their own trials because they died in prison. Giles Corey died sticking to his principles. He didn't want to lie. He knew he wasn't a witch. But as the sheriff just said, he may have been trying to keep his property from being confiscated. He apparently wrote a *last will and testament* in prison that wasn't legally binding."

John interrupted. "You mean to tell me I could accuse someone, and they could hang them based on me claiming to have seen a farm animal leap? Isn't that... lame?"

Nora answered, "You're right. All it took was for someone to say *I saw my goat bleat in the middle of the field, and knew it was Missy so and so* Missy would be arrested, and perhaps then she accused more people, and possibly she died in prison. If Missy made a plea of *Not Guilty* they would hang her, and she would cling to the truth she wasn't a witch."

"This is serious." Reynold said in a hushed tone.

"The governor of this region was appointed by England, uh... Named uh, Chips, or Phips, and he assigned his lieutenant governor as the head of the court. I think his name was William Stoughton. Other judges are John Hathorne, Jonathan Corwin... Reynold, you remember the house we drove by earlier today? That sheriff was Judge Corwin's brother."

Reynold's attention hadn't been on the houses they passed while driving that morning. "House?"

"You're kidding me. You pass by an amazing three-hundred fifty year-old house, and you don't notice it? Didn't you wonder why they call it the witch house?" Nora wondered if the people next to her ever had their eyes open at all.

Nora continued, "Nathaniel Hawthorne changed the spelling of his name by adding a *W* to disassociate himself from his equally famous yet shameful great grandfather who was a judge on these trials. This history isn't a good one. History books called it the *witch delusion* for a reason. It's why people thought Arthur Miller paralleled McCarthyism with this exact period in history. Both used unfounded accusations which led to persecution, not justice. The people who were jailed suffered miserably. One innocent who died in prison was only a few months old. She was born and died in prison. If they survived imprisonment, they hanged by walking up a ladder, then they walked off on their own."

"So they weren't burned at the stake?" John asked.

"No, that's a common mistake. The women and men accused of being witches were hanged, not burned in this case. It was equally inhumane as burnings. Compare to the hangings of the 19th century where the person would break their neck immediately after falling through a trap door. These people walked off ladders and choked to death, which was slower and horrible."

After a few seconds, John spoke, "So no watches in public, and no tablet computers. I wonder what would happen if I took out my cell phone and made a call?" John wasn't joking.

Reynold had an idea. "Remember the startup company thing I bought last year? I kept making you play with them. Then we both realized that the chances of us being off grid would be impossible? Well, we're off grid until Samuel Morse is born." Reynold reached into his jacket and proffered the battery for John. "It can provide four days of charge for your phone, and turns it into a two-way radio, and allows us to send text messages to one another without a cell signal. In case we split up, all you have to do is plug it into the phone. It loads software automatically, allowing the user to text or talk to the other device or through the software."

John took the battery and said, "We are not splitting up. I'll plug it in now, but we're sticking together." After a couple of minutes of playing, both phones could send messages, and they put them back into pockets. There were only two people they needed to communicate with. E-mails, text messages, phone calls, and social media seemed like a waste of time. Current status: *probably screwed.*

"How do we proceed?" Reynold was curious if John or Nora had any ideas.

"What do you mean?" John asked.

"Well..." Reynold said, "couldn't our existence cause ripples in timelines? Couldn't we kill a lot of people from our germs like Columbus did? Just by being here, and now, we're... I can't believe I said this only a day ago, but testing the limits of causality?" Reynold was being honest.

Nora's eyes hardened more. "First, Columbus was over five hundred er... two hundred years ago. So people's immune systems have mixed it up with Europeans. Second, we have to be very careful with interactions. All this history happened without us before, so if we stay out of the way, it'll happen the same way. Also, we must be careful, because we're living in an age without the three A's."

John looked puzzled. "The three A's?"

Nora replied, "Antiseptic, Antibiotics, and Anesthesia. We get hurt here... ur... NOW... even an amazing doctor probably won't wash his hands, and will kill us with germs from his prior patient. Not to mention ignorant to the doctoring we're used to. They don't know what a germ is... oh and they probably use parts of frogs and roots like, believe it or not, a witch doctor in our time." Two very concerned faces stared back at her.

John said, "Nora is right. We could cause some serious damage to our world if we interfere, and if we get hurt here."

"Let's stay here. We'll be hungry in three days, but it'll be safer. We can capture rain for water. There are plenty of leaves. We can make them into cups to drink rainwater. Without pesticides and pollution, the fresh leaves on the trees are clean." They all agreed. They could die of boredom in the three days before they returned, but hopefully not from accidentally poisoning themselves.

Nora looked at Reynold and braced herself for one more item to help them blend in. "Reynold, you will have to fit in more. I think you must give John your jacket to wear. I must find a head covering of some kind. Both you and John will need to cuff your pants to reach above your shoes. John, when you put on Reynold's jacket, make sure your shirt collar is above the jacket so your white collar is visible. In addition, cuff the sleeves of the jacket."

Reynold took off his jacket and used a pocket knife to cut away some of the white liner of his super pocket sport jacket and handed it to Nora as a makeshift head bandana.

After a few moments of field upgrades to their apparel, they were all closer to the fashion style of this time period.

From a distance, their clothing wouldn't give them away. From up close, everything would. Their teeth, their skin, and their eyes all revealed the healthiest people during that time period. They may as well have antennae on their heads, and silver outfits.

Nora added, "One last thing. Reynold try not to walk... so tall. Maybe slouch or something?"

Reynold, throughly exasperated said, "So, to sum this up: We're different down to our molecules because we have antibodies and viruses that could kill the people around us if we breathe on them, or if they - god-forbid - breathe on us with their dragon breath. We have to avoid contact with them for fear of possibly messing with our futures and our history. In a little over three days, the thing that got us into trouble will charge itself enough to help us go back to our time, as long as the wormhole allows us to enter it again. But there's a chance we're trapped forever in the most odiferous place with no indoor plumbing, electricity, or internet access. Meanwhile, I am not an accepted part of society, nor will people treat me equally for hundreds of years, so who knows what sort of reception I will get if I show my face again or walk with an erect spine. We talk strange, look strange, our teeth are way too white, not to mention we have far too many of them than anyone here and now, because the three of us have used tooth brushes, or in our case teeth brushes, mouth wash, and floss. On the plus side, Newton is alive in England and has a lovely job and may hire us as assistants if we're nice to him. If we can't get back, let's see if we can catch a Renaissance festival, or as they call it *now*. We may go crazy playing with tenses for a few years if we don't die trying to re-invent the things we miss the most. Please let me know if I forgot anything."

Nora and John heard "blah blah blah we're dead, blah blah blah blah we're really dead blah blah blah."

The three sat on the roots of the trees, leaning against them in silence. They easily fell asleep in the complete darkness and calm.

They slept soundly and didn't remember their dreams. They were oblivious to their surroundings until they heard a twig break the next morning, shocking them into the waking world and redefining the meaning of present tense.

10

JUDGEMENT LOST

After resigning from the court, Nathaniel Saltonstall became a recluse and stayed in his home in nearby Ipswich until he couldn't stand the horrible news any longer. He returned to Salem to see what he could do. Rumor of Giles's lack of a plea boiled over to his town quickly. Bad news seems to travel like the speed of the sunlight. He checked into Thomas Beadle's Tavern and walked to the jailhouse to see his friend lying under the rocks placed there by the process of *peine forte et dure*. This was an ancient law from the *Standing Mute Act* written in 1275, under which they place one stone at a time on a prisoner to elicit a plea to his crime of guilty or not-guilty. Nathaniel knew Giles was a proud man, but he was also an OLD STUBBORN fool. Nathaniel thought, "Torturing an eighty-year-old. How horrible."

Now Nathaniel looked at the three strangers, observed their behavior, and was transfixed. They had witnessed as the life drained from his friend Giles Corey, whose only crime was remaining silent in the most ridiculous miscarriage of justice he had seen in his entire life.

When Nathaniel resigned as Judge from the Court of Oyer and terminer four months earlier, he gave no reason. He found it ironic that the English translation of *oyer et terminer* means *to hear and determine,* yet nobody was listening, and they were killing the innocent. Nathaniel was afraid of becoming the court's next victim and escaped since he knew nobody listened. It offended his soul when the court sentenced a woman to be hanged without real evidence of a crime. Now eleven people were dead because the court allowed using evidence they had manufactured to fit the crime. Dreams. Being sentenced to death based on the supposed dreams of awful children. Nathaniel knew all evidence being generated after a crime was nothing but lies.

Everyone around Nathaniel had gone mad, insisting that logic and justice had nothing to do with the world they built in this new country. He had to separate himself from that madness. He didn't want his name associated with them, as the trials had the potential to contaminate all definitions of justice. Justice is based on the truth, and about balancing the scales. Justice isn't about reinforcing lunacy. The governor chose him for the court for his integrity. He had quit for the same reason.

The judges assigned to the court were great men who were individually affected by the downturn in the economy and relentless defense against Indian attacks. They wanted justice for their individual losses. Successful men couldn't fail, so it must have been the work of the devil. To them, Satan was running amok in their close-knit community, causing their strife. Nathaniel knew the judges believed they were doing the right thing. He had to change their hearts and knew he was ill-equipped for that task.

He stared at the strangers in fascination, almost forgetting why he stood across from the jail. As he snapped back to reality, he watched Giles being tortured without a trial. The judges he sat with were now accessories to murder, and he seemed to be the only one to understand this. He had had enough and became compelled to stand up to the court put in place to eradicate witchcraft.

Nathaniel knew witchcraft was a tremendous sin. The sinners in Europe were hanged or burned by practicing a demonic faith. But here, when there's not a shred of evidence other than a child saying, "I dreamed about so and so putting my name in the book of demons," somehow intelligent people had become convinced to murder. He had to draw the line. These young girls weren't helping matters. They needed to be punished for their involvement. How would he alone convince anyone of this? If something possessed the girls, couldn't their testimony be false? Why wasn't the devil also putting the testimony into them? Madness. The double and triple negatives angered Nathaniel.

Without credible evidence, pleading guilty meant something had forced the accused to lie without proof of any witchcraft being performed. Someone tells you that you're a witch, and that's the truth? Backed up by misbehaving children, CHILDREN who should be helping their families tend their livestock, fields, and chores. Not sitting in a court playing games. Salem and the surrounding area was wasting away, along with justice.

There was no evidence found at the property of the accused. No eyewitness. Nobody is awake to witness your crime. Only recounted dreams, and girls that would have fits around you while testifying, or someone would suspect and accuse you of being a witch. They used spooked animals as evidence of witchcraft. They're animals, and can't testify. Question any of it, and you become the convicted, then accused. That is not justice. That is insanity.

When they convicted Bridget Bishop, Nathaniel argued with the other judges saying, "IS THIS PATHETIC DRIVEL ENOUGH TO KILL A WOMAN?" They didn't want to hear it. The unknown force hypnotized and convinced them of the only thing they could do. Eliminate it.

As the townspeople watched the life drain from Giles Corey that day, these three strangers distracted him enough to make him realize they were very different. The African man dressed differently. He didn't look like a servant. He's definitely not a slave. That black man seemed proud, and an equal to the two people around him. Nathaniel had never seen that behavior from a slave. Nathaniel didn't believe in keeping anyone as a slave. He also objected to turning families into indentured servants to pay off their travels to the New World. But this was only his opinion. This black man acted differently. He also seemed taller because of his proud stance. He whispered to the two others, and wasn't subservient to them. He stood stoically. How strange. It's dangerous for the black man to act free in front of the crowd. The others he spoke to didn't fit in either.

The three strangers stood slightly behind the gathered townsfolk. They might be the key to helping him heal the sickness in these towns. It had only been four months since Nathaniel became involved. Everyone in the surrounding towns was topsy-turvy while finding and accusing witches. No crops were being harvested, people weren't focused on keeping their livestock healthy. The people became engrossed in the horrible drama that overwhelmed their lives. They may freeze to death if they don't snap out of it and chop down trees and cut up wood for fires before winter. This will be their destruction if it doesn't end.

As the final moments of life drained from Giles, he had a gut feeling that these strangers would help him. His instinct tingled, and he knew he would convince them, and they would help put an end to this horrible nightmare that had sent these surrounding towns into a tailspin. Why would anyone accept this as justice? Now eleven people had hanged by the neck, dying horrible deaths. George Burroughs recited the Lord's Prayer, then walked off the ladder where he hanged until he breathed no more. Forty-five minutes he hanged before he gasped his last breath. That he could utter the Lord's Prayer was proof of a miscarriage of justice. This was impossible for a witch to do, even with Cotton Mather attending, and reassuring the crowd that the devil recited this to him. How could the devil even speak these words? Cotton's father, Increase Mather said, "... focused responsibility on the people of New England at large, and yet looked to individuals for the means to solve the problem. It encouraged the individual believers to attend to the state of his or her own soul regardless of what might be happening in the world." Can he be so cut off from these trials to ignore the sins of the judgment itself? The Governor was too busy fighting Indian forces; Nathaniel had to act.

Nathaniel's deposed the active governor of the Dominion of New England, Sir Edmund Andros in 1689. This ended with the Governor being jailed, which angered England. Andros's tyrannical behavior had been too much for the colony to bear, turning Massachusetts into a state governed by the military. Nathaniel served on the council of the revolutionary government that continued until a new Governor arrived in May of that year. Increase Mather had returned with him from England with a more robust charter for the Massachusetts colony, and his return to administering Harvard. The colony now had to adhere to the laws of England and ignore the laws created by the colonists. Increase Mather advocated for the colony, and England appointed the Puritan Sir William Phips to be their new governor. They rejoiced at the return of normalcy, not realizing that the chaos had only just begun. Governor Phips had his hands full.

Nathaniel stood perplexed. Where they were from? The African man had a jacket on, dressed more formally than the other two people. The woman wasn't dressed in pious looking clothing, but more like a peasant. It was outlandish, scandalous attire for a woman. She seemed to deduce something and led them into the woods. A slave not acting like a slave, and a woman not acting as a proper woman in public. Nathaniel's wife treated him differently in his house, but she had her place in public. This was bold behavior.

Nathaniel watched the three strange people walk away from the scene. The townspeople noticed them for their differences, but they were in too much shock from the horror they just witnessed to address the strangers. Since they are outsiders, they won't be worried about being accused. The townspeople can't charge someone whom they don't know. Nathaniel only had scraps of ideas about how they could help him put an end to all of this, but their presence gave him hope. The strategy remained unclear. They would be more willing to help because they have nothing to lose. They would not be persecuted as he would. Nathaniel had to convince them.

Nathaniel observed that as they walked away, the strangers glanced nervously at the townspeople. They walked past the group of trees behind the jail and disappeared inside them. What strange behavior, Nathaniel thought. Israel Porter will not be pleased people are on his property and may chase them away. After watching them go behind the trees, Nathaniel walked parallel to the wooded area to overhear their conversation, but failed. He knew how to locate them, and would return and plead for their help tomorrow morning.

Nathaniel was obsessed with ending this witch crisis and hoped he had found his solution. He foresaw the townspeople accusing each other endlessly until everyone was eventually guilty of witchcraft. He had stood up to England without remorse, nor fear, but now he couldn't stand against his neighbors, who were accusing each other of being witches since they saw them in dreams. The mob mentality, combined with false information, sent chills down his spine. How was the process going to end? He couldn't think past the current idea, which was to use these individuals at any cost. After that, maybe fate would be his friend and help him out. Nathaniel only had a clear idea of the big picture. He would make contact and convince the outsiders to help.

Nathaniel returned his thoughts to the use of folk magic through the touch test. It was like using witchcraft to prove someone a witch, which meant the tester was a witch trying to see if the other person was a witch. How could this be legal? Or fair? These women had been tortured enough already by having someone examine all of their skin for witches' *teets* where the *familiar* or witch's animal could suckle. When working on a farm, people developed scars and marks incurring injuries received from the hard labor. Why would anyone that called themselves a Puritan think reviewing a person's naked body was permissible, when within their own households, that wasn't viewed as holy? He couldn't let his name be associated with these proceedings.

He had spent time at Bridget Bishop's unlicensed tavern for a drink or two. It was a raucous place, but fun. None of the other taverns played shovel board, and he was good at the game. Nathaniel felt responsible for not preventing her from hanging. She was harmless, and people were coercing the girls performing the touch test to skew the results. Perhaps the people in the village didn't like Bridget because of her clothing? Perhaps they didn't like her because she was different? She was a free spirit. It was enough to make him quit serving on the court.

Nathaniel was ashamed of his short time on that court and felt obligated to stop the proceedings without endangering himself and his family. He worried that someone could harm his sons. Even if the townspeople hanged him, his children would grow up without their father.

Nathaniel would appeal to the three people to help.

Nathaniel walked to Beadle's Tavern on Main Street, just past the Common Ground, and entered. He walked into the main room and socialized until they served dinner, ordered a beer, and had lobster and mussel stew. Although the bread was warm and comforting, still he had watched his friend die only hours earlier. His mind kept recalling that moment, upsetting his appetite.

Once finished with his meal, he asked Thomas Beadle if there were extra rooms available. Because the court was not in session, the remaining rooms reserved for the judges were available. Since the strangers seemed to be staying in the woods, he thought they needed a more comfortable place to sleep.

As he walked upstairs to his room, he drafted his plan of action. He would try to talk to the strangers privately without alarming them and pray they wouldn't reveal his subterfuge. He was afraid of the backlash because he was well known. His goal from now until this horrid court was disbanded, was to prevent more people from being accused.

Brother was against brother, families were against families. He couldn't wait for everyone to come to their senses. The court needed to determine the truth, and the people in jail needed to be given fair hearings without the use of this touch test or spectral evidence. Everyone deserves fair treatment, no matter what they look or act like. Everyone needs to see that this court is a sham.

He wrote in his personal diary, then predated the next page, as had had done since he started keeping a diary as a boy. Nathaniel wrote Tuesday, September 20th for the next day's writing. He read a verse of the Bible by candle and went to sleep.

When Nathaniel awoke the next morning, he had breakfast in the tavern, and set out back to that patch of woods next to the jail, he prayed that they would listen to him and help. His plan was better than waiting for chaos to become order. That would take too much time.

He entered the patch of trees and stood for a few moments, watching the three strangers as they slept soundly. He decided it was time to begin and found a thin branch that had fallen from one of the surrounding trees and put his foot on it, making a loud snap.

11

TO NATHANIEL'S SURPRISE

John's, Nora's, and Reynold's eyes flew open when they realized they were not alone. The sound of the breaking twig woke them like the best alarm clock on the planet. Reynold felt his heart skip a beat.

Nathaniel still had his foot on the twig, satisfied that he had their undivided attention.

"I'm very sorry for disturbing you. I'm Nathaniel... Nathaniel Saltonstall. May I ask why are you sleeping on Israel Porter's property?" Nathaniel inquired. "'Tis a good thing he's visiting his family in Boston, or else he'd be quite furious right now. He's an excellent shot with a musket, you see." He talked in the most *matter-of-fact* voice he could, so as not to accuse his future allies. Calling on his experience in the military, he needed to motivate his soldiers.

John's eyes widened in shock. "Uh... Hi Nathaniel... Nathaniel." He realized he had said his name twice and knew he only had ONE first name. What's his last name? DUH.

Reynold panicked about germs, and interacting with a person who had passed away over three-hundred years before he was born, and wondered why nobody in the *now* wanted to clean themselves. Everything he does might cause ripples in history. "That plan didn't last long," he said aloud. This *holy cow* moment had removed a majority of Reynold's speech filters.

Nathaniel responded to Reynold, "I... don't understand what you mean. You seem too disorganized to be executing a plan. Where are the three of you from?"

John, Nora, and Reynold now showed fear in their eyes. Nathaniel knew he may have just set his plan to involve these people back. He blurted out, "Oh no, please don't worry," but then slowed down for his audience as he continued, "I am merely... curious." These people had to help him.

Reynold thought how little this man had washed his hands, thought of famous germaphobe Howie Mandel, and made a fist bump to greet him. This only caused Nathaniel to look at it quizzically and made Reynold feel like he was from another universe.

Nathaniel said, "Are you holding something... in your hand, for me to catch?"

John opened his eyes wide at Reynold trying to stop him from waiting for his return bump and said, "We're from... out of town and didn't have a room at the local... uh... hotel."

Nora looked terrified, then she elbowed John in the ribs and quickly interrupted, "TAVERN... he means tavern!"

John winced from the blow and continued trying to avoid any gaps in the conversation. "Yes Tavern, and we just wanted to uh... relax after traveling for a half hour."

Reynold tried to cover John's second blunder by saying, "Uh, hours. We traveled for hours." How long did it take to walk rather than drive anywhere? Could a horse gallop on these terrible roads?

Nathaniel tried to soak this all in. These people spoke

strangely, and he couldn't recognize where the accents came from in England. They spoke with accents that made them stand out. There was a familiar hard *R* in their speech, and missing elements he couldn't put his finger on. He had heard no one like them.

John continued, "I'm John Milners, a... professor at Harvard, and this is Nora... my... uh wife, and this is Reynold, our... uh... man-servant." John knew Harvard's first graduating class was in 1642. This was a good cover story.

Reynold gave John a dirty look. He wanted to transmit, "Those are MY formulas and calculations that got us here, buddy. I'm the professor. You're a damn lab rat." Turn the filter back on, captain.

Nathaniel responded nonchalantly in Latin, "mala tempora currunt."

Six eyes stared at Nathaniel. At that moment, Nora, John, and Reynold proved how terrible they were at improvisation. What a terrible cover story, John thought.

John had never studied Latin. He only knew the Latin names of chemicals. He remembered how a smug language student had made a twenty-five minute long speech in Latin on the day of their graduation. Nobody understood that speech. That student was kind enough to carry on the three-hundred-seventy-five-year-old tradition of making a speech in Latin at the graduation. John had read they had to argue their thesis in Latin before making the final speech. Nobody understood what side that person was arguing for. Did anyone know? Did he know?

John responded with a croak back of his throat. Nora and Reynold didn't have the internet to look up that phrase. John appreciated that Latin student, and wanted to ask, "Should we slug that guy?"

Nathaniel sighed and continued in a carefully modulated tone. "What that means is *bad times are upon us.*" He paused, thinking about John's introduction, and explained why he didn't believe it. "You are not a professor at Harvard. You would need to teach lessons in Latin, Greek, Hebrew, Chaldee, and Syriac. To pass the entrance exam for Harvard as a student, you need to be proficient in Latin and Greek. I don't think you know Latin. I myself graduated from Harvard and attended many of the ceremonies, including the first honorary doctorate recently given to our current President, Increase Mather. You don't look like anyone who's attended Harvard with me. This African man doesn't seem like a servant, he's far too... confident. He does not seem to be a person who takes orders from anyone. My father spoke out against slavery in 1645, and like him, I'm glad he's a free man. You also don't seem like dishonest people, so I should hope there is more to your story."

Reynold's eyes went wide. They. Were. So. Screwed.

John's mind was reeling. He was caught in a bad lie, and his mind failed to issue a better one. They were prepared to sit for three days without a back story. John thought, "Damn it, I LIVE in Salem, and work at Harvard, and have the paychecks and electric bills to prove it."

Nathaniel could see he had frightened the strangers, and he changed to a less confrontational tone. "You look like you've traveled a long time. Please join me back at the tavern where I am staying and we can discuss yours and my situation. I need your help, and it is of little consequence to me where you are from. What matters more is your willingness to help. I'm sure you have heard what is happening. You also witnessed yesterday's horrific event, so you know how desperate the times are."

Nora, John, and Reynold were astonished. They were staring at their worst nightmare. They didn't want to interact with people. Time travel seemed complex enough without worrying about changing the past. If this guy writes *met with three people from the twenty-first century, they seem nice. I wish I had an auto-driving horse like the cars they mentioned. Oh yeah, what's a car?* they were screwed. If they did anything wrong, they could change part of history, and they needed to avoid that at all costs. Nathaniel stood in their way of making a clean getaway. This guy had read their expressions, understood they didn't fit in, and was far more familiar with customs than any of them could ever be. Was this the only way they would survive? They had to be careful.

Nora's mind raced. She wished she could write backstories that sounded believable, but the three of them were literally out of time, and she was a history professor that liked her internet access.

Reynold began, "Sir, we're sorry, but how can we help? We're not from around here and don't know your... uh, local customs?"

"I am sorry," Nathaniel started, "I am not trying to corner you into anything. However, you are here. Unless you have horses someplace, I do not see you leaving except on foot. You are sleeping in the woods, that can not be comfortable. As you saw yesterday, our court just tortured someone using an ancient law unused since the thirteenth century without a trial for remaining mute about his plea. You must realize that the world has gone completely mad, and justice is nonexistent. I cannot get directly involved, as they will quickly retaliate, accusing me of witchcraft, and hang me, or accuse members of my family. By now, this news has reached England. My instinct tells me the three of you can help."

Reynold started, "We're really not sure how we can help. We are obviously not from around here. We know what is happening and want to help, but are hesitant to get involved." Reynold imagined putting his crossed fingers behind his back.

Nathaniel had never talked to an African person as an equal. It was intriguing. Reynold was the most intelligent of the three. Although the people in front of him weren't educated enough to be accepted into Harvard, he still had a hunch they could help. "The townspeople do not know you. These girls making accusations would need to give evidence of you to the courts. Since they have never seen you before, and the court is not in session this week, you are safe. This court must come to an end. Please understand that I trust you not to accuse me of witchcraft. I think you grasp that with your strange dress and appearance, you three are outsiders and are conspicuous. I can advise you on what you need to know so you can help. My intuition tells me you can help."

John's brain remained locked up, unable to contribute.

Nora looked at Nathaniel and said, "Look, sir, we are... travelers. We can... try."

Reynold ran scenarios in his mind. Nora said not to interfere with history, and now she wants to try? What if they changed something? What are the repercussions of changing history? No scientists were ready to test these circumstances. Talking to people out of time. Technically, they were out of time. Every moment was needed for calculations, verifications, and documentation, but taking out a tablet computer was too dangerous, not to mention the lack of wireless networks. How could they figure out if their actions changed history? Would they even know?

John wondered, how could they help? Why did this guy

approach them? True, they were outsiders. Could they do anything without suspicion? More likely the opposite. Just as Nathaniel had noticed, they would be singled out and everything they did would cause distrust.

Nathaniel pleaded, "Please come with me, and we will talk more at the tavern, hopefully in more private surroundings in my room."

They followed Nathaniel. Somehow, they trusted him.

They looked to the right and saw the *North River,* which was enormous. Wherever they looked, they looked with eyes from a different time. Re-shaping the landscape in their minds, they remember both views of the same place. The *Washington Street* they saw now was narrower, but it occupied the same place as the road they knew.

Nora walked over and noticed Reynold gliding like a Harvard professor and not trudging like a servant. She elbowed him as a reminder, giving him as wide a gaze that said, "DUDE," as she could. Once she realized that she was a little hard in her correction, she turned to Reynold and said, "Oh wow, can't you see all the differences?" She asked, trying to be vague but still talk about their surroundings.

Reynold rubbed his ribs, slouched a little, and glowered back, acknowledging that he understood.

Nathaniel turned and looked at his three strange charges and asked, "What do you mean, differences? Isn't every place you visit... different?"

John tried to save the conversation from getting ugly. "What they mean is there are... differences... and similarities to where we come from and this town." Nathaniel looked baffled by this terrible explanation.

They walked away from the North River and were transfixed by the openness of the sky due to the absence of tall buildings. Everything was spread out. Each house had a miniature forest on their land. The road had rocks of all sizes and dirt looked horrible and never meant for any wheels except for slow-moving ox-carts. Few tires would survive. Only horses or oxen could use these roads. Horses couldn't trot quickly but walked as if the speed limit were slow. The properties defined it with short stone walls delineating where one property began and another ended. Many houses didn't have real windows and used wood shutters instead. Glasswork was costly and came from England. The roads were so rocky and unkempt, there was no need for speed limits and stop signs.

As they walked down the middle of the street, they approached a brick building that looked official, but it was unmarked. Nora stared at it as if looking at a ghost. "Mister Saltonstall?" How should she address a man in this now? She felt as trapped as Reynold. They were both second-class citizens. *Seen and not heard* ran through her mind. Thank you, Susan B. Anthony. She continued, "What is this building?"

"That's the Town's House. They have been holding the witch trials upstairs," he replied.

Nora made a mental note of the paintings depicting the Salem Witch trials on the ground floor of an unnamed open building.

With the door open, Nora could see small desks arranged with children sitting at their desks. It'll be some time before someone yells about the wasted heat escaping out the front door. She imagined the conversations. "HEY! Were you raised in a barn?" "Why Yes. In fact, I was raised in a barn. It's the 1600s, silly." And then they would laugh and laugh. She was surprised by the lack of a spring mechanism to close the door, and she wondered how it stayed open. DUH. The building stood stoutly in the middle of the street. The fact that the witch trials happened in that building dominated Nora's thoughts.

They walked around the Town's House and continued toward a square area about seventy-five yards behind it. In the square stood two pillories, one empty and the other occupied. A man stood with his head and hands locked on the top. He had soiled himself. He slouched uncomfortably, and was sobbing openly. He looked like he was in terrible agony. They had just left him locked in place by the neck and arms in the wood stocks. Reynold stared aghast and thought, "This isn't funny. How long had that person been in that thing?" He'd seen the wood pillory at amusement parks, had even taken amusing pictures with his head and hands inside them. He wasn't laughing now. This looked awful. Leaving a person locked there just didn't seem right. This man had been there at least a day, and was shivering from the cold, and must have been starving. People would walk over, spit on him, yelling "SINNER!" One person threw a potato at him, which hit him on the hand, and he cried out, "OW!". This was torture.

Behind the pillory was an area that looked like an open square at the intersection of the streets. A thoroughfare crossed the street they were on, and a four-inch by four-inch post with the name "Ye Main Street" painted on it stuck out of the ground. There was more visibility in some places than in others because of the number of uncleared trees on properties.

Nora turned right and looked down the offset part of "Main Street" and saw the familiar gray wood house they had passed earlier. Was it only yesterday she and Reynold had driven to the office they had met John. The one house that existed in both time periods now looked commonplace, except that in this time it stood taller than the buildings surrounding it. It was one of the few houses that had windows instead of doors. The house appeared to be less than three-hundred yards away. It was clearly visible now from this spot as it had never been in her lifetime due to the modern buildings blocking it. In their time, this was the crossroad of Washington & Essex Street.

Nora's eyes were wide with recognition. She whispered, "John... Reynold... that's the Wi... uh... um... Corwin House."

John and Reynold seemed unfazed by her revelation. It looked like a wooden gray house in a sea of wooden gray houses. Granted it was a little taller, and the diamond shaped windows gave it a distinctive appearance. The Corwin house had been restored using original blueprints in 1944, so it looked the same in both now's.

"Is it cool because it's over there?" Reynold asked.

Nora's eyes filled with daggers and she mouthed, "NO."

Nathaniel looked on in curious fascination. Why are they so interested in houses? Very strange. Don't they have houses where they are from?

They followed Nathaniel who turned left, onto Essex Street, or "Main Street" as it was named in 1692. The three travelers stared at the loud, bustling market in front of them. Salem had blocked off parts of Essex street in the 1970s to make it into a walking mall. Here, over two hundred seventy years earlier, the street looked nearly identical with the same type of activity, except everything had far more *elbow-room*.

They walked up "Main Street" and passed the Meeting House, which looked larger and more stately than the Town's House. Why weren't the trials held in that place instead?

The amount of activity splayed out before them was overwhelming. On one pushcart, rabbits, pheasants, and other meat hung on wooden hooks behind the person selling them. The animals on the hooks were today's hunt. Other people sold their wares from pushcarts and shouted to get passersby attention yelling, "EGGS, CHEESE, MEAT PIES, FOR A TUPPENCE! TWO POUNDS OF MEAT, SIX SHILLINGS!" The cacophony of voices filled the streets.

Some carts overflowed with clothing and handmade items, such as candles. Even toy makers with crude looking horses and wooden soldiers hawked their wares. Horses drank from makeshift troughs next to some of the carts. People rode oxen that were pulling carts. They were slow, but they could walk on the streets and pulled like mad. Where did they come from?

John noticed one or two children held poppets, and a nearby cart had dozens of them with prices in front of the merchandise. He thought, "Gosh, if I had a video game here, these kids would go nuts. If he had electricity, their parents would go nuts. If I showed them Tetris, they'd explode in front of me."

John leaned into a gawking Reynold and Nora and said, "I betcha I could sell my smartphone with a game running on it for a million bucks here." Reynold and Nora gave John an annoyed look. "Okay, OKAY!"

Reynold was in germaphobe hell. He wondered how he could look brave while walking amongst the veritable petri dish of people standing around him without freaking out Nora. These people haven't bathed in... aw, shoot, forget giving them the benefit of doubt. THEY HAVEN'T BATHED. Their teeth also looked horrible. How can these people be alive and chewing? He was using all his willpower to resist running back to the woods where they had sat happily before all these malodorous people invaded their privacy. Didn't they understand what grew under their nails? At least the ones that had all their nails. And these people should floss like... a lot. What sat between that guy's canine and incisor looked like a piece of meat still on a bone. Was it even dead? If they didn't make it back to their time, he would invent floss, toothbrushes, toothpaste, toilet paper, showers, and hot water heaters. Reynold didn't care about timelines and time travel issues, he wanted convenience and comfort.

They passed by more pre-cooked foods on other carts, and since they hadn't eaten in over a day, the three of them looked on and salivated.

They walked past a place on the left side of the road with a sign that said *Ships Tavern*. Raucous people kept emerging from the building, singing and staggering. One visibly ill patron walked out and retched for a long, long time. Nora whispered, "You go sailor dude." Another walked outside and didn't even stop drinking his bottle of rum or whatever as he turned away from them and made a remarkably high urine stream. As disgusting as this guy was, he owned it. "Thanks for not facing US with that, mister sailer dude!" she thought. Nora brushed off the repulsive encounter and moved on. Nora whispered, "I hope Beadle's Tavern is not like this."

As they walked through the central town market, it seemed much like a market in the Middle East. Merchants bargaining with their customers, some taking money, most taking barter. So many people selling different things they'd made. Men's hats, women's scarves, dresses, lace, wigs, ruffled shirts, and blocks of soap. Others sold household goods such as brooms and other tools. People even pushed elixirs as cures for ailments. An apothecary would suggest things to people that would clear up various aches and symptoms.

One stand had a very elaborate wooden box on it. It was very ornate and had carvings that must have taken hours to create. John asked, "This is beautiful, but what is it for?"

Nathaniel looked at him flabbergasted and said, "That is... a Bible box... don't you have this in your home?".

John nodded, then grunted his reply, "mm hmmm. Yeah. Mine is less... fancy."

They walked on, looking at the amazing display they observed, and lost track of time. They savored the moment and let everything soak in.

Nora looked longingly at the food and asked Nathaniel, "We're very sorry, but someone robbed us. We have no money to pay for anything, but we're starving. Could you buy us some food?"

Nathaniel replied, "We'll be able to eat at the Tavern just past the common grounds over there. They serve dinner after dusk." He pointed just to the left of where they were heading. "I... know the owner." He leaned into the three of them and whispered just loud enough for them to hear, "He's a good friend of mine, and is also opposed to the injustices being inflicted on innocent people. We need to get you off the streets before people get more..." he paused for effect, "curious."

Translation: they had to get off the grid ASAP. The longer they walked around in public, the more they were subject to scrutiny and suspicion. Damn. How much did this guy decipher?

Reynold was struck by how clear the sky looked. The fresh air was polluted only by the smells of the intense eye-watering body odor of people they smelled in close quarters. Their breath wasn't anything to write home about, either. Stephen King could write dozens of horror novels just about their lack of hygiene. These people washed far less than Nathaniel, which seemed impossible. The tantalizing smells of food were drowned out by the mind-altering body odor. Which was maybe why they weren't hungrier? Kings and members of the aristocracy would rub rose petals and other flowers under their noses when they walked amongst the common folk.

As she walked, Nora drank in her surroundings. She had seen blue skies before, but this blue looked brighter and seemed to be in higher definition. She didn't realize that the haze she saw in her time didn't need to be there. Lack of pollutants in the atmosphere made colors pop. There were still clouds in the sky. The previous night before falling asleep, she had thought of how many stars she could see as they appeared somehow enhanced and pronounced. This was better than any planetarium she had ever experienced. Without light pollution from any place on the planet, the night sky looked dazzling.

All three looked at the damaged faces around them, many of which were scarred from various injuries, or from yellow fever to smallpox infections which these people had fought off and survived. Nora wondered if anyone had been inoculated against smallpox. Inoculations for smallpox weren't popular since one out of one hundred people would die from introducing a milder form of the disease. When did they even start to inoculate against smallpox? Were the Chinese people doing this?

The townspeople's faces and eyes showed they had lived through harder times than Nora, John, and Reynold had ever known. They were far younger than their countenance made them seem. Real life started sooner for these people. Nora wondered how much more the three of them stuck out, with the absence of scars and weathering on their own faces. Her complexion wasn't flawless, but compared to the surrounding women, she could be a socialite.

Fishermen showed off their morning catch, and allowed lobsters to walk across their tables.

The townspeople occasionally glanced at them, but they turned their attention to the deals they were making from the street vendors. The shoppers weren't interested in the strangers.

Nora was in her element. She had spent all her life studying history, and now she literally stood within it. She wished she could take out John's videophones and capture everything around her. Nora wasn't worried about being stuck here anymore. She observed the surrounding people with delight. Once she saw an old woman, who looked to be around ninety years old, but her more weathered features probably hid her true age. She thought, "Was that woman one of the original Pilgrims?" Her next thought was that she should corner and interview the woman, recording her responses so her voice could be heard. "What was it really like for you? How did you survive the first horrible winters? Why did *you* and your family make this treacherous trip to the New World?" Nora also considered how her colleagues back at Harvard would feel if she told them she didn't just study history, but had experienced it first hand and recorded it on her phone. Her days in academia came to a crashing halt as she remembered she was standing in history. Actually, she was standing in *now*. This *history* hasn't happened yet. Was she out of a job? Could she teach current events instead?

She was ecstatic. Most women from this period read, but most likely had never written unless they needed to do so. So many of their voices were unheard in the present. The earliest woman's diary discovered was written by Mehetabel Chandler Coit, who started it when she was about fifteen. Her mother was, or IS... damn these tenses... Elizabeth Chandler, and she wrote one of the first known published poems by a woman. Maybe they were walking around this market with Elizabeth or Mehetabel right now?

She decided that as far as first dates, this would be impossible to top. "Oh thanks for taking me to a restaurant and a movie..." she imagined herself saying. "Gee, thanks for taking me to a museum, and some coffee and a snack." "Oh, thanks for taking me to a Harvard vs. Army football game for some delicious dirty dogs and to watch a bunch of nerds that hopefully won't get hurt playing against enormous mutants bred for destruction." "Oh, why didn't that do it for me? Well, my last boyfriend took me back in time to experience something I've been studying all my life." Boyfriend... BOYFRIEND... wow... I... like Reynold, she thought. How many people have shown their historian dates a good time like THIS ever before?

Lost in thought, Nora did something she didn't think was dangerous, and reached for Reynold's hand to hold. Upon feeling her fingertips, he enjoyed holding her hand for a moment. Reynold's spine straightened up for the first time since being corrected by Nora. Then he realized what she was doing and looked at her with his wide brown eyes as he let go and hunched over again. He smiled ever so slightly and gave her an almost imperceptible *no* head shake in warning. Nora knew that interracial relationships wouldn't be accepted in public for another... 270 years? Living history and understanding it were two different things. Something Reynold had wanted for a long time would need to wait until they were in private.

Behind them, they heard a commotion which startled

them back into reality. The crowd parted as three men on horses galloped by without the slightest regard for people's safety. One was the cane-wielding man they saw yesterday, pushing Giles Corey's tongue back into his mouth. The sheriff didn't look pleased as his eyes zeroed in on Reynold.

12

TAVERN *NE B&B?

As the four of them walked down *Main Street* together, Nathaniel wondered where these strangers came from. He usually walked through the market in minutes. They took their time and gawked and pointed and touched everything. They seemed uneducated since they didn't know Latin. They acted as they had never seen a market before. How strange. Could they be aristocracy from another country? Governor Phips didn't know how to read before the age of 21. Perhaps there was no need for them to know Latin? Had he made the mistake of deciding to trust them? Would they be discreet in their help? Would they be able to help resolve this situation? That would be the real challenge. Strange. He still felt they would help despite their deficiencies in any social skills. These outsiders might be able to accomplish something he couldn't. As outsiders, they would be unaffected by the accusing children and townspeople in the long run. They may persecute them after they helped, but he needed to take that chance, even if it were selfish, not to mention the possibility. He wanted his troops ready for now, not later.

They walked down a more residential area, devoid of the bustle of the carts, although peddlers were approaching the buildings, calling out sing-song announcements of their wares. "Flowahs git yer flowahs!" Nora, Reynold, and John could barely understand him. That peddler didn't have a discernible "R" in his speech.

They saw a sprawling field with hills and tall grass behind these houses. It seemed familiar, but at the same time, it wasn't. It looked like Salem's common area. The common area was an enormous field with paths to walk through in their time. Where did these hills go? Who took them away? That common area seemed like its own ecosystem. It looked like a swamp with hills that contained a pond. Nora closed her eyes and pictured the area, and she could see nothing but some trees planted in a pattern surrounding this large field bisected several times by paths to make walking easier from one part of Salem to the other. Here it is a moldy smelling swamp, with old trees, some dead, some living. Many with spots on the leaves. Strange that. Perhaps it was GOOD that someone took this icky area of standing water away. The hills in the area stood a little taller than the two-story houses. The landscape of the area looked very different in their "home" time. Did they grind up these hills to fill in some areas, and expand the shoreline, or even smooth out the landscape? It reminded her of rough-hewn regions of a third world country more than anything she had seen.

This place had not yet become a city. It was a bustling town.

They passed houses, with the common land behind it on their left, and approached a large three-story building that bustled with a lot of energy and activity. A sign in front hanging from an bracket against the side of the building said, *Beadle's Tavern.*

John, Reynold, and Nora glanced at each other with wide eyes. This looked like a hopping place. The sign seemed humble. In modern times, the sign would be large, neon and blinking. People flowed in and out of the building wearing smiles. The horror and persecution of this period described by Nathaniel and Nora somehow was suspended in the market and at this tavern. John thought, "People gotta eat."

Nora got a spark of an idea. Behind them was a path, with a wood post on the corner marking "Ingersoll's." Her idea would keep them on the street a little longer, but she needed to beat sunset, and she HAD to look for this one house close to here. The end of the road was sixty yards away, only a two or three-minute walk. "Hey guys, I wanna look at something-follow me for a few minutes."

Nathaniel's eyes widened at the brazenness of the woman taking charge, but he gave a resigned glance as the three followed Nora down this narrow street that could only fit maybe a single horse. They walked until the end, where they encountered another wood post, which said, *Water Street.* John and Reynold were following as Nora increased her pace. She wasn't running, but she was certainly on a mission.

She made the left turn on "Water Street" and walked along the edge of the town. Before making the right turn ahead was a short pier where a ship was moored. Just at the head of that pier was a guard shack that looked like it could hold perhaps four guards, and a pair of soldiers with muskets stood guard next to it.

To their right, fifty-feet away was the customs house. This was a substantial brick building that looked a lot like the Town's House and was also three stories tall. Tall buildings stood out like looking at red on a field of gray. The brick building looked official. John said, "I guess, this is where they collected taxes for goods entering this port?" Could this be an international port?

They passed a field on the right and continued walking a few yards. They saw what Nora was looking for. Another three-story home that seemed out of place amongst the other buildings, especially since it had three distinct smokestacks. The windows differed from the Corwin house with its diamond-shaped windows; these were more normal-looking square windows. Nothing was out of the ordinary except that it had two more fireplaces, and a third floor.

She stood there and marveled, while John, Nathaniel, and Reynold wondered what she found so amazing. The house was enormous, but why was it special to her?

She explained to Nathaniel. "You see, there's a building where WE come from called," she paused for effect, turning to Reynold and John and changing to a sarcastic tone, then continued, "... the *House of the Seven Gables.* Remember guys... er, gentlemen?"

Reynold and John had to muster up their best *ah ha* faces to respond. "Oh sure, that place," Reynold said, and wondered why it sounded familiar. Hadn't Nora been grading papers about that place? Was it a book? Reynold then forced back a little laughter. He got it. A *which* hunt. Reynold plus humor equals laughter. He could get used to that.

Nathaniel looked at Reynold and John and merely shrugged. "Hmph." These people were odd. Why were they so fascinated by houses? People built houses all the time. Strange. Anyway, there were only five gables he could see.

Nora resisted an urge to throttle them all. Why weren't

they excited about this? She could understand Nathaniel not getting it, but the other two weren't jumping out of their skin. They lived in Salem, for crying out loud!

She marched back down the street, backtracking along the same route they had taken to get there. Reynold hurried to catch up with her.

As Nora and Reynold walked a little ahead of Nathaniel and John, Nathaniel touched John's arm. "I don't want to offend you... but the woman you introduced as your wife earlier seems to... like your servant Reynold."

John spun and responded, "How... How do you know?" What were the clues he hadn't picked up on? Is this guy clairvoyant? This guy was a master of languages, hunted for his food, fought in wars, and had graduated from the same school HE did although hundreds of years earlier. But John loved using search engines, while this guy was perfectly fine without one. Wow, he felt grossly inadequate. He repeated his question. "I mean, how do you know she... likes Reynold?"

"She seems more frustrated by him than you. My wife gets frustrated with me all the time, and she loves me. I sometimes think that is a man's purpose, to frustrate our wives," Nathaniel replied. He didn't say it with any sarcasm. He merely said it.

Nathaniel fascinated John. This guy was pure genius. If he ever heard a stand-up comedian utter that phrase, he would roll on the floor laughing. He could still take Nathaniel down at *Star Wars* Trivial pursuit and felt just a little better about his master's degree from Harvard because of it.

Nora and Reynold were ahead of them, walking side by side. Nathaniel and John quickened their pace to catch up to the other two. It was so strange to walk on streets that had never seen a car. The houses were more cluttered in this area. It felt like a suburb. How many people lived in American now? Two or three-hundred thousand? Salem had over forty thousand people living in it when they had left the day earlier. In this *now*, everyone has to supply themselves with the means to keep their families alive, in this still untamed land. Every house had a farm, although some were larger than others. Almost all had barns. They even had trees on their property because they needed fire wood to heat their homes in the winter. What did modern people grow besides herbs for their salads?

Walking up the street back towards Beadle's Tavern, their growling stomachs grew louder. They needed food and drink. Filling their nutrition tanks became necessary in order to think clearly.

They were so distracted by their surroundings and didn't realize the passage of time. Reynold didn't dare check his smartwatch. You don't appreciate time while watching it.

They took a moment to absorb the rectangular shaped building they were approaching. Three stories tall, it had six windows with square panes above the second floor. The two windows on the ground floor in front and four on the side had their shutters pulled in. Behind the building was a barn for the guests horses. Also in the back there was a pair of small structures that looked like the house *Caractacus Potts's* father lived in from the movie "Chitty-Chitty-Bang-Bang." The wooden structures were narrow and seemed raised. One door had a carved a crescent moon, and the other a full moon.

John asked, "Nathaniel, what are those small buildings... behind the barn?"

Nathaniel looked with astonishment at John and replied, "Those... are... privies. Were you... injured on your head during your journey? You've never seen nor used a privy?"

Nora was annoyed. She would let the other two men ask stupid questions and correct them later. "Um, no sir, maybe John and Reynold may have, but I did not witness their injury." She received scalding looks for that response. Reynold liked Nora a lot, but if he was going to get sassed all the time, maybe bachelorhood wasn't so terrible.

They entered and gawked at the bustling activity. The place was warm and inviting. At the Ships Tavern, many people were singing rhythmic sea chanties, while at this tavern, one person played the violin in the corner. This place was upscale. A few people played cards. John ignored his hunger while he investigated what game they were playing. He eavesdropped for a few minutes. He observed that the cards had no numbers on them. One man had a pile of coins in front of him. He put his three cards down, and said what sounded like French, "Vingt-et-Un." What did that mean?

John returned to where Nora and Reynold still stood and absorbed their surroundings and asked if they had heard of *Vingt-et-Un.*

Reynold looked at him and said, "Twenty-One? Could it be Blackjack?"

Nora thought, "Didn't Cervantes feature that game in Don Quixote?" She wanted to take out her phone and investigate, but resisted the urge.

The next room they entered had long benches and tables of the same length. The fire was blazing hot, but the hearth was inviting and as large as a closet. They had been outside for two days and needed to remove the chill from their bones. The trapezoid shaped fireplace had a short wall behind the fire with two angled walls facing out to the room.

There were bricks below and behind the fireplace, and some copper pots hung on the left next to the fire. The fire was very hot. The blackness behind the fireplace streaked up the wall toward the chimney, where the flames had burnt carbon scars into the wall. Against the wall on the right was an enormous shelf for items waiting their turn in the flames. The large fire had two pots over it. One was huge. Someone easily six feet tall would only need to stoop a little to stand in the fire's place. On both sides of the fire were two brick ovens built into the wall. There was also a similar oven lower to the floor, closer to the flames. John surmised that the different locations were for different cooking temperatures. The oven on the right had several loaves of bread already baking, caused a fantastic yeasty smell to permeate the room. Against the wall of the room were two oil lamps suspended by *L* brackets. Their table had a few lit candles on it.

The room was tall, with exposed ceiling beams and solid walls. From outside the building, it looked like a wooden structure, but the interior walls comprised rocks with cement holding them together. This place wasn't going anywhere.

A woman dressed in a loose white top and dark wool dress walked over and asked, "Drinks, dearies?"

Reynold's eyes went wide and didn't know what was available. "No Water, No Water, please no water," his brain pleaded.

Nora saw the hesitation and said, "Three ales please and today's special." She figured she had better order for them before they asked for a *soda* or something equally strange. Hmm. Maybe she'd have an after dinner mead. The honey-wine must be fantastic.

Nathaniel looked at Nora sharply. A woman ordering for

men? Most unusual. He said to the bar wench, "Yes, a fourth ale, please. And please tell Thomas to add this to my tab. Please bring today's stew for everyone."

Reynold became concerned about his allergies. Should he ask about salt content? Did anyone ask for anything lightly salted? Oh no. Could he get an ingredients list? How many calories did the stew have? JUST DON'T TALK.

The woman who took their order walked over to the fire and scooped their dinner out of the cauldron and into plates over the large fireplace, grabbed a loaf of the bread at the oven, then went to the bar and fetched four tankards. Her two dexterous hands held it all with ease and placed it in front of them. Within just a few minutes, they had their drinks and their bowls of ox stew. She placed an additional bowl of stew next to them in case they might want more, and they did. They were hungry. John thought, "There's no menu?" but was happy to be eating anything other than Chinese food. Thomas Beadle prided himself on hiring only the best cooks that would find all the shrapnel from the day's kill, so customers didn't eat bits of a musket ball. It was why customers came back. Beadle's stew was the best.

The ale was light tan, and the flavor of the *hops* was pronounced. They made the drink with more molasses than anything they had from modern brewing methods. It contained citrus flavors, had both toffee and caramel undertones, and was also chilled and refreshing. A benefit from living north of the equator, and using the coolness of the ground and burying the beer filled casks. It was ambrosia after a day without drinking or eating. Since Reynold wasn't a regular drinker, he felt the alcohol warm him faster than the fire.

The slightly salted stew tasted terrific. The meat was very tender. That wasn't far from the truth. Since the cooking temperatures weren't as high as modern stoves, so the stew sat over the fire for many hours.

The stew had a flavorful brown sauce with mushrooms as its base. The corn and carrots were also sweet. They enjoyed the freshest vegetables they had ever tasted.

Reynold thought, "Hmm, wonder how much it costs to stay here?"

In December 1693, the total bill submitted to the court by Thomas Beadle for reimbursement was 58 pounds, 11 shillings, and 5 pence for all the services rendered during the trials. Beadle didn't detail the bill for the court. They used rooms at his Tavern for some prisoners, the out-of-town Judges when the court was in session, the barn for their horses' lodging, and occasionally they would even interrogate the accused in his front room opposite from the bar and food area. The court didn't hesitate to pay him for his *service* to the community.

This tavern was teeming with activity. People were talking louder and louder as the guests consumed more alcohol. They all seemed to understand that drinking water was more dangerous than drinking alcohol. What the heck, it also thinned their blood and made the lack of entertainment choices bearable. It also made people attractive using beer goggles. Early colonial life was impossibly hard on a person's face and eyes.

Two men smoked pipes at the table next to them. Nathaniel spoke to them, and they put their pipes away. Damn! who was this guy?

The four of them sat and enjoyed their surroundings. They didn't talk much over dinner, as they were famished, and slightly dehydrated since they hadn't had liquids in over a day and a half. The beer quenched their thirst, and the saltiness of the food made them drink more beer.

Many people walked over and interrupted Nathaniel and caught up with him. Travelers were a source of news from out of the area. The guests stared at the strange-looking people who were filling their faces with food and drink. Oddly enough, the travelers didn't seem to mind the three asking questions. Occasionally, they would nod and grunt when acknowledged by the people talking to Nathaniel. They learned their lesson. Loose lips sink ships.

John was buzzed. Reynold arrived at a *toasty* buzz and progressed further as the beer got tastier and tastier. His eyes became a little glassy. John asked the waitress, "Miss? How much for another beer?" as if he had money to pay for anything. Oh no, the alcohol made him give away too much information.

"Dearie, calling me MISS. Looking to butter me up like a piece of bread, are you?" said their waitress, showing a few missing teeth and a thick British cockney accent. "A Hay-penny is all it is gov'na. -N- Yer 'ost, is taking care of it. Yer a chahmer you are."

John thought, "I understood hay-penny... was that even English? Was the hay-penny part of a Christmas song in the lyrics? Was that more or less than a penny? *if you've no penny, a Hay-penny will do* so a hay-penny for a beer? Was that a type of penny? How can there be a half of a penny? Also, what's an *'ost?"* John didn't understand her at all. Why did he talk to her?

They could drink for years for a single dollar. If he shared the beers with Reynold, he would only have three and a half years of beer since Reynold would rarely partake. There's no drinkable water here. He will get sloshed if he doesn't control his drinking. He thought that reaching into his wallet and taking out a bill with the picture of someone who will not be born for forty years may not be cool. "Here's a buck lady!" Not the best move.

Reynold drank infrequently. Being in control of his faculties was far more important than getting drunk. He had better watch himself, or he'd reveal their innermost secrets every single day. Reynold amused himself by thinking about a scene from *Back to the Future Part III*. "And in the future, we don't need horses. We have motorized carriages called automobiles." He allowed himself to smile a little. How many had he had? Just the one he was holding.

Reynold drank and wondered how he would maintain control of his senses. He never drank. How was he going to build up his tolerance?

John thought Reynold was just... well, a wuss as far as drinking. Wait... he realized why the waitress perked up by being called miss. Was he supposed to call her a *wench*? And if he called that woman a *wench*, would Nora kill him on the spot, vaporizing him with a single look? Have three days passed yet? He couldn't even touch the gizmo he created that got him into this mess here.

John conjured up a mental image of the device in their pockets and silently yelled, "Charge, damn you!"

13

FASTING AND PLANNING DAY

John pondered their circumstances. The three of them were glassy-eyed and ready for bed. Drinking beer needed to become commonplace. People could watch them staggering around and silly all the time will become suspicious. The residents must have solid steel livers. Their blood alcohol level must have hovered above legal limits all the time. It's a good thing no cars are available. You can't charge a horse rider with drunk driving if the horse knows how to get home.

Nathaniel looked at them and said, "I'm going to hit the hay. We will discuss our strategy tomorrow."

John and Reynold's eyes popped out. Did he say hit the hay? Nora whispered, "they make the beds out of hay." At that moment, John and Reynold perfected their *ah ha* looks.

What was their next move?

From across the room, the sheriff of Salem stared at a black man acting free. Was he free? That didn't matter. Freedom didn't mean he had rights. Why wasn't he in the barn with the farm animals? This was strange. A freed negro man interacting with the rest of society. First witches, and now this. Servants and slaves had their place. The other two people distracted him, but he saw Nathaniel Saltonstall sitting with them. Why was he back in town? Saltonstall sat on the same Court of *oyer et terminer* that his brother, Jonathan Corwin. Nathaniel had quit after only two weeks. Those four people were very suspicious. They walked over to Thomas Beadle, talked for a moment, and proceeded up the steps to their rooms. George thought he would need to ask some questions.

As Reynold, John, Nora, and Nathaniel trudged up the steps, Nathaniel said, "I'll knock on your door tomorrow morning. Thomas said the corner room upstairs next to the stairs was yours. I'm just next door."

They half walked, half staggered to their room and were surprised at how much it reminded them of a bed-and-breakfast, not an inn. It was just a regular house with rooms. The noise from downstairs echoed everyplace.

They were cozy from excess beer consumption and exhaustion. They entered a bedroom which had no lock. The contents included one full sized bed, a small set of shelves, a bowl of fresh water (who knows what was living in there) a clean white towel, and a tall ceramic black pot with a wide opening on the top, which stank.

John and Reynold were visibly disgusted with the repugnant pot. Nora said, "It's a chamber pot."

John's face said it all. He had to ask, "What do you store in a *chamber pot*? It smells like... shit. Why not keep a vase for flowers?" His face was near it, his nose almost descending into the wide mouth of the pot.

Nora looked at him and responded as plainly as she could without making him smash his face into the edges. "Do you see any sinks or bathrooms in here? There's a reason it smells *crappy*."

Reynold grasped this new concept and said, "Buddy, back your face away from our room's communal bathroom."

John turned to meet Reynold's and Nora's gaze. Hopefully, John was so buzzed, he might not remember this portion of the night.

Nora said, "I'll take the floor, you guys. Sorry to make you share the bed, but... it's far too soon to get chummy." John and Reynold sharing a bed. This will be interesting.

John didn't argue and fell on the bed making a floof sound when he landed. The hay beneath the goose feather mattress was the box-spring. He passed out on the bed near the wall. It was their first night of horizontal sleep. They were getting acclimated to their current *time-zone*, but it was still hard to recognize what time it was by their body clocks.

Reynold gave Nora his pillow, folded up his jacket as a substitute, then Nora kissed him. Reynold relaxed into the moment and let his mind go numb. It was their first kiss and was unmistakable. Reynold plus Nora equals bliss.

Nora stretched out on the floor, put her head on the pillow, fell asleep, and snored lightly.

Captivated by the kiss, Reynold thought, "Wow! This is really cool," and burned the moment into his permanent memory storage. He listened to her soft snores for a few minutes, soaking in the day, and thought, "Good thing she fell asleep first, cause she'd hear me snore."

Reynold cleared his head and realized this was the longest he had gone without an inhaler since before being diagnosed with asthma. The absence of pollutants was excellent for his lungs.

In the next room, Nathaniel took out his diary, chronicled the day's activities, and predated the next date in the book. No matter what, the days will continue. September 21st.

Nora woke up first the next morning and tried her luck at the privy outside.

The plan was to walk downstairs and out the back door of the tavern. Easy. She descended the steps and saw someone stoking the fire in the dining room. The tavern was calm. What time was it? How do people make appointments in the mornings? Nora imagined someone saying, "Whoops, missed my alarm. Wait, it hasn't been invented, so no problem."

She hadn't brushed her teeth in days, and that was getting annoying. She felt she had the dreadful combination of grit and slime on her teeth. Did I kiss Reynold with this breath? Oh God. What is HE thinking?

She opened the back door, and the cold struck her face like a million needles. "CRAP ON A CRACKER THAT'S COLD," she said. Maybe the thunder mug in their room wasn't such a bad idea. Although the idea of two physicists staring at her as she squatted over the pot wasn't giving her a good vibe. Maybe good second date material but definitely not first. Could she declare the start of the second date yet?

The smell as she approached the privy was horrible. Tomorrow. When will it be tomorrow? Is that dang gizmo charged yet? As she approached the wooden buildings, she considered the two doors. One had a full circle or moon cut out in the door at eye height, and a crescent moon shape on the other door. Weird, she only remembered the crescent moon shape on outhouses. As she approached the privies, a man emerged from the full moon shaped door, and a woman emerged from the crescent moon door. In the near future, the crescent moon privy or outhouse would evolve as the only survivor. She never studied the history of bathrooms. Crappy study, if anyone asked her. Gales of mental laughter.

As she opened the door she thought, "Oh joy of joy." If she ever saw a highway rest-stop ever again, she would love and cherish it. She resolved she would set aside a lot of time to get truly emotional over her next meeting with a modern commode. After the initial mental preparation, she found that it was smelly, but as Beadle's tavern was more upscale, she was hit in the face with the smell of what she guessed was lime and pine. She remembered her lime from using a campground outhouse once. Which was her last special experience? She wondered, was this where the pine smell originated from? On one side of the confined space, she saw a large bucket of white powder, the lime, complete with a makeshift wood scooper. On the other side was the bucket of pine smelling aromatic wood-chips. Next to the hole was a pile of cloth strips. She realized what they were for. The smell was worse outside than inside. STRANGE. She marveled at the rough looking raw wooden seat. Will she get splinters? Did these women have tougher bottoms than modern women? "Oh hey Reynold, could you be a doll and help me pick the wood slivers out of my butt?" Oh sure, more demoralizing first date moments.

She completed her task and returned to the room. As she opened the door, Reynold and John started to wake up.

"Hey where did you go?" asked Reynold, rubbing his eyes.

"You see, they have a coffee shop downstairs, so I asked Martin the barista to make me a large cappuccino. I connected to their hotspot and received my E-mail since we didn't pay extra for the internet in the room. You know, they spelled my name as *Nero* on my cup... not even close... not even close."

Since her sarcasm was lost on the two sleepy men, she said, "Ok I lied, I couldn't get my E-mail using their hotspot.

This fancy place has an outhouse. Reynold. Please give me your hand sanitizer right now. I'd like to shower and gargle all of it." Reynold saw the fire in her eyes, hurriedly found the pocket where he stashed it in his jacket, and handed it to her.

Reynold said, "Look, I am so sorry breakfast sort of got extended."

Nora replied, "Yeah, you should be sorry... bringing a history major back in time. It's so terrible viewing history while it's happening... I will never breakfast with another physicist ever." Her broad smile punctuated the sentence.

They needed a day and a half more, and the green lights of their devices would light up. Halfway home. None of them dared to look at Elmer. It would not speed up the charging. Shaking and tapping it was tempting.

Reynold looked at her and said, "Hey... thanks for that kiss."

Nora thought, "Oh no!" Reflecting a moment, he said, "What else did I do?"

"Snore... just a little," Reynold replied.

Inside Nora's head, a little voice said, "... oh no." Her eyes went wide, and said out loud, "Snore... I don't snore." and she wished the matter would be quickly dropped.

John sensed the tension building, and jumped in by saying, "You know, just spit-balling here. We will need to return to the exact same spot in those trees to find that wormhole if it hasn't collapsed." Good change of focus. Hi. I'm John, couples counselor.

"I still think we are holding it open by being here." Reynold replied, "But hey, we're the first people in history to traverse one. Maybe we should leave a note before we leave, so our family will know we tested something, went back in time, then tried to return, so they know what happened to us. Or maybe they'll tell us to bring thicker jackets and a port-a-potty next time, and suck it up buttercup, 'cause SCIENCE."

Nora began, "I don't know how we can help Nathaniel, and if we do, what will we change in the future? I really don't remember his name being mentioned more than once, nor if he did anything notable in history. Maybe his children did? If we change that, could our time change? We have done nothing of consequence yet. Nathaniel said the court isn't in session this week, so I don't know how things could change. Tomorrow is September 22nd, and eight more people will hang. If we stop that, we may change thousands of people's lives in our *there and then* - if and when we get back." She added air-quotes around there and then.

John turned and said, "Thousands? Really?"

"We're about eight or nine generations away from our *here and now*. Man, this past tense/current tense conversation is driving me bonkers! Anyway, if each family has two or three kids, we populate our time-zone with thousands of people that may not have existed. How many become president? There's a story about a servant who fell overboard and was rescued on the Mayflower voyage. He's a direct ancestor of the Bush family, who contributed two Presidents and a governor." Nora wondered what sort of craziness they were playing with.

Reynold said, "We really can't help him that much. Just observe and make sure we don't get painfully dead." He still had the printout of the gravestone in his pocket. The stone had Sept. 22nd 1692 for the date of death for both he and Nora. This was serious. Maybe things they do will get them killed tomorrow? Yet somehow, he didn't feel worried about it. It hovered in the back of his thoughts. For some reason, he had confidence in their success. It might be a long time before anyone could appreciate what they accomplished. He did enjoy spending time with Nora, and she had kissed him goodnight. That gave him inner strength. He was in heaven. Amazing what self-assurance does to a person. He was worried about how to surpass this first date.

They heard a knock on the door. "It is Nathaniel. May I come in?"

"Sure." Nora was closest to the door, and she opened it. The room wasn't big, but still offered privacy for them to talk. Nathaniel walked in with his hat under his arm and launched into his idea for a plan.

"We have little time. One person has confessed to being a witch and has been spared from hanging. So instead of hanging ten tomorrow, they will only hang nine."

Nora leaned into John and Reynold and whispered, "That is weird. The numbers don't jive. Like I told you before, they hanged eight people, not nine on September 22nd. Maybe we've already changed history?" John turned and looked at her. What could they have done?

Reynold said, "To confess to a crime and be spared execution. Strange."

"Not exactly. They are still in jail, but they now need to accuse another as a witch." Nathaniel had seen this pattern earlier. Claim innocence, get convicted. Then hang by the neck until dead.

"How are we going to help you?" Nora began. "This is a terrible thing. But we're not from around here and have no discernible skills to contribute to this fight. We can't overpower anyone, and we are unarmed."

Nathaniel looked defeated, bordering on emotional. He spoke slowly, almost in a whisper. "It is terrible to know so much about something and not be able to help. I am a man of means and have survived wars and many, many fights.

Each day here, we're living well. It's not like it was when the original settlers arrived, nearly freezing to death one winter without provisions. This is not about fighting the environment, nor the Indians, nor are we fighting the English or French. We are fighting ourselves. I was part of the force that deposed the governor only a few years ago. I did that with the passion of a tiger, yet now I stand mute. Afraid of being accused and killed for speaking the convictions I share with many of the townspeople. No, we're accusing each other of... air? Breathing? It is ridiculous." He drew in a deep breath and continued, "I... watched a friend of mine draw his last breath the other day because he stood his ground. Martha and Giles Corey aren't witches. They are good, God-fearing people. But this disease people have picked up is in their minds. Is it making men and women crazy over land? Over their livestock? Over status? It is impossible to see what motivates these accusations, or even if there is a desire to stop it. I'm at a loss, and I'm probably thinking so much about it that it turns my thoughts into knots. My gut and instinct tell me you three people can help bring an end to it. You may walk, talk, and look differently. And if I may speak honestly, you aren't the smartest three people I've met..."

At this, John and Reynold looked at each other and were sorely tempted to show him Elmer, thinking, "Oh yeah, well, what do you think of the magical blinking yellow light on this thing, kind sir?"

Nathaniel continued, "... but you seem to have an innate understanding. Maybe you can help eliminate this evil. Many people are opposed to what is being done, but are afraid to speak out because they will become the next victims."

Nathaniel drew a deep breath and considered his next

words, but was out of them. Salem and the surrounding villages and towns had gone crazy. As far away as New Hampshire, people were accusing each other of witchcraft without evidence. Salem was the epicenter of an endless disaster. He gazed at them in despair.

Nora looked at Nathaniel and said, before he could continue, "We'll figure out a way to help."

Thomas Beadle interrupted her next thoughts by banging on their door. Thomas said, "Nathaniel. You and your friends need to get out quickly."

14

SHOT THROUGH THE HEART/TAKE ONE TABLET

Nathaniel snapped to attention. His emotions disappeared as he stood up, ready to command his troops. He said, "Gather your things and follow me."

Reynold scowled and put on his jacket. He felt their attempt at subterfuge failed.

They opened the door and followed Thomas to the back stairs, then walked down as slowly as they could to avoid raising suspicion. Fortunately, the offset tavern exit shielded them from view by design to ease getaways such as this. They walked to the barn and stepped through the side entrance.

Once they were inside the barn, they followed Thomas and Nathaniel toward a stall with a horse standing in it. Thomas said, "Quickly!" as they joined the horse in his private stall. The horse shifted position briefly and scrutinized everyone walking by his post. He distrusted the newcomers invading his personal space.

Once inside, they closed the stall door. Thomas looked

at his horse and commanded, "Abigail, sentry." The horse returned to the door and draped his head outside to greet people if any entered the barn. All five of them were now hidden where they stood. Two lanterns hung on the wall, already lit.

Nathaniel said, "Thomas, you named a stud after your neighbor's wife?"

Thomas replied, "She's a nag... and so is he." The horse whinnied at Thomas for this response.

Thomas moved a barrel filled with horse manure, revealing a hidden door in the floor. That barrel should have weighed hundreds of pounds.

Nora, John, and Reynold stared at the door in awe. Thomas said, "False bottom barrel. We replace the top with fresh droppings daily," he nodded at Nora. "She could probably move it... Abigail helps me fill it." Well, at least he's not using another horse's manure. That would make Abigail feel bad sharing the stall with unfamiliar poop. They looked down at the dark wooden staircase he had revealed.

Thomas took one lantern and handed it to Nathaniel. He said, "Keep them safe. George Corwin is looking for the black man. Seeing him in the tavern last night made him angry, besides all the witches he is hunting. I have drawn that dog off the scent. Now it's up to you." They walked down the steps with more confidence now that their way was lit and their eyes acclimated to the darkness as they followed Nathaniel.

They descended the steps into a large storage area under the foundation of Beadle's tavern. It was like an underground world.

Where were they? Why would Beadle's tavern need a secret basement? What was happening in Salem that people needed all this strange subterfuge? Why was Thomas hiding this?

Nathaniel gestured toward the back wall, at the entrance to a tunnel that was wide enough to fit two people side by side. They were passing underneath the streets they had been on yesterday when they walked into the front entrance of the tavern. "Come. We're under the tavern. Let's take the tunnel."

"What is this for Nathaniel?" Nora's brain was practically on fire with questions. Are Thomas and Nathaniel a pair of master smugglers? What were they smuggling? Why?

"Shhhhhhh, follow me. I'll explain." Nathaniel's eyes were very serious.

They walked along the impressive stone tunnel.

They walked for a few minutes in silence, then heard the sounds of crashing waves.

"Ok, we're safe here," Nathaniel announced softly.

John finally asked, "What is all this?"

"Years ago, the governor was taxing us at an alarming rate, filling his pockets. He turned most of the colony into a... military state. Soldiers were everywhere. The money wasn't even going back to England because he was stealing it. We were under great duress. So a lot of the goods that came in from ships were off-loaded before it became taxed or tariffs levied on them by that customs house we walked by yesterday."

Nathaniel continued, "So Thomas was nice enough to help by building the storage area under the house and above his barn when he first made the tavern. This way, taxes that burdened ships coming into Salem were... shall we say, eased? It also helped when we were stocking ships. The filled ship might not have all the goods taxed."

"Who else knows about this tunnel?" Nora asked.

Nathaniel had to trust these people now. They were inside a very important area that had helped people in Salem, and most of New England, for years. A secret delivery tunnel for black market goods. He replied slowly, "Besides the men who helped us build it, only a few trusted merchants know. Maybe fifteen ships' captains at most, and a few members of their crew."

Nora the historian was now looking at an unknown history.

The silence lasted quite some time. Nathaniel broke it by saying, "Sheriff George Corwin isn't a man to trifle with. He visited children after hanging their parents and confiscated and sold their property to pay for their jail costs. He's a young, driven, and vicious man."

Nora replied, "That's horrible. You become an orphan, and in horrible debt. Even though the parents are innocent."

Nathaniel asked, "How do you know? I said there's no evidence of witchcraft."

Reynold replied, "Because there is no witchcraft. You said it yourself. It can't be proven."

They sat quietly waiting for some sign.

After sunset, the tunnel was barely lit by the hanging oil lamp. They listened to the splashing of the waves and waited. Nothing to do but wait.

Nathaniel said, "We need to make a presence of ourselves, and stop the hangings tomorrow." He knew they had no weapons, nor an army to let the convicted out of jail. Tomorrow they would hang nine people, Salem's largest group of accused since the trials began. The Court was traveling to condemn other people accused of witchcraft. Repeated in the surrounding towns, it spread like a plague. The pieces of the puzzle didn't fit. It was impossible to sway the minds and then get everyone out of jail. The injustice had to stop.

Reynold responded, "I don't know how we can help? If this Corwin guy is after me, then we can't help. Really, I can't. I don't know how to help if I'm a wanted man drawing attention because of my skin color." Acting against history could be dangerous. Not acting could have consequences. What was the right answer? Are there parallel universes? Broken timelines? Could they stop people from existing? Create a future person who becomes another Hitler from their interference? This wasn't his class, and students were not in front of him. He was out of his element. What was the next move?

No one spoke for a while as they considered Reynold's point. He asked, "How long are we going to stay here?" It was dark outside. Reynold grew angrier about being singled out because of his skin color. More questions popped up in his mind. Was avoiding interfering with history going to be enough? Or had they already interfered?

Reynold looked ahead to where the sound of the crashing waves directed them to safety. What was on the other side? Despite the relaxing sound, the cave felt like a prison. "Guys, let's get out of here. I don't think we're being chased anymore."

They reluctantly agreed, and Reynold led the way forward. They proceeded to the end of the tunnel and approached an iron gate which opened underneath the pier. The opening was behind a rock, hidden in plain sight.

They looked both ways and quietly crept out. The moonlight and stars lit their way. The hairs on the back of their necks stood alert.

As they walked up the beach where the pier met the street, they felt they were not alone. A single guard wearing the familiar *red-coat* British uniform was standing at attention, guarded the pier. An empty ship tied to the dock waited patiently for its crew to return.

"Guys, should we split up?" John was sure that splitting up was dangerous, but it was less dangerous than being jailed or interfering with history.

Without realizing their poor coordination, nor of a positive or negative response to his statement, Nora, John, and Nathaniel walked one direction, and Reynold walked the opposite direction toward a field next to the pier. As he walked, the guard called out, “HEY! You! Slave! The sheriff is looking for you!”

Nora, John, and Nathaniel froze. Reynold ran.

The guard shouted again, "Slave!"

"What the heck!" thought Reynold. The guard's attention was on him, and completely ignored John, Nora, and Nathaniel.

The guard thought to himself, "Nickolas, why did I draw the short straw for this horrible shift?” He shouted, “Halt slave or I will shoot,” emphasizing every word.

Nickolas jogged toward Reynold. British soldiers always had their guns ready for the first shot. His musket training was complete, and his accuracy was the best in his unit. He loaded his rifle earlier that day in anticipation of any action. To make sure everything was fresh in his gun, he would fire it at a target at the end of a shift, dig out the musket ball, and re-use the shot if the ball wasn't too damaged, or bang it a little with a hammer to get it back in shape. Musket balls were expensive, and he wasn't reimbursed nor resupplied, so he was careful what he shot. That morning he inspected his musket, starting with the flint. He pulled the trigger, and it created a spark against the frizzen to ignite the powder through a small gap. He pushed it back to cover the pan where the powder was loaded. OW. That damn thing was hot. Next, he measured out the precise amount of gunpowder from his first powder-horn, and poured it down the end of the musket barrel. Nickolas took a piece of cloth out, dabbed grease on it to perfect precision, and placed the musket ball into the center of the now greasy patch of cloth. He took the musket ball in the patch, placed it into the tip of the barrel, and used the push rod built into the gun and shoved it as hard as he could until it was firmly against the powder charge. Then he took out his second powder-horn, which was filled with finer powder pouring it into the open frizzen again. This packed the coarse and fine powder behind the musket ball. When the flint strikes the frizzen, the coarse and fine powder will ignite launching a half an inch ball at its target at half the speed of sound.

Reynold ran away from the guard and his shouts. Hard to believe he had traveled back in time to feel like a third-class citizen. His jacket wasn't helping him, loaded with his daily supply of stuff. Running for your life hauling extra weight wasn't easy.

Nickolas commanded, "In the name of the King, halt!"

John and Nora were helpless. They were too far away from the guard to distract him now, and too far away to prevent him from shooting Reynold. They stared in shock as everything happened in slow motion.

Nickolas's target was seventy-five yards away. He was an excellent marksman and had to stop the slave who was defying his orders. He took aim, raising the gun a few inches to compensate for the distance. Realizing a wind was also coming towards him and slightly across the right side of his cheek, Nickolas adjusted, further shifting the aim of his gun up and to the left. He could no longer see the person he was aiming at through the sight at the end of the barrel. The whole gun was blocking his target from view, but he knew from experience he would be accurate.

Nickolas closed both of his eyes to avoid blinding himself by the explosion that was about to happen inches from his face and squeezed the trigger.

Reynold spun around to see if John, Nora, and Nathaniel had reached safety while he drew the attention of the guard.

The flint struck the frizzen, and the explosion created pushed the gun barrel against his shoulder with a hard punch. Nickolas opened his eyes to see what had happened to the target. He saw the negro's body jerk backward while his chin jolted forward. Bullseye. It cost him a musket ball, but this shot was one for the record books. He wanted to jump for joy to celebrate the accuracy of the shot, but this was serious business. He had seen no one survive a shot like that.

John, Nora, and Nathaniel watched in horror as Reynold's head jerked forward. They saw blood splatter outward. This was a direct hit. John gasped when he saw Reynold's chest covered in blood.

After witnessing many clean musket shots, Nathaniel knew there was nothing to be done. Reynold was gone. If he wasn't dead from the shot, he would pass away from the day-long agony or the attempt by the doctors to save him.

"COME ON! Your friend is dead. The guard is about to reload and fire at us. You can't help him; you must help yourselves." Nathaniel focused on getting out of harm's way. They would fight another day.

John was stunned. With smaller bullets in the 21st century, there would be a chance at that distance to survive. With a large ball, even at its slower muzzle velocity, that shot must have caused a lot of internal damage. The blood on Reynold's chest was obvious.

Nora managed to run. They hoped to return to Beadle's Tavern and stay in the room and hide from everything. She reminded herself of the missing A's - anesthesia, antibiotics, and antiseptics. She had started the day in *serious like* with Reynold, and just witnessed his death.

15

BACK TO BEADLE'S

John, Nora, and Nathaniel were beside themselves. Reynold was dead. The blow to his chest was an obvious kill shot.

Once Nathaniel got them back to the main street, they attempted to slow their run to a less conspicuous walk. Sheriff Corwin rode by on his horse, and they hid their faces. Corwin wasn't looking for them, and without street lamps, he didn't recognize them.

Their hearts pounded. If they were caught, they may not get back. The jail was a dungeon. It may not have had torture devices from the Middle Ages, but it must be dreadful without heating, cooling, bathrooms, or human rights. They had no money nor land to pay for the miserable accommodations. Every day in jail was paid by the accused. This was a nightmare.

What were they going to do?

All hope of helping the accused witches drained away. They trudged in silence towards Beadle's Tavern. Their feelings were so different from that morning when they awoke, rested and optimistic. Now they could barely put one foot in front of the other.

There were no video cameras, radios, nor phones, so John and Nora didn't exist. George Corwin was suspicious and obsessed over an escaped slave. The others remained safe until they opened their mouths because they couldn't be arrested for their thoughts. John and Nora stuck out, but without a crime visibly being committed, they were just people walking. What could they do now?

Nora couldn't process what had happened. The loud bang rang in her ears, as if it had happened next to her. The bright flash lit up the gunman's face like a spotlight. It etched his face in her mind. She saw him behind her eyelids with every blink. She replayed the moment in her brain. Reynold spinning around to look for them diverting the gunman so they remained safe. Reynold falling down, covered in blood. He saved their lives.

Nathaniel snapped them back to the present by saying, "Let's get a drink."

"Drink? Our friend is DEAD Nathaniel, Dead!" John retorted.

Nathaniel said, "Sorry, this... happens. Mortality isn't something you can predict. Friends die, people die. Your friend caught the sheriff's attention. He's not looking for us anymore. Let's try to remain on our task so we don't suffer the same fate." Nathaniel was commanding his soldiers to continue the fight, no matter the cost.

Nora looked on in shock and whispered, "How? What is the purpose? We're risking our lives, and one of us gave his already."

Nathaniel replied, "I don't know. I told you this morning, I didn't know how you could help, but I still believe your presence here must mean something. These are terrible times. I have never seen such indiscriminate torture. Everyone is a suspect. The conditions in jail are horrible. This is an infection of the town's heart that isn't caught through disease, but through thought. They are convicting based on their desires, not what's real. This is a fight for the truth. The only way to save ourselves is to keep moving forward. I'm more determined to stop this madness. Especially for your friend's sake. People may use this method to spread lies and kill more people. It's a war of morality in the end. How much can a person accept, and sow lies? These people who have been accused and hanged have pleaded innocent, have not been found nor proven guilty."

John's patience was gone. He was reticent to fight for a cause that wasn't his. He replied, "Nathaniel... what difference can we make? Reynold was the smartest one of us and could make the best argument to change their minds." If only his friend were alive so he could admit that to his face. "This isn't a battle we will win by attacking someone or something. We have to change people's attitudes. People are looking for the easiest solution to their problems and are blaming their neighbors. It's human nature. It's never about thinking how they can find a solution to their troubles, it's how other people are causing the problem. People will point, but they will never empathize with the person they are pointing at. They immediately dehumanize them because they are the problem in their mind. How can we change people's minds? The people they accuse are guilty. They can't get out of it. And these judges are the most respected men in Massachusetts. How are they going to be made to see things differently? You said yourself the court isn't in session right now. When will they begin again? How long can we hide out before we're discovered? We also must leave tomorrow."

Nora spoke without hearing the argument going on around her. "I'm so sad. I can't do this. I started this day feeling gleeful, and to be thinking about Reynold's death like this is not how I expected it to end. How can you expect us to continue where we left off as if Reynold's death was meaningless?"

Nathaniel's mind was spinning. He needed to reassert his control and rally his troops, or else a mutiny would end this battle before it truly began.

Nathaniel tried a different approach by making it personal for them and accepting blame for Reynold's death. "Your friend is now another victim of this horrible mess. It is my fault for leading you three upstairs in the tavern. Reynold should have stayed in the barn with Abigail."

John was mad now. "WHY! What did he do?"

Nathaniel explained, "It doesn't matter if your friend was free or not. They regard any black person with suspicion. Unless you are at the Ships Tavern, servants aren't allowed to sleep in rooms. I did not think about it because the more we talked, I almost," he had to choose his words carefully as it was strange to him "stopped seeing him as a negro. I can't explain it. He was your peer, and... he became mine. Your friend differed from any black man I've ever met."

Nora and John had never seen Reynold differently. They were accustomed to an integrated society. This here and now became their reality. Until this moment, it had been easy to brush off the differences. But this terra firma remained under their feet, and they had to stand on it.

They headed toward the tavern, now needing all their energy to reach their destination rather than talking in the street. Everything took concentration. Nora was no longer excited to be observing history. It hurt her to think about it as tears rolled down her cheeks, tracing painful channels from the corners of her eyes. This time period was now something to loathe. Reynold was dead. The image of his body lurching backward from being shot was etched in her mind. The blood on his shirt and jacket, equally so.

During traumatic experiences, the mind creates indexes to that exact occasion. Moments that indelibly plant themselves like mature oak trees, visible from a great distance. It's always able to refer back to them without hesitation. A smell, look, noise, or a sensation help bring emotions and thoughts to the surface. Nora and John now had images of their friend spinning around, looking toward them, then being jarred backward by the invisible force of the musket ball hitting him in the chest. Both could rewind in slow motion how he spun, jumped backward, then fell on his back with his chest covered in blood. Although surreal because it only happened a few minutes ago, she knew she would soon need to take time to cry an awful lot.

John was watching his feet move. Don't step on the rock. Don't step on the enormous livestock crap. His brain was awash in thought. Memories of his friend flooded his mind. So many happy memories. What was he going to do now? Like Nora, he was too numb to devote too much emotion to this problem. Through his clouded mind, he had a vague awareness that he had to keep his feelings together.

How were they going to help Nathaniel? Were they going to wait for part of a day tomorrow when both his and Nora's devices completed charging?

Suddenly, John's brain lit up with a big neon sign bringing him back to the present and thought, *Oh no!* He remembered Reynold had more technology in his jacket pockets than anyone he ever knew. He had secret pockets for all of it, and his dead, lifeless body was sitting in the middle of a field filled with things that won't be invented for hundreds of years. They should worry about this! Should he go back to collect it all, so people aren't blasted into the future as far as the invention of technology? Or would they simply bury him?

What would they do with Reynold's body? Would they place him in an unmarked grave? Would someone guess his name? They could not identify him, he knew that.

Identify him. IDENTIFY HIM! That damn gravestone with the Hebrew. Was it past midnight? He needed to protect Nora. The stone's inscription had Sept. 22nd 1692 as the date both Reynold and Nora's death. John dared not bring this up with her at the moment, as it would freak her out. He had a small fraction of doubt because today was the 21st of September, not the 22nd.

John's thoughts overwhelmed him. He took a deep breath to plan his next actions. Moments ago, his heart was racing. Other than movies and video games, he had never heard a gun fired, much less a musket. Without light pollution around to diffuse the blast, the flash was bright. It burned into his brain like a hot iron. He blinked his eyes and still saw a glint of green as if a lightning bolt had gone off near him.

John couldn't imagine a moment without Reynold.

John knew a little about survival. He knew they had to stay off the grid.

John saw Nora walking and had no words to say to her. John couldn't think of conversation starters. The person who brought them together was gone. They were together, yet alone. If they couldn't leave this *now*, they would need to become much closer to survive. Could they talk about anything other than Reynold? How do you strike up a conversation with someone who had horrible memories as a catalyst? It's the elephant in the room. What would Reynold want us to do? How would he protect Nora? Could they help Nathaniel?

The next day he would insist on going back to the outcropping of trees, and as soon as the LED's glowed green, leave. How were they going to reconcile this equation, and balance the thoughts and emotions over the past day? Or with Reynold gone, would the equation ever balance? Three went into the wormhole, and only two returned.

They approached Beadle's Tavern. Only minutes ago, Reynold had been alive, and they planned their next move. Now, this terrible gloom hung over them.

The tavern seemed empty. They were late for dinner and couldn't partake in today's stew. The bar was closed. Food for tomorrow was cooking over the fire, the bread was baking distracting them with the yeasty smell.

How could they think of food? How could they think of drink? Human instinct. Their hunger pangs made them feel guilty.

Reynold's death weighed heavily on Nathaniel. He thought of Reynold as a new friend.

They walked up the steps of the tavern and ascended the staircase toward their rooms.

Nathaniel looked at Thomas's and shook his head *No.* Thomas's eyes widened at the realization of what happened.

Thomas knew this wasn't good. His bar wench overheard George Corwin repeatedly saying, "That escaped slave." The black man's behavior and his presence enraged him. The sheriff was a tough man, but he respected Thomas's position in the town, and his help with the courts. Thomas still had favors he could call in to get out of trouble, but seldom needed to redeem them. His involvement in the community of Salem led them to name a street after him. The people who built the tavern knew to keep their mouths shut about the tunnel leading to the docks. People kept Thomas' secrets out of respect, not fear.

Once he saw the stricken faces of the people entering, he knew why they looked beaten. Either Corwin had jailed the black man or killed him.

John, Nora, and Nathaniel ascended the stairs, walking to their rooms in silence. They had nothing further to say. They could repeat their words from earlier, but they knew they weren't alone here, and the walls had ears. They had to watch themselves.

Nathaniel entered his room and closed the door. He saw the lit candle and a pitcher of beer waiting for him. Nathaniel had arranged with Thomas to be woken up early, so his *alarm clock* was a tankard of beer. Drink a lot, and he'd need to pee in the morning. The combination of the sun hitting his eyes, and the beer would wake him up early.

Nathaniel took out his diary. He never wrote his secrets in his diary, only notes to help him recall everything that had happened that day. If he didn't write it down, he might not remember. But he was keeping tabs on these developments. Someday, someone would ask what happened, and he wanted to explain it to them, without hesitation. He wanted to do this. Nathaniel took out his quill and ink and wrote down the events of the day. Once completed, he dated the next day to be sure he didn't miss it, else he could forget a date in the calendar. After the last entry, he wrote Sept. 22nd. He finished the beer and went to sleep.

John called dibs on the floor as they entered the room. Nora needed to sleep somehow. Tonight they were part of history, possibly polluting it.

John made a mental note to wake up early and return to that spot where they had seen Reynold fall, find his body, say a prayer over him, and remove all the technology from him. Perhaps he should bury him. How was he going to move him? Where would he get a shovel? Could he borrow one without raising suspicion? He set the alarm on his watch to vibrate just after sunrise at 6:45am. Reynold and he synchronized their watches Monday after Nora told them the exact date and time. He hadn't thought about the time in days, and now it was to wake up and look for Reynold's body. For Reynold.

He needed to take care of this for Nora. He knew she could have a mental breakdown at any moment. She had really liked Reynold a lot. John had a morbid thought. When their devices were charged, did he and Nora need Reynold's body to balance out the equation with the wormhole, cancelling out the negative mass? This was Reynold's area of expertise, and he missed his best friend to think clearly. It was too much for John to think about. His mind was moving very fast, but the combination of emotional and mental stress caused him to fall asleep when he laid down on the floor.

When they entered the tavern, they hadn't noticed the soldier behind them pushing a cart.

16

MEDIC!

Sheriff Corwin had alerted Nickolas to the negro and his traveling companions just before his shift started. This negro concerned the Sheriff. When he saw him, it was his duty to apprehend him. These were his orders. Nickolas had warned the negro several times, then announced his intentions before firing. He was in the right.

After Nickolas watched the man fall, he bolted toward the motionless body. While standing over the bleeding man, he realized that something was amiss. The blood was everywhere, but the rhythm of the breathing was... normal. This man was asleep.

He examined the body so intently that he was oblivious to his surroundings. Sheriff Corwin rode up on horseback, startling Nickolas. Corwin barked, "If he survived, bring him to the jail. If he needs a doctor, we'll arrange it after tomorrow's hangings. If he doesn't survive, knock on Reverend Higginson's house for last rites, and arrange burial." And he rode off. Gone as quickly as he had arrived.

Nickolas watched as the sheriff rode off and muttered under his breath so only he could hear "You are welcome, sir. Only a few people in the colony could have made that shot, sir... ever your servant, sir."

At that moment, Reynold jerked to a sitting position, gave one incredible gasp, and fell back down, unconscious. Nickolas stared with amazement at the negro now. There had to be a fatal wound to his chest some place, based on all the drying blood. Nickolas searched the man's body for injuries.

He saw the musket ball entry point on the jacket and opened it to inspect underneath. The red stained white shirt was obvious even in the dark. The man's breathing seemed even and regular. No rasping sounds, no signs of distress, just the sound of sleeping. He unbuttoned the shirt carefully, trying not to get the blood on himself, and saw his chest hadn't a scratch on it. Nickolas leaped to his feet in shock and pointed his now empty musket with bayonet at the body. He was gobsmacked. He cursed then prayed in his confusion.

Nickolas stared for a full minute as the body was laying immobilized. He knew he had to follow the orders given by the Sheriff. He was reticent to touch the blood. He wiped the excess off on cleaner parts of the victim's clothing, praying he wouldn't become a witch. This man could be the devil himself.

His proof was that he showed no sign of injury from a musket shot true to its target, and he healed within seconds of the soldier's arrival at the body. This was enough proof for him.

Until that moment, Nickolas wasn't convinced the search for witches made any sense. In the seven months he had stood guard during the trials, listening to countless hours of testimony by the witnesses, and watching the girls carry on making their strange noises in the courtroom, he had thought, "Why aren't I being affected by the people on trial as well?" The other people in the courtroom weren't bewitched during the confessions, only these young girls. If you stand in front of a cannon when it fires, everyone hears it for miles. People in the way of the cannonball are either instantly killed, or sustain injuries that make them succumb within hours. How was something that powerful ignoring the rest of the people in that courtroom except the girls? Nickolas didn't take their testimony seriously. In contrast, this man had healed instantly after being shot. What other magic could this man do? Nickolas didn't want to find out. He commandeered a cart to move the body so he could be away from it as soon as possible. Merchants often left their carts around, so he would borrow one and bring the body to the jail, as ordered.

Nickolas returned to Reynold's sleeping body and maneuvered the cart into place, lowering the back of the cart next to Reynold's head. He grabbed Reynold's jacket and dragged him up the inclined plane, reducing the weight by half. It pleased Nickolas that he avoided letting the blood stain his clean uniform.

After loading the body, Nickolas pushed the cart toward Main Street and made a left turn, walking past Beadle's Tavern.

The Sheriff hadn't paid Nickolas in weeks and wasn't happy with the extra work. He was less than thrilled to be carting around someone who could wake up and bewitch him. He needed to be efficient and quick. Nickolas's anxiety grew with each step towards the jail as he became convinced that Satan himself was in the cart. He was obsessed about how this man could have survived being shot in the chest. He had shot the devil, and it had no effect. That was the only answer. This was clear evidence that this person was the devil and Nickolas wasn't taking chances. Nickolas quickened his pace toward the prison. He didn't care that his victim groaned during the bumpy ride.

He made the right turn onto Prison Street, pushing the cart over rocks and debris. The roads were suited to people, oxen, and horses - creatures who had eyes and could avoid obstacles. Wheels were not helpful.

He still had to give a report to the commanding officer at the jail and return the cart where he borrowed it. Would he need to report how his prisoner survived the shot? He hoped not, for he could not explain it. Then he needed sleep before tomorrow's long shift due to the hangings. They wanted extra guards for the executions. Dorcas Hoar confessed, so there were only nine to hang tomorrow. Nickolas would still need to work.

Nickolas was convinced that the townspeople needed to trust their magistrates. He thought to himself, "Average people don't know what's good for them. How can they doubt such successful people? They understand things better than we do. They want to protect us, and we should respect their authority and their wisdom. These judges have all the wealth in the colony. How could they have gotten all that wealth without knowing a thing or two? They know that Satan invaded our town."

Nickolas recalled hearing confessions telling of a *black man* invading their dreams. The black man sleeping in the cart had to be him.

He was perspiring by the time he approached the jail. What time was it? He really needed sleep before his next shift started. He also couldn't wait to put distance between himself and this man.

The two guards outside the jail were friends of his, but

Nickolas was all business upon arrival. "I have the devil to drop off!"

"The Devil, you say?" said the closest one. "How do you know?"

Nickolas turned to the cart and showed them Reynold's body, exposing his bloodstained jacket and shirt. The open shirt revealed no visible wound. Reynold was obviously sleeping soundly.

"I shot him in the chest. He has no wounds now, though the ball pierced his jacket. Look!" He pointed from a distance, afraid to touch the blood again. Could the blood bewitch him? Could it curse him? "I... wouldn't touch the blood, just in case..." Nickolas said to the guards.

"This witch turned at the last moment, and I shot him square in the chest from about seventy yards. He went down hard. This must be the black man the girls dreamed about during the trials," reported Nickolas. He was sure.

The officer was a powerful man, but nervous around the devil. Holding the lantern closer to Reynold's chest, he could clearly see the hole in the jacket, the blood stains, and the uninjured chest. The devil slept and snored in front of him. He'd need to get him into the cell as soon as possible and deal with it after he returned tomorrow. The evidence was clear. He will explain to the court about this man when the trials resumed.

This was one of the finest jails in the colony. No one had ever escaped from it. They built the jail recessed into the ground for more protection. Nobody could dig out nor in. There was no need for bars on the windows, as the openings were only an inch high, letting in air. Every time it rained, the jail would flood, giving the inmates more rehabilitation for the crimes they had committed. That would also help clean the cells. The cell doors were six-inches of oak with an iron central core and spikes on the inside, preventing the bravest of prisoners from loitering on the other side when they opened inward. Hearing the locks tumble would make prisoners scramble for safety. They had imported the locks from England, and only a specialist could make the keys. According to the manufacturer, nobody in the Massachusetts colony could copy these keys.

Nickolas had successfully incarcerated the runaway slave and found Satan at the same time. The Sheriff would be even happier about this catch now.

Judge Jonathan Corwin would be proud that his brother had caught the man responsible for all this witch trouble. Maybe the town could finally pay all the guards.

Nickolas and the officer lifted the devil's unconscious body making sure not to touch the blood. This officer was as nervous as Nickolas now.

Sheriff Corwin rode up to the jail and smoothly dismounted. He saw the men holding Reynold's blood-soaked body and asked, "How is he alive?"

"I don't know, sir," Nickolas responded. “He must be the devil himself!" he continued.

George Corwin gestured to the men holding Reynold and grunted a reply of "hunh." Despite having instructed Nickolas to bring the black man here, it annoyed Corwin at yet another body in his jail. He opened the door to the jail and let the two men carry Reynold's sleeping body inside. Corwin took out the second key and opened a cell, gesturing to a place on the floor to deposit the prisoner.

The front door and all cell doors used separate keys. If you escaped your cell, you were standing inside a locked jail.

The guards brought Reynold in and placed him face up on the floor. There were no beds. The cell was cold, damp, and reeked. They placed Reynold's head next to the slop bucket, which needed emptying. It was overflowing with grotesque sewage. This prisoner deserved it. He was the devil. The guards backed out of the cell and Corwin locked the cell, then the outer door of the jail.

The other prisoners leaning on the walls were malnourished and underweight. They were no match for well-fed, healthy guards. There were only two unchained people in the cell. The woman said weakly, "Who is he?"

"I don't know," replied the unchained man. "I thought I heard the guard say he was the devil? Maybe he's just another witch. You would think with all the witches they captured, one of us would conjure up something to escape."

The jail was closed for the night, with only the light from the moon shining into the cell they were in. It was at that moment, a glint was slightly visible from the key around Reynold's neck.

17

INCARCER8

Reynold was in pain. His chest hurt like hell, and he rubbed it subconsciously. His nose was being overpowered by horrific smells, the olfactory glands overwhelmed to the brink of calamity. Acrid smells of feces, rotting food, death, decay, rotting rats, and a host of other unidentifiable things were mixing to engulf his senses in ways he had never experienced in his life. Before that, the cadaver lab was the most malodorous place to invade his nose. Awful. The smells from formaldehyde and rotting flesh was awful. This was thousands of times worse.

Reynold opened his eyes inches away from a bucket filled with overflowing human waste and vomited uncontrollably. He was in hell.

After catching his breath, he sat up again, knowing he added significantly to the stench. For good measure, he vomited again.

He sat up and caught his breath. Reynold blinked out the fogginess in his eyes and assessed his surroundings. He rubbed his chest and reviewed his damage now that he returned to the waking world. What is this horrible place?

He remembered turning around, and then a flash of light. After he passed out, people must have taken turns hitting him in the chest with a baseball bat. Probably a lot of people.

As memories flooded back to his fuzzy mind, he grabbed onto the last great thing his brain could remember, being kissed by Nora. Ok. With that memory, anything could be tolerable. He made a mental note not to sweat the small stuff anymore. Although... this really sucked.

Clarity returned to his brain. He was SHOT. He reached for his chest again and made a more accurate damage assessment. His chest really smarted, and he didn't think he had any broken bones. Why was he sticky? He looked down and saw a lot of red stains. I was shot in the chest? He only felt tender in his chest. His ribs hurt, but nothing stung. Had he been shot, he'd feel more than sore. Did a doctor save him? Where was the wound? Was he bleeding out? Maybe he had nerve damage? He reached under his shirt and felt no blemishes on his skin. Just a lot of muscle soreness. Probing with his fingertips, he found no holes in his chest. So the dried up crusty red goo wasn't blood. Where did this sticky stuff come from? Did someone ELSE get shot in front of him? He touched his jacket finally and found the hole in the pocket where he kept his inhaler. Reaching into that pocket, he felt jagged pieces of the destroyed inhaler. "Good thing I'm not desperate for it," he said to himself. He needed to jot down a complaint to the company that made them and cheered himself up by thinking of ways to complain and get a free replacement. *Your product is not musket proof!* I'm using an alternative brand until you take corrective safety measures! Hey, wait. I'm not musket proof. Did this thing save me?

When the Heart And Lung pharmaceutical company

made a miracle drug for people with asthma, the company created one of the first gel that could become aerosolized for that purpose. The gel had an incredible shelf life and gave triple the applications compared to the competition. You only need a few of these inhalers for long trips. When they developed the product, the gel was clear. They added the color red, which helped track its progress through the lungs during FDA trials. Because of the long approval process, they went to market with the color as part of the product.

Nickolas's shot pierced Reynold's jacket crushing the inhaler, causing it to burst. This impact slowed the musket ball.

Elmer was hidden in the inside pocket of his jacket, held shut by velcro. Behind it was Reynold's tablet. Elmer was charging until the musket ball created a hole slowing it down further. This shattered the two capacitors John made days earlier. Reynold's *Elmer* was incapacitated.

The company that produced Reynold's tablet fielded complaints about the product bending. So the engineers strengthened the aluminum alloy. The new material was stronger than aircraft aluminum. Once satisfied with its tensile strength, they released this new version with faster processors and better graphics. Marketing the new version, the company emphasized that this version of the tablet was the most powerful in both computing power and physical strength.

The musket ball had slowed down enough to create a dent on the outside of the tablet, leaving it fully functional. In its final act, the musket ball dropped harmlessly into Reynold's pocket, deformed and inert.

Reynold's hands searched for more damage. If that guy shot him in the chest, he'd be dead or dying, and other than the fact that he had contributed to this HORRIBLE smell that surrounded him, and the soreness one would get from the cast of "Stomp" practicing on his chest, he was nowhere near death.

He frantically searched his jacket pockets. His hands went into the inside chest pocket and found the hole in Elmer. He also felt the dent on his tablet computer. The tablet company is getting a five-star recommendation. It had saved his life again. First, when he had a significant project and used the tablet instead of his laptop computer to complete it. Now it had literally saved him. Go tablet. Go tablet. He would have to complain to John later about it saying, "All of this is your damn fault, and now I have a DENT in my tablet!" He was sure he'd empathize. He felt around in his pocket and found the deformed musket ball. Well, he could help the company that produced that tablet computer by giving them another bullet point for the website. Ha "bullet point" good one. His spirits raised a little.

He considered taking his phone out of his pocket for more light, but sitting in a room full of... wow... full of what? In his haste to check over of his personal health, he hadn't taken in his surroundings. Two people watched his movements in complete fascination. He was as foreign to them as they were to him.

Looking around, Reynold saw moonlight coming in from a thin opening near the top of the room. The opening was enough for ventilation and light. Precise measurements were difficult to calculate in the darkness. If he stood, he could touch the ceiling. The ceiling was dark wood and looked solid. He saw that the walls were made of stone and cemented between the rocks. The door had metal spikes. Where was he?

People leaned against the walls and looked like they were chained up. What the heck? THEY'RE CHAINED UP.

He was in a jail cell. What did HE do? More memories flooded back as he recalled the chase and his attempted escape.

Where are Nora, John, and Nathaniel? Oh man. DEEP BREATH. OW, OW, OW. One more deep breath... OW. Less pain. Reynold's muscles were sore, that was the pain in front of his ribcage. It would go away soon. This HORRIBLE smell wasn't going away, and he contributed to it. He wished he hadn't given his hand-sanitizer to Nora. When was that? Today?

How would he get out of this? Would he be able to find Nora, John, and Nathaniel? He twitched when he thought of calling them, but set that thought aside. He wasn't going anywhere.

The people chained to the cell walls were catatonic, not moving, nor interacting with anyone at all. They sat chained against walls. Based on how he felt, he understood their despair. Then again, it was... what time was it? These people could freak out if he turned on anything electronic. Reynold cheated and held his watch against his chest, turning the watch crown to show the current time, dimmed. If the people thought he was a witch for surviving being shot in his chest, they would flip out if he showed them a cartoon character watch face dancing, singing, and telling them the time in twenty languages. Showing a digital watch face could be disastrous.

The watch face showed *6:18am, 09/22. He wasn't sure if knowing the time changed anything, but he remembered the discussion about today's hangings. Was he about to hang? He wanted to get out. Doesn't Monopoly have a get out of jail free card? Concentrate damn you!

Reynold reviewed this ghastly place. All his physics knowledge wouldn't help him. He was sitting in a sturdy cell that looked like an armored tank would dent itself if it rammed it. The cell door was solid oak, covered in pointed spikes, and opened inward since the hinges were on the inside. The hinges opened at the top, so there was hope. But the door closed flush with the surrounding wall with a quarter inch gap at most. So unless the door was open, they weren't coming off the hinges. Clever design.

Reynold was in despair. He was chilled to the bone, and his last meal was days earlier. He had just vomited out a bunch of nutrients, so he was a few days from starvation, in a fetid jail cell. Terrific. Reynold minus... ok, forget the damn formulas. Reynold felt like he was going to die in this cell.

Wait, could Nora and John try to spring him from this hell? Did they have something with which they could grab the jail cell bars and yank them out so he could crawl to his freedom? Wait! No jail cell bars nor window. One inch opening. No need for bars. Did they think he was dead? He remembered seeing them run away, so he hoped they hadn't been captured. He began to panic but forced himself to calm down when he realized breathing faster only brought more revolting smells into his nostrils. CALM DOWN AND THINK. Nora and John weren't in jail with him.

Did he have any assets? Could he use his dented tablet computer as a fulcrum under the door to get it off its hinges when the guards opened it? No. That was an awful idea. The spikes in the door would kill the person it fell on. He felt badly enough about his own incarceration. The chained woman across from him would be a casualty of such an attempted escape. He also had many warm feelings about the tablet now that it saved his life again. He wasn't taking it out even to inspect it. Wrong tool. Besides, in his few days left, he wanted to watch whatever movies he stored on it to cement himself in his original time period.

THINK, REYNOLD. Could he try subterfuge? Overpower the guard? Then what? This is a jail. Would there be additional doors to open? He heard no guards, but that didn't mean there weren't any. Reynold made another attempt at a calming breath. He had laughed at Nora's *which hunt* pun, and he was part of it now.

A man and a woman sharing the cell with him stood unchained and watched Reynold with curiosity.

The woman walked over, picked her hand up and poked Reynold's left cheek. "HEY!" Reynold responded to being poked. "I'm awake!"

"No, he's here. He's not a dream. Why did they arrest you?" she said.

"I... actually... I don't know. What does that mean? Am I going to be tried?" Reynold responded.

The man replied with a thick accent, "Well, ye're the first negro in here. The girls have said a black man was haunting their dreams as a specter. Maybe they think ye are that man?"

Reynold's despair grew more pronounced.

The burly man walked closer and whispered, "How... how did ye survive being shot? It looks like ye were shot?" he said with a gruff but concerned tone.

Reynold said, "I... I don't know." Since he only had part of the facts, Reynold wasn't fibbing.

The man said, "I've never seen a man sit up from a shot like that... Ye're jacket and shirt are covered in blood."

Reynold considered his next words carefully. Well, he didn't want to be trapped in an escape proof room with people thinking he's the devil. How could he respond? How SHOULD he respond? He didn't have Nora to consult, nor John to complain to, or watch him screw up and feel better about not being the one in the hot seat.

"I... don't understand it myself, but I'm thankful. I promise you." Reynold slowly stammered out. Now what? "What... are the awful smells?"

The man said, "Have ye ever traveled by sea? The smells could be the slop bucket ye woke up next to, or the uneaten food rotting in the corner, or the dead rats, your vomit, or the..."

Reynold interrupted, "Ok, ok, ok. The stinkiest place ever. That was a dumb question. I am sorry for asking that. Really, I am." Reynold was trying to make conversation but realized he was getting ill from the disgusting smells. He had the beginning of a headache from lack of food and felt queasy from hearing all that was fueling the putrid odor. That wormhole had better be open, or else he would find it and open it with his bare hands. He wanted to find John and choke him. Reynold said, "What the hell was I thinking? It'll only feel like three minutes passed. Ha." Why he was wasting time and thinking about that? He had to get out of here.

The burly man looked at Reynold. He was unsure how to respond, so he tried sizing him up. This stranger they brought in had a strange accent, he thought. Was he an escaped slave? He didn't speak, nor act like a slave. He acted more like a seaman. The only place blacks were equals was serving aboard ships. Being at sea was such a tough occupation. Because of that, all ships were integrated.

Reynold looked beyond the two stupefied people standing in front of him.

The woman turned to the burly man and said, "I don't understand it. They accuse us of being witches, and here this man is covered in blood, but not wounded? Maybe this is an example of the devil's work," she said, baffled.

Reynold looked at her and said, "I'm as much the devil as you are."

They were the only three prisoners not in chains. Reynold asked, "why aren't we chained?"

The woman replied, "They ran out. There are hundreds of imprisoned witches in jails. Are you... an escaped slave?"

Reynold was despondent. He was resigned to the fact that soon he would die. The chill from the damp, horrible smelling cell was invading his limbs, causing him to shake. Reynold shivered so quickly, his legs and arms grew an endless supply of goosebumps. He wasn't feeling well at all. He thought of the man in the stockade... wait... Pillory... who soiled himself. That man stood there and wept. Nobody checked on him. Nobody. They were alone in the jail without guards.

This was a low point in his life. Reynold was always a nerd. Last time he felt this low, he was sent to the dean's office in junior high school, after someone had noticed the front page ripped out of a library book. The assistant librarian sent him for punishment. He sat, crying uncontrollably, repeating, "It wasn't me, it wasn't me," but she didn't want to hear it. She had accused Reynold, and she felt justified for the harsh punishment. The head librarian heard about it and walked into the dean's office, and told him that the book's front page was ripped out years earlier. Now, Reynold didn't have the energy to cry.

He looked at the two people and took a breath. He spoke slowly, "I'm... not the devil. I'm definitely not a slave. Whatever I am presumed to be guilty of, I'm certain there is no evidence whatsoever of me doing it. I am stuck here, and if I don't get out, I shall be stuck here forever. Which... is harder to explain, and say to... anyone here." Reynold sat up. The two people stepped backward, and the woman looked at Reynold's chest. What was she looking at?

Reynold continued, "This cell seems impenetrable, the walls are stones in cement. I have nothing to break through any of it. The ceiling is solid. I wish I carried something larger than a pocket knife. That lock doesn't look friendly, and the door looks scary. The opening in the wall giving air and light is too narrow for anything. We could at least slide the dead rats out, but getting the nauseating rat smell out of here seems like a waste of our time since we're being pelted by so many other smells. I have three friends out there somewhere that may need me, or even if they don't need me, I need them right now." Reynold wasn't so much talking to the people looking at him, but laying out what was causing his despair. The two prisoners looked confused, but the woman saw something that distracted her.

"But," she said, "YOU have the key." She emphasized *you* so he would understand.

Reynold thought he was dreaming. Was his uncle in a woman's body sharing a cell with him? How did this woman know the depths of his passion? His desire for the truth. Did she know about his obsession with the truth and the facts? Reynold looked at her, "Why do you think I have the key? I have absolutely nothing that can help us get out."

"No, I said you HAVE the key." and this time she poked Reynold's tender chest, but something hard, brass, and special blocked her finger.

18

OUT OF THE FRYING PAN

Many years earlier, Reynold's uncle George attended an out-of-town seminar. As he was also Reynold's godfather, he had often felt bad for not doing more for his godson. He had to make sure Reynold knew that he loved him, and was an important part of his life. He wanted Reynold to succeed, seeing he had such incredible potential. Potential is only a seed. He wanted to push him in the right direction. Uncle George knew if he had the right tool, he could make his godson focus like a precision laser. He needed to plant a fire inside Reynold's belly, like the one that his godfather had planted for him years earlier. It seemed too harsh to pick him up by the collar and scream, "Don't screw up kid, just don't screw up!" What could he do? They had no family heirlooms to pass down to Reynold, and he knew he needed something significant. Perhaps uncle George only needed to repeat the same conversation his godfather had given him? No, no, no. Reynold needed a talisman. Something to remind him to focus. Should he get a genie lamp and have him rub, rub,

RUB it? No, that was a terrible, horrible cliché. What an awful idea. Reynold took everything SO literally. NO. He needed something to give Reynold a constant reminder.

So George took a break from the seminar in the exotic land of Newark, New Jersey, and thought about what he could do for his godson. As he walked by a jewelry shop window, he saw a beautiful brass, antiqued skeleton key on a leather necklace. He walked into the shop and bought it. He would see Reynold after this trip, so the timing was perfect. Now all he had to do was remove it from himself and give it to Reynold. His uncle will always be with him. Instant heirloom. Just add water.

Reynold took the key from around his neck and placed it into the lock, then turned it. The lock gave no resistance, and he heard the familiar click indicating the lock had opened. It was ironic that the company that created the key 300 years later had never manufactured a single lock. The graphic designer, Robert, walked into his boss's office with a grand idea and handed her the sketch. She held it up and said, "You know what? I'd buy this myself! Design it and have our manufacturing guys make it!" and they sold hundreds. Old style key pendants on a leather necklace.

The older woman hesitated about leaving, worried about being recaptured. Reynold said a phrase he'd heard in the movies. Was it cliche? Certainly. Was it true... yes? Did he picture Kyle Reese saying this to Sarah Connor? Yes! They opened the jail cell with Reynold's key and met no resistance. Nobody was stationed inside. The jail was impossible to escape, and nobody cared about the inmates. They were guilty because they were in jail. Within one hundred years, the constitution would require that a person be considered innocent until proven guilty. That might not be a perfect system either, but at least it was one where innocent people were not tortured because they plead not guilty. The people being hanged in a few hours plead not guilty. All of them. Pleading guilty was no picnic, since life in jail was truly terrible, but it was life. The public had realized that pleading innocent led to certain death. Pleading guilty led to significantly more accusations and filled the jails to over-capacity.

Reynold departed with the only unchained people. To unlock the other prisoners required a unique tool, which they didn't have. The other inmates were barely conscious and sick from malnutrition. The elements slowly killed them. They were catatonic. They weren't conscious enough to acknowledge that anyone was sharing the cell with them, or if they were still there. The missing people may have been perceived as ghosts to the remaining inmates. Reynold looked in the other cells for his friends, and after not finding them, he locked the cells and approached the outer door of the jail. Was it this easy? He had never picked a lock before, and now he was breaking out of jail. Technically, this was walking out of jail, so he still hadn't broken out of jail. If he were ever to return to his *here and now,* he needed to thank his uncle profusely. He knew uncle George wouldn't believe his story, but dinner was in order, and maybe he would buy him a lifetime of his favorite meal, dessert. He walked over to the jail's exit, used his key on the jail's outer door, and it clicked just the same as the other cells. Was he a magician? Lucky? He had been prattling on about his despair when his cellmate pushed on the key on his chest. It hadn't registered that it could be useful for anything except unlocking his goals.

The craftsman that created the doors for the Salem jail had sold extra keys, manufacturing them with slight differences. He told the buyer that each key and lock combination was unique. Since they were Puritans, they trusted the tradesmen and believed him. In reality, they could have used any keys given to the warden on any of the doors. The technology creating specific tumblers wasn't used for these locks. In addition, Houdini wouldn't be born for another 182 years.

Since there were no cameras to record their escape, nor guards, Reynold worried less about being recaptured. But he needed to lay low.

Reynold and his two escapees now stood in the same outcropping of trees where he, Nora, and John arrived three days earlier. Reynold regarded his partners in crime. This woman was feisty but exhausted. She was desperate for proper nourishment and a lot of care. The burly man was roaring for adventure, and Reynold punched his ticket. He was responsible for these people.

"Who... are you sir?" Reynold asked.

"Captain John Alden," he replied.

Reynold asked, "Where will you go? What will you do? Will you stay here in these woods? These trees would give you adequate cover. The sun will be up soon."

John Alden looked at Reynold without hesitation. "I'm heading back to London on one of my ships. I'll stay for a little while, trading, and getting more goods to bring back. Then I will return. That's what I do. It's been years since I've been to England, but the Caribbean seems too close to escape this madness. I'll be safer where I can work, then bring back goods to trade. By the time I return, this nonsense will probably have faded. For all I know, they'll hire me for more charter work for the battles being fought. They need my company to ship things to and from parts of the colonies. They were asses for accusing me of being a witch."

Reynold didn't hesitate, but took out a piece of paper from his back pocket, turned Captain Alden around, using his back as a writing surface. This paper had been in his back pocket since the conversation with John and Nora. He turned the page over and wrote in script on the back with his prized Parker fountain-pen. "Dear Isaac, Cheers! Signed, RW, JM, and NF". His fancy pen wrote like the quills they used around this time. Causality needs to trust him.

After writing the note, he turned the captain around, and said, "If you are at all in my debt for getting you out of jail..."

Captain Alden interrupted, "Actually that woman pointed to yer key to get us out of jail... technically we owe her..."

Reynold quickly said, "Never mind that. Please deliver this to Isaac Newton. He works in England, probably in London for the government. Hand deliver this directly to him if you can."

Captain Alden paused and said, "Yes. I can do that. I have friends I can ask. I will deliver this. Be safe. Don't get into more trouble." And he strode off with a captain's swagger. You would have never known he was weak from malnutrition. He was commanding, tough, and resolute. John Alden had resources. He'd be just fine.

Reynold looked at the woman. Frail, yet determined. He had such a hard time guessing her age, since wilderness living seemed to age people. She looked at Reynold and said, "Thank you. My husband, Thomas, has been working diligently to get me out, and yet you simply walked me out of jail. I don't even know what to call you?"

Reynold said, "My name is Reyn..." and he stopped. He

knew he had seriously interfered with history and he needed to be careful. He had written the letter to Isaac Newton as vaguely as possible just to say *hi*. You know, if you're in town, look me up? He didn't put their names on it, just initials. That seemed safe. But he felt worried after letting two people out of jail and interfering with this timeline. Were there now split timelines? What did Nora say a day earlier - thousands of people could exist in the future timeline if he prevented people from dying? He had to consider all his steps from now on. No more being a hero and saving anyone else. He couldn't leave these two people. They weren't chained to the walls. They would have died from the freezing cold. They were coming with him, and he didn't regret letting them out of jail. But he couldn't tell her his real name. Nathaniel already knew his, Nora, and John's names, but this was different. They had to interact. His actions saved this woman's life. But she couldn't change the future. She was a much older woman. How could the fact of her survival change the outcome of the future? Reynold thought about it a few moments more and answered, "My... name is Rey." It was a nickname. Not traceable. Perhaps he should have told her his full name, but he stuck to his guns. Now throwing caution to the wind, he took the leather strap that held the key from around his neck, gave it to her, and said, "Now you have the key. I've had this most of my life, and now I'd like you to have it." What the hell, he thought. He didn't need it anymore.

She never thought this moment would come. She was in jail for what felt like an eternity, with her husband paying for the privilege of keeping her there. He fetched food for her, and kept her as healthy as he could, considering she was in jail, and he wanted to free her. She was now free thanks to the kindness of a total stranger. She teared up and sobbed, "Rey," she had to get the words out, "my name is Mary, Mary Bradbury, and I will say a special *thank you* to you every day, even if I can't say it directly to you. If I'm captured again, I will have breathed fresh air which I thank you for. You have saved me from the gallows." They nodded to each other, and then she walked away. These people weren't into hugging. Not even a handshake.

Reynold got the chills. He remembered that Nora said only eight people hanged on September 22nd. Nathaniel said ten people were scheduled to hang. Did he fulfill history? He needed to tread lightly.

It felt amazing to stand in the same grouping of trees he had been in only a few days earlier. Every breath he took was ambrosia compared to the jail cell. He didn't notice his hunger anymore. He didn't even notice the manure smell. The air was fantastic.

According to Reynold's watch, it was *6:42am. He rotated the crown backward to darken the screen, and the watch was again an obsidian bracelet. He placed it around on the inside of his wrist to make it less conspicuous. It looked like a black leather bracelet.

After setting his watch to vibrate in an hour, he sat down on the familiar tree stump he had been sitting on days earlier and prepared to take a nap. He was a now a fugitive, and needed to make sure he remained incognito until they were ready to leave, but how would he leave? Elmer, the device that had brought them there, or in this case *then*, sat destroyed in his pocket. Alone in the woods, he took it out to examine it. It now had a stylish new hole, and an LED that was now blank. Well, John had made it. Maybe he could resurrect it? He put it back in his pocket and thought, "That's nice." Nothing could worry him now. He was too happy being out of jail. He also knew, without access to serious technology to fix it, he could be in trouble. But he was giddy. He had the key around his neck the whole time. And now Mary had it. The guards hadn't thought to search him before putting him inside that dungeon. They hadn't wanted to make any more contact with him than necessary. Maybe they wouldn't make the same mistake twice. Then again, why should they? If they searched him, what would they think, if they found his now dented tablet on him before imprisoning him? Would they even be able to turn it on? Had he downloaded any music onto it? Was everything he had so virtual that he believed he'd have access to the internet all the time? Well, that had been proven wrong.

Wait. He took out the emergency communication device for when he and John were off the grid. Reynold plugged it into his phone, and composed a text message and proof read it. He wrote, "I'm safe and napping in our favorite group of trees. I'll explain when I wake up." Reynold hit send and passed out.

John's phone vibrated with Reynold's message, and his phone's alarm at the same moment. Missing the message, John woke up, quietly exited their room, descended the steps and walked out of Beadle's Tavern, hoping to find Reynold's body. Moving on autopilot, he made a left turn outside the tavern and made the right, heading toward the docks. Once he reached them, he searched the field where Reynold was shot. The grass was tall in various places, and so he spent time searching. John found a red splotch in one spot, and the tracks of a cart next to it. They have Reynold's body. He plodded back to the tavern and wondered if he should tell Nora.

Nora stirred as he reentered the room. "You looked for Reynold?"

John replied, "Yes. They've taken him and may have buried him."

Both passed out again from mental and physical exhaustion. There was nothing else that could be done.

An hour later, just fifty yards from where Reynold slept, several guards began their morning shift at the jail. Nobody would take a headcount until they wheeled the cart to the front of the jail to collect the prisoners being hanged.

19

PROCESSION TO GALLOWS HILL

John and Nora slept for a while, then awoke and sat in silence. Their shock seemed like it would never wear off.

John never saw Reynold's text. He had quickly let go of his electronic life. It didn't occur to him to check for missed messages. There was only one piece of technology that concerned him, which was the LED on Elmer. Why check it? He thought far less about technology without Reynold. How would he tell his parents, "Your son died by musket fire in 1692," when he saw them again? If he saw them again.

Nathaniel knocked on their door and asked, "May I come in?"

"He is so... damn... polite," Nora thought.

Nora said, "Sure."

Nathaniel walked in and said, "The execution will take place soon; we should proceed to the grounds." This was a matter-of-fact. Nathaniel's plan had evaporated, and he didn't know what to do next. He only knew he had to follow the events and hope for something to alter their outcome.

They needed to be part of the action if they expected anything to change. This was his last attempt to stop the madness.

Nora composed herself and said, "I... don't want to watch nine people die. I can't do that. Is there something we can do without witnessing that anguish?" She wanted to change all of this, but knew she couldn't. Nora thought hard about it from a historian's viewpoint, struggling for the impartiality her profession sometimes required. This was an opportunity for modern eyes to witness this moment. Despite not wanting to watch, she still had a duty to see it.

Nathaniel looked at them. He drew in a deep breath and said, "Perhaps you are right. We should go to those grounds, but after delaying for a while." Nathaniel's grand scheme from days earlier was now a distant memory. It had all been for naught. By involving them, he may have gotten Reynold killed with no effect on the outcome. Guards were surrounding the prisoners, and John and Nora were unarmed and untrained. Nathaniel needed an army.

Reynold woke up in the woods and determined his current level of hit points and damage count as if he were a character in a video game. His chest ached from having been pounded by the musket ball only hours earlier. Reynold was hungry, thirsty, yet gleeful for having walked out of the most disgusting place ever.

He had never considered himself a germaphobe, but knowing what germs can do, he had never liked them one bit. Reynold was desperate to spend a month in his brand new shower in his house. He was sure he would be patient until the last fifteen seconds of that long three hundred year wait to install it again. That is the moment he would have a full-on hissy fit until he could enter his shower and clean himself from everything that had happened over the past three days, probably crying with absolute joy.

He had no floss, no toothpaste, no mouthwash. When he had awoken in the jail cell the night before and spent what felt like an eternity vomiting, he felt he compromised his breath forever. For good measure, he spat out as much saliva as he could to remove some of the intense halitosis. Could he pause this first date with Nora to run and shower in acid to remove the layers of his polluted skin?

No, he wasn't a germaphobe, but he thought it could become a great hobby if he ever made it back to his own *here and now*. Maybe find a few conventions where everyone sealed themselves into their hotel rooms after meticulously steam cleaning, bleaching, and testing the air quality with calibrated sensors. Now that would be a party.

He took out his frenemy, Elmer, and looked at it again in the light of the early morning. John will need to pull a rabbit out of a hat to repair it. The hole was clean because of the heat from the musket ball. Elmer and Reynold's tablet computer had saved him. Thanks, John.

The red gel from his inhaler had hardened on his jacket and shirt, so he scratched and flicked it off. After a few minutes of scraping, the jacket was acceptable. That's a relief. There are no dry cleaners yet. Those stores should open in the late 1800s? He was sure he had coupons.

Unless you were next to Reynold, the jacket's dark color hid the remaining stains. The shirt needed washing and still had a significant amount of red dye on it. If he held the jacket shut, he could hide the shirt. He still had to conceal himself. He disliked having a neon sign on him saying, "Here's the freak who can't die! Maybe try stabbing and poisoning him!"

A crowd had formed in front of the jail, which he had

emerged just hours ago. He felt safe in the trees since the attention was on the front of the jail where all the drama was taking place. The people became raucous. Some yelled, "Witch! Let them die!" while some shouted, "They're innocent!"

The scene captivated Reynold. He stared with his mouth agape. This was madness. Stark raving madness.

Several guards with red uniforms and muskets shouldered stood at attention like statues. A slow-moving cart came into view, pulled by an ox. The building obscured only part of the cart. The beast pulling it was standing ahead of the cart, facing south towards Main Street.

Reynold had learned from personal experience that the exit to the jail was on the corner, so he watched the proceedings from the safety of the trees. Humanity was going crazy in front of him.

George Corwin strode up with what looked like a ring of keys in his hand. Reynold smiled and thought about the key that opened all the doors. Corwin withdrew a rolled-up piece of paper from under his arm and read:

"Hear ye, Hear ye. The following nine prisoners are officially remanded to gallows hill to be executed, hanging by the neck until dead! Hear ye Hear ye! Fetch Martha Corey, wife of the deceased Giles Corey."

Another guard appeared, forcing a frail woman up the ramp into the cart. The crowd couldn't contain themselves. They had witnessed Giles's passing only days earlier. Some people still shouted, "She's innocent!"

This infuriated George Corwin. He regarded the crowd sternly as he threatened, "Do ye want to join them?" The crowd became silent as the protestors knew this was very serious.

A guard pushed the weeping woman up the ramp into the open cart.

George Corwin shouted, "Hear ye Hear ye! Fetch Mary Etsy!"

The guard disappeared for only a few moments, then walked out of jail with another weak gray-looking woman, and proceeded to push and shove her into the cart.

Corwin yelled, "Hear ye Hear ye! Fetch Mary Parker!"

The guard left and returned with yet another sickly prisoner.

It seemed like a cruel joke was being played on these poor people. First abuse, then death, which you longed for after the terrible treatment.

George Corwin turned his head to the air, "Hear ye Hear ye! Fetch Ann Pudeator!" They pushed another catatonic person into the cart.

Corwin shouted, "Hear ye Hear ye! Fetch Alice Parker!"

Reynold thought, "This is all madness, they are all innocent!" and became angrier.

George Corwin yelled "Hear ye Hear ye! Fetch Wilmot Redd," then "Hear ye Hear ye! Fetch Margaret Scott," then "Hear ye Hear ye! Fetch Samuel Wardwell." Three more zombies were loaded into the cart.

The court sentenced Dorcas Hoar to death on September 9th. She had confessed a day earlier, changing her plea to guilty and spared her life. So she remained in jail.

They determined that Abigail Faulkner was pregnant, and they gave her a temporary reprieve until after the birth of her baby.

George Corwin shouted "Hear ye Hear ye! Fetch Mary Bradbury!"

When the guard returned, he was visibly agitated. He

whispered into George Corwin's ear. Whatever he said enraged Corwin, who kicked the cart's wheel violently and repeatedly. The sound echoed across the field between them with a loud "crack, crack, crack!" The Sheriff had to stop for a long time before he calmed down.

Eight people executed instead of nine, and Reynold had saved one, maybe two. Was John Alden intended to hang today?

Reynold absorbed Sheriff Corwin's rage like a solar panel. As a rule, Reynold didn't take pleasure in making people mad, but this was a special moment. Each kick Corwin delivered to the cart's wheel filled Reynold with happy, healing thoughts. "I did that," he thought, and smiled. For some reason, Corwin spun around and looked toward the trees where Reynold crouched, causing him to duck down. It took a few moments for Reynold's heartbeat to return to normal. Reynold sought lower ground to further shield himself from the casual observer.

Until that moment, Corwin had been unaware that three prisoners had escaped, and he was now melting down in front of a crowd of townsfolk. The guard had no evidence to explain how the three prisoners had disappeared. Nothing. Not even a scratch on the walls, much less a tunnel that would have taken years to dig. Reynold was so grossed out when he left the jail, he used his elbows to close the doors, leaving no fingerprints. That technology wouldn't be discovered for hundreds of years, anyway.

Reynold heard a different banging sound and peeked out from behind the tree to see the source. They placed the ramp for the prisoners on the back of the cart. What a clever, efficient design, Reynold thought.

Once the guards secured the back, the ox pulled forward, bringing the eight standing people in the cart with him. The prisoners' hands were loosely tied, but they seemed so weak they didn't even try to break out of the ropes binding them.

People lined the streets, many jeering at the prisoners and many others yelling, "LET THEM GO!" This was a divided town. Was this a teachable moment for them? Don't get caught? Don't get accused? Did they realize how close they were to being hanged with their neighbors?

The seven women and one man standing in the cart were pale, haggard, and in a great state of despair. The crowd kept rippling with murmurs and shouts as they rolled toward the main road.

The guards beside the cart held their muskets with bayonets attached and were ready for battle. Although the prisoners would not be escaping in their condition, if a fight broke out, the crowd outnumbered the guards, and they were understandably on edge.

The procession moved slowly, allowing Reynold to find adequate hiding places along the route as he followed it. He had forgotten about the message he had sent to John only a few hours earlier saying he was staying in the woods. Reynold's priority was witnessing this and somehow trying to help. In his gut, he felt his friends were safe.

On Prison Street, Reynold watched the cart move out of view, rolling toward its goal, and the crowd parted to let it through. Reynold changed his position so he could continue to follow it undetected. He didn't see guards, so they didn't see him. He would stay in the shadows as far behind as possible.

Once he had the procession back in view, Reynold saw the cart get stuck on a rock on Main Street, and one soldier leaned his musket on the side to shove the cart with his shoulder.

After they freed the cart, the musket fell on the ground, and the soldier picked it up cursing. Nickolas immediately placed it back on his shoulder and continued marching alongside the cart.

Most of the prisoners had ceased sobbing and were taking in their surroundings. The air was fresh, and their faces were being touched by a sun some of them hadn't seen for months. Their last moments wouldn't be spent in the foulest jail, and that was soothing. This brief journey seemed like a dream to the prisoners, although they were restrained and were being pelted by things thrown by the crowd. They were on their way to salvation, and divine forgiveness, even if the towns people didn't forgive them. They began to pray amongst themselves.

The cart proceeded toward its goal, Reynold taking pains to follow well beyond the last person in the crowd. Reynold wanted to be late. Seeing the guards armed with muskets caused his chest to throb. He kept his distance.

The procession passed the pillory Reynold had seen days earlier. The cart rolled toward the house known as the "Witch House," which was Judge Corwin's house. Screaming towns people lined the streets. After some time walking, they made a right turn onto a long road that led to a bridge over the North River. By now, Reynold was only marginally good at hiding while keeping pace, but the whole town's attention was on this execution. This grisly moment had brought their lives to a halt. Reynold wondered why they were fascinated by the macabre scene.

As they proceeded up the hill and crossed the bridge over the North River, the cart became stuck again. It took considerable effort to move. One person in the crowd claimed to see the devil holding the cart back from its goal.

The ox had trouble keeping its footing with over eight-hundred pounds of people standing in the cart. After crossing the bridge, they arrived.

John Alden noticed how the town had emptied and followed the cart head towards Gallows hill. He noticed the man who saved him the night before and kept his eye on Reynold, hanging back. He was newly freed from jail, and had no desire to return.

The crowd gathered around the area where the gallows was erected. Since it was one of the higher points in town, it was visible from a great distance.

Reynold found an outcropping of trees where he could hide and watch the precariously erected platform. He was within earshot of all the action. Now he just had to be silent and observe.

John Alden watched Reynold's actions and thought he was a fool for placing himself nearly at the center of the place they wanted him the night before; The gallows.

20

INNOCENCE LOST

The guards stood next to the gallows to prevent the townsfolk from interfering with the executions. Nickolas's shoulder was still smarting from shoving the cart, but he stayed alert for any disturbances, either from the crowd or his commanding officer standing next to him.

Reverend John Higginson was an official witness representing the court. He was also there to hear confessions of the accused made on the gallows. He wanted these witches to be hanged quickly so he could make the three and a half hour horseback ride to Boston where he was to report to Samuel Sewall and the other Judges and discuss their next court dates. The Reverend needed to declare the proceedings fair and just in the eyes of the court.

Robert Calef, a witness to all prior hangings, also stood in the crowd. Robert was a Boston merchant, and would finish work, close up shop and head to Salem on hanging days. He was furious watching the miscarriage of justice carried out before his eyes. He wasn't sure what he could do. He was one man, against an agitated town, armed soldiers, and powerful judges. If he spoke out, he risked being accused. He had made it his quest to absorb as much as he could about the trials and their consequences. Robert never thought the hangings would end.

Reverend Nicholas Noyes was convinced Salem was filled with witches and Satan himself. He wanted to eradicate his town of evil. Today would be a great day to remove more of *them.* They were afflicting this town, causing endless strife. The neglected crops and livestock were evidence.

The guards led the seven women and one man off the cart and pushed them up to the makeshift scaffold. The condemned waited for their turn to step off and hang themselves. They each had to walk off the ladder on their own and in rare instances, needed to be pushed to their slow death. The eight people walking off the gallows would take nearly an hour to stop suffering and breathing their last breaths. A few years earlier, a hanged man was removed from the rope still alive, requiring the executioner to use a sword to behead him.

Martha Corey was the first to stand, pleading her innocence to the crowd. She was more upset about being excommunicated from the church than being accused as a witch. The fact that her husband was now dead from remaining mute rather than giving a plea only three days earlier weighed on her heart. She was a religious woman, seventy-two years of age, and being a Puritan and part of her church was special to her. She had been outspoken about how the afflicted girls used as star witnesses were lying about their baseless accusations. Then two of those girls accused her of witchcraft. She continued to declare her innocence and was convinced she'd be vindicated once the girls were proven to be liars. Until the last moments of her life, she still fervently preached to the crowd and graciously prayed for them.

Mary Goody Parker was fifty-five years old. Widowed in 1685, her husband left her the land and wealth that was collected by George Corwin to pay for her time in jail. Mary's accusation came from William Barker Senior, when he was tortured to confess and accuse others. Though there were several Parker women in the area, the court magistrates took it upon themselves to issue a warrant for the arrest of Mary Ayer Parker without making sure they had the right woman in custody. Her daughter also had been convicted of being a witch. She looked at the crowd and staunchly declared her innocence. The raucous crowd didn't agree and jeered back at her.

Mary Warren accused Alice Parker of murdering her mother. Mary herself had been orphaned at an early age because of the many conflicts between the Indians and the villagers. Giles Corey came to Mary in her dreams and she accused Giles of witchcraft. She worked for John and Elizabeth Proctor. They told her that if she had any more fits and fell into the house fire, she would not be saved. Miraculously, Mary's fits ceased, giving pause to the proceedings, raising questions of their validity. This made the other *star witness* girls angry, and they then accused Mary herself of witchcraft. After Mary was back on board with her other accusers, she accused John Proctor, who was hanged on August 19th. Alice Parker declared her innocence to the crowd, only to be yelled at and mocked.

Mary Warren accused Ann Pudeator. Ann was a lovely seventy-four-year-old woman, a midwife who had helped deliver many of the children in Salem, some of whom accused her now. Mary Warren and other girls accused Ann of presenting them with the devil's book, which they claim they were forced to sign. The authorities saw grease in Ann's house, which they considered "witching material" but it was actually ingredients she used to make soap. Ann also collected children's poppets. One of those poppets held her pin collection, which she used to sew garments. This was the sum of the physical evidence against her. The girls claimed her spectral form appeared to them, causing them unrest. The star witnesses accused Ann of causing her second husband's first wife to pass away before meeting him and then caused him to pass away. They accused Ann of almost killing John Turner, owner of the house that Nora, John, Reynold, and Nathaniel were looking at only days earlier. They also accused Ann of making a man fall out of a tree. Throughout it all, she maintained her innocence, but her declarations fell upon deaf ears.

Wilmot Redd was an unpopular fifty-eight-year-old woman. She complained about everything and filled the ears of anyone who asked her about anything. She steered the conversation to what bothered her most about her neighbors, town, and her life. Mary Walcott and Mercy Lewis accused Wilmot of *sundry acts of witchcraft* and the girls fell into fits around her while she gave testimony. When asked why the girls were disturbed by her, she would only reply, "they are in a sad condition" while watching in horror at their masterful performance.

Nathaniel, Nora, and John had reached Gallows Hill. Nora still had no desire to witness the hangings and only stayed to avoid suspicion. They remained on the outskirts of the crowd to prevent drawing anyone's attention.

Abigail Williams went out in the woods in January with her sister Betty Parris and Tituba, the servant that migrated with them from Barbados. Abigail, Betty, and the girls from town came over and played exotic games with Tituba. Since

Tituba grew up in a world different from a Puritan's, she always had interesting stories and games to entertain them. During that time, Abigail had the first of many grand mal seizures. Abigail was the first girl from Salem given a diagnosis from a doctor of being afflicted by the devil. She suffered violent seizures that would also cause her whole body to become rigid. Betty Parris saw the attention her cousin received while seeking doctors to cure her and imitated Abigail to avoid punishment for being caught in the woods. Betty couldn't be happier with the results, which kept her from her chores. The other girls in town realized they could avoid duties and punishment in the same way, and they followed Abigail and Betty's ingenious lead.

At that same time, Reverend Samuel Parris increased the quantity of fire and brimstone in his sermons. The town had stopped paying him, and he interpreted the interference with his success as the work of the devil.

The girls accused Tituba of witchcraft. Tituba wanted to protect the girls because she loved them. They tortured her until she confessed to whatever they wanted to hear. They gave her the answer, "confess and save yourself," so she did. Tituba had many stories from her time in Barbados. All she had to do was recount them to the Judges which kept her out of trouble. The court remained transfixed by her testimony and saw the root of their problems.

Abigail was having many seizures and couldn't remember what was happening to her. After they abated, she worried about being disgraced and she spun stories for her uncle to protect her backside and cheeks from injury.

Judge William Stoughton, Judge John Hathorne, Judge Jonathan Corwin, and Judge Samuel Sewall, and Reverend Samuel Parris all believed an external evil force was acting upon them. After massive losses of property, and failed investments after the losses inflicted by governor Edmund Andros, and the many conflicts within the regions, the judges assigned to the court believed some external force was impeding their success. Something ungodly was acting upon them. How could such successful men suffer such financial losses? They came to this country to worship in the Puritan way, something they had been denied in England. They were trying to make their religion as pure and natural as possible. After being presented with what they considered to be overwhelming evidence that the Parris children and all the other children were beset with something otherworldly, the diagnosis given by that doctor was the answer to their prayers. The doctor's proclamation meant that there was evidence of the devil, and thus the seeds of an epic disaster were sewn.

Judge John Hathorne took the role of prosecuting attorney. In the late 1600s, it was illegal for lawyers to accept money for issuing advice about the law. So the accused couldn't defend themselves nor could they hire lawyers. Each initial question from Hathorne intimated the presumption of guilt. If you were accused, you were guilty and couldn't declare innocence. You had no choice but to confess your sins. After a certain point, the townspeople accused figured out this pattern. So they confessed and accused someone else so they could live. This resulted in jails being filled with witches waiting for a court date with the highest ranked judges in the Massachusetts colony.

Mary Warren saw this as an opportunity. John Proctor beat her when she didn't do her chores properly. He also beat her because of her involvement in the trials. As a servant and a woman, Mary had no rights. But if she were afflicted with witchcraft, Mary could end her torment and exact revenge. So when Mary saw her friend, Abigail

Williams, avoiding chores and persecution because of her seizures, and Mary imitated them flawlessly. She then accused as many people as she perceived had wronged her. She was a star witness to crimes she told the court she dreamed about.

The girls in the region, being clever, saw this pattern long before their Puritan parents, townspeople, and judges.

Spectral evidence helped convict Margaret Scott of witchcraft. Spectral sticks supposedly hit some people, and others claimed to be chased around by Margaret's ghostly presence. These stories of Margaret Scott appearing in dreams as a specter were the court's only evidence. The accusers didn't feel guilty because all Margaret had to do was admit she was a witch, and accuse other people, and she would remain alive. Instead of lying, however, Margaret stuck to her guns and pled innocent to all charges.

Margaret stood on the gallows and shrieked, "Why are you doing this to me?" and the crowd became silent. She was enraged and criticized the crowd. "you're murdering me based on the fanciful dreams of girls!" The crowd had their attention on her. Until this moment, the prisoners weren't fighting their plight. "I am an innocent, god fearing woman, as pure as all of you, and I stand before you about to lose my life, making all of you murderers! Thou! Shalt! Not! Kill!"

The crowd watched silently. Anyone that disagreed could be convicted of witchcraft, and anyone that didn't was guilty of murder. This was very uncomfortable, and it was getting worse. The crowd were listening to the indicted convicts. It was clear they could be the next victims standing next to someone pleading innocence, or in a jail rotting to death.

Nora and John watched the crowd go from an ugly mob

to silent dread. Margaret amped the crowd up but stunned them into muteness.

William Baker junior was accused of performing witchcraft. He confessed under interrogation, and accused Samuel Wardwell, his wife Sarah, and their daughter Mercy of witchcraft. It was inconsequential that William's actions cost the life of someone else, since his life would be spared. Since Samuel Wardwell knew the confession they tortured out of him was a fabrication, he retracted it. In his heart, he knew it was wrong. He could never live a lie and claim to be a figure of the devil. And if his family survived, they might have no assets, since Sheriff George Corwin would seize as much property and goods from the accused. If you weren't killed on the gallows, you could die from being destitute after the trials. Sheriff Corwin seized the Wardwell's one hundred eighty-eight acres of land.

On the gallows, Samuel Wardwell tried to articulate his innocence, but smoke from the pipe of the executioner was so thick, he choked and coughed. His last words were snuffed out, and nobody heard them.

Mary Etsy and her sister, Rebecca Nurse, were accused of witchcraft. The court hanged Rebecca on July 19th two months earlier. The accusing girls, upon encountering a woman as intelligent and eloquent as Mary, imitated her motions during her testimony as if possessed. If Mary moved her head, the girls would move their heads. Judge Corwin asked Mary Etsy if she was in league with Satan. She replied emphatically, "Sir, I never complied with Satan, but prayed against him all my days." Judge Hawthorn had serious doubts about her guilt. The court realized this could just be a game the girls were playing. So they released Mary Etsy, declaring her innocent for two weeks, only to arrest her again based solely on more accusations from the same girls.

On the gallows, it was now time for Mary's last words. She was eloquent. She began, "I refuse to ask for my own life to be spared, for I know I am condemned to die and my appointed time is set. And the Lord knows it is, and he knows my innocence well, so likewise my death is as meaningless as it would be on the great day we are all called back to the Lord. I question not what the judges have done, nor my accusers, nor even the afflicted. So I stand before you and I repeat that I will not plead my innocence before you. My desire is to ask that you do your utmost in the proper discovery and detection of witchcraft and witches. I pray you stop spilling innocent blood. For by unequivocally knowing my own innocence, know you are in a very bad way. If you feel you are being driven by the Lord in this work, I beg that you examine the confessing witches much, much more. I am confident they will be judged for their acts with a harshness befitting their crimes. I know nothing of the ways of witchcraft, nor the devil, nor does anyone up here on these gallows. So I am here now to say farewell to my family and my children. And pray for everyone's salvation, as you should all seek that out."

Her words stung the people in the crowd as each one of them acknowledged the painful truth that they each had a hand in this anguish.

As all eight walked off their ladders and hanged there for a full forty-eight minutes before the last one stopped writhing. The sounds of sucking, gagging, and seeing the bodies thrashing was horrifying. The human body can take so much abuse before it breaks down. Muscles continue to contract, including the heart, long after the brain shuts down. Although some victims may have been brain dead only a few minutes after the air was choked out of them, their bodies continued twitching for quite some time.

The crowd stood motionless. What started as an afternoon of morbid entertainment was now their terrible reality. The townspeople had separated themselves from the guilty, but now they had faces and families. This moment reached their hearts. They were ready for something.

Nora and John were frozen in place in the spectacle of the eight corpses dangling before them.

Reverend Nicholas Noyes said for all to hear, "What a sad thing it is to see eight firebrands of hell hanging there."

Nathaniel Saltonstall was next to John. The soldier in him was unable to fight and became resigned to the courts and the inevitability of the hangings. In his mind, this would continue until nobody remained in Salem.

Reynold couldn't take it anymore. He was trying to remain as still as possible, not to interfere. He felt the sweat form on his palms and on his head, and he knew he had to ignore it. The sounds of dying had finally ceased. Eight people hung lifeless. It suddenly sank in that he was trapped here in this misery forever now that the device that got him here lay dead in his pocket. Nora had warned them that any interference could be dangerous and could add thousands of people to the timeline. But some of those people could be great, or some could be monsters. Reynold couldn't remain silent. He saw Nora and John in the crowd and decided that he couldn't let them stay in 1692 for him. Reynold had to make a stand. He would accept the consequences from here out. His racing heart slowed down as he worked out the details.

Reynold stood up and walked toward a higher section of the grounds parallel to the gallows until he was higher than the crowds. No longer hiding, he needed to say what was on his mind. He had to make them understand. He was enraged by letting these eight people die to fulfill history.

Now he wouldn't move from this spot until he made his point. Even if they attacked him.

John Alden seeing Reynold reveal himself made him instinctively hide behind a large bush. He thought, that damn fool will get himself killed! He could barely see him through the branches, but there he was.

Reynold used his best theater voice and said, "How are you so sure that the firebrands of hell aren't the ones who just killed eight innocent people?"

Nora, John, and Nathaniel looked at Reynold as if he were a ghost. They gawked at a man they grieved hours earlier. How was he alive?

George Corwin was enraged. The negro standing there had disappeared from his jail and may have freed two other prisoners. He would stop him once and for all.

Corwin was a trained marksman and rarely missed his targets. He could control his breathing and heartbeat, so his shots stayed true to their target. Nickolas was one of his best marksmen, yet he had failed to kill this man the night before. That man was alive, uninjured, and standing feet away from him drove him to the brink of insanity. His existence was a curse. George Corwin took the musket Nickolas held on his shoulder, and in one smooth maneuver, he swung the stock to his shoulder and aimed for Reynold's chest. There was no breeze, and he was only a few yards away. The shot would hit his target with precision. If the people weren't still too shocked at witnessing the death of eight people, they would be impressed at the sheriff's marksmanship in killing a ninth.

Reynold stood still, unwilling to show his fear. He watched as the raised the gun, which he realized was aiming at his exposed chest. There was no tablet computer to block incoming projectiles now. Reynold braced himself for the inevitable pain that was moments away. Maybe he wouldn't feel anything? Perhaps the end would be quick?

With the gun now aimed directly at Reynold's heart, Corwin spoke above the villagers. As angry as he was, his voice was passionless as he declared, "You will bother me no more, you devil!" With Reynold in his sight, Corwin closed his eyes to the blinding flash and pulled the trigger.

Stupefied by the shot, Reynold was transfixed by its flash like a deer stunned by headlights instead of running away.

The explosion from the musket fire created a flash that people could see for miles.

When John Alden saw George Corwin fire, he immediately turned his head and strode toward the docks to board his awaiting ship. He couldn't watch Reynold's death.

Nora and John still reeled from Reynold's reappearance into the living world, only to see him sent back into the land of the dead. Nora turned away when she saw the musket raised. The surrounding faces become illuminated by the deadly flash.

21

STOPPING THE MADNESS!

Nora looked away, but John just closed his eyes. Watching their friend die a second time would be harder than the first time. Nora saw the bright flash reflecting off the faces of the people looking at Reynold, and it replayed over and over in her mind like a horrible, endless looping movie. People around her were still, and their expressions grew more surprised. Their eyes grew wider. Were they so perverse that this seemed amusing to them? She said, "That's my friend you're watching die! He doesn't deserve it. He did nothing wrong! Just because his skin's a different color? Do you devalue a person's life because they look different from you? How DARE you!" Their gazes agitated Nora. She couldn't contain the feelings of revulsion for people that could cast aside another's life for their own.

John turned to Nora and said to her, "Nora. You gotta see this right now." John reached into his pocket for something that was now important.

Nora became enraged with John. She replied, "What the

hell! He's your best friend and now he's..." As she turned around and saw.

Reynold was on his feet. His shirt had bloodstains, but no more than before. His exposed chest didn't have a mark. He was standing upright and uninjured.

She gazed at Reynold and said, "How..." The tears in her eyes dried up. She didn't have enough energy to replace them with happy ones and was having doubts that the day of emotional highs and lows wasn't over yet. Perhaps she should bank a few of these feelings for later.

Sheriff Corwin stood frozen like a statue. Seeing Reynold through the smoke from the musket he fired, which was still raised and pointed at his intended victim, he couldn't bring himself to lower it. He was looking at his target only yards away, who stood unblemished. Unharmed. Although Reynold was shocked, he stood motionless and stared back at him with defiance.

Reynold mentally organized what he was about to say to the bewildered onlookers. He was dehydrated. He was hungry, unkempt, and exhausted. He needed to get through to this crowd. All of them. He had a temporary advantage from their astounded reactions and needed to act fast. Reynold had to capitalize on his newfound lease on life before the viewers figured out that this accident of fate left him alive. He wasn't questioning his survival, but was grateful for it. He was convinced he was a goner when he saw the Sheriff aim and shoot the rifle from such a short distance.

The bang from the musket was still ringing in Reynold's ears. He began in a raspy voice that somehow had strength. Reynold said, "Someone once said, *silence encourages the tormentor, never the tormented*. Now it's time to listen and to question everything we have done, and everything we have allowed to be done. We are all acting as both tormentors and tormented. And I can't stay silent anymore."

"Why should we listen to you? You're an escaped slave!" shouted someone in the crowd.

Nickolas was standing at attention. Sheriff Corwin still held his gun. He felt he had to speak out, remembering parts of the witness testimony he had heard while at the trials. Some of that testimony convicted the people who had just hanged. "You are the black man from the girl's dreams! You are Satan himself! I am convinced of it! I shot you last night, and yet you survived! A guard and I placed you in a jail made of oak and solid stone walls. You disappeared from the jail, passing through those walls like a vapor! This morning the cell doors were still locked, and the walls undamaged! How did you survive being shot just now? I loaded that musket only hours ago! How did the musket ball pass right through you? You are the escaped negro slave! You are the devil! You are the devil!" he yelled with a menacing growl in his voice.

Reynold had something he could capitalize on, so he took a breath. He started so matter-of-factly he surprised himself with his tone. "Is this how you judge me? By my skin color? You form your decisions based on how a person looks? We are all alike in thousands of ways, but my skin color makes me guilty? Justice should be blind, not deaf! Eight innocent people are hanging here, making you all murderers, and you dare judge me this way? I didn't kill them. If you don't want to listen because of my skin color, then close your eyes. Shut them tight! You won't see me, but you must hear what I have to say. You are not ready for this battle about my color. What I'm about to tell you has no relevance on how I look. It has everything to do with our empathy. No matter what, I'm built the same as all of you!

All of you are different. You all have different colored skin if you really take a hard look at yourselves!"

Reynold inhaled and exhaled then said, "You are so angry at all these perceived enemies that you've lost your way... You accuse me of being the devil, but why aren't I judged as an angel instead? Is your perception of what you think of as right and wrong so damaged that you concluded I am the devil because of my skin color? If you want to judge me the devil ask yourself, would the devil survive being shot? Couldn't an angel do this? Would the devil be able to pass through the walls of a jail? Couldn't an angel pass through walls? Would the devil be able to make the musket shot pass through me right now in front of all of you as witnesses? Couldn't an angel do this? Why must you see the bad in people and refuse to consider the alternate possibility they are good people? It is this mindless judgment that infects all of you!"

"You hanged eight people. The first thing I think of is the commandment *thou shalt not kill*! You ended those lives, and they all had families who depended on them. How many other lives have you destroyed through these miscarriages of justice? Are you so confident about your verdict that you need not worry about your judgment when you all meet your makers? Will each one of you pass from this earth so clean as to be absolved of this horrible sin? How do you expect to receive absolution with nineteen lives gone from this earth, convicted with no hard evidence? Why? Because they declared their innocence, and you deemed them guilty before they even testified?"

"The woman who bared her soul to you by saying farewell to her family said you should reexamine the girls who are making the accusations, and she's right! These girls are children and aren't aware of the magnitude of what they are doing or saying. This was a game for them! Have none of you been manipulated by your children when they wanted or didn't want to do something you asked of them? Or they had their own personal motivations, but none of that is enough to condemn someone to death! The girls were telling you about their dreams, but they're only dreams. Voltaire said, *Those that can make you believe in absurdities can make you commit atrocities.*"

"Each one of you is deluding yourselves into thinking you are doing the right thing, imagining injustices where none existed. These eight people hanging are just like all of you, and you each need to ask yourselves, how did they get there? Perhaps you should wonder if you are next. Will you plead guilty and force yourself to lie, or plead innocence and hang? That is the danger you face now. This constant state of fear is all-consuming because a person will always look or act differently than others. If you keep persecuting the *different* people, there will be no one left!"

"Each of you had a hand in this. Each of you! You also had a chance to stop it. What you are doing to your own neighbors is a crime against humanity. These are your brothers and sisters. You share a bond of surviving. You will need to atone for this for a very long time. It will take an ocean of holy water to wash away these sins. What if you are never granted absolution? You will never have enough time to show faith and atone for your sins, so when you are judged by your maker, you will still have the stain of this crime on you. No, no, no. You all need to live a long time and repeat over and over how sorry you all are. Each of you needs to balance that fear of righteous retribution with as much caution as you can. You will be judged, and that judgment will be harsh! Do not count on future acts of piety to prevent it! You cannot escape it. It will come. You are gambling with your fate right now! Are these actions how you want to be judged for all eternity?"

"Do you feel safer now that these people are dead? How are you going to get by without these eight people? All of their lives touched yours both directly and indirectly. They contributed in some way to the survival of the community. They're gone now because someone claimed they saw them in their dreams? You found a poppet with pins in a woman's house? That person annoyed you? Each life lost is like burning down a library filled with information you can never recover."

"Eliminate a single ingredient for bread, and you end up with something tasteless and inedible. Each one of you is an ingredient for your success! Will the bread rise without yeast? How will it taste well without salt?"

"Even as you judge me unfairly for being a different color, you judged them the same way. Maybe the reason wasn't as obvious as my skin color, but possibly you didn't like some of these people? Maybe you envied some of them for their successes? Were you feuding with them? Maybe you're allowing your hatred to guide you, instead of using compassion and understanding? Or maybe your motivation is greed? Isn't that the reason you turn to religion? Why are you using religion to guide you toward the devil instead of seeing a way to protect yourself, or to bring joy to your soul?"

"As much as the devil can exist, so can angels. If a man were standing here performing miracles by healing the sick and comforting the poor or elderly, would you judge him the same way? What if he made a blind person see? If he turned water into wine? Would you fear him and then hang him for being the devil?"

Reynold had their attention. They weren't looking away,

and they weren't closing their eyes. Even the guards were listening to him.

He took a breath. His chest heaved up and down and he continued. "You see the devil in everyone, but why? Why do you assume evil is constantly among you? You can't keep seeing only the bad, because there is so much good in this world. You don't even have to look hard to find it."

"Your families left everything behind to seek a better life. You or your parents spent months on a ship risking their lives to do it. You didn't know what you would find here. You didn't know whether one wrong turn would end your lives or whether a paradise would welcome you. You have journeyed to a new place, in search of what? Religious truth? Freedom? Land? What are you doing here? Why are you spending so much time persecuting each other? How are you viewing the world around you with these clouded eyes? You're distracting yourself from your goals with this foolish business of seeing evil in your neighbors. You have an opportunity to shine here, and you're wasting it, wasting it on mindless destruction, and a misguided desire for revenge!"

Reynold took a breath to regain his composure. "I'm... disappointed that this is how we began. This land is a gift, an absolute gift given to you. You're missing out on this opportunity to expand your horizons and take advantage of a place with tremendous natural resources and things you have never seen before, and you're wasting it. What happened to love thy neighbor?"

"This place is a new land, and you will have to fight for it. You are always going to fight for it! Because it is right, and it is good. It is so good you would die to protect it. To protect this fertile green land. And have better ideals to live up to.

Because sometimes, you will ask, did we come here for the right reason?"

"Many of you bravely got on ships to come here and form a new country. Maybe there was even an opportunity to gain wealth here. Maybe there was a chance for success?"

"Hammurabi's law is an *eye for an eye, and a tooth for a tooth, and a life for a life*. Did you treat these eight people fairly? Their lives mattered. Did you decrease your chances of survival by killing them? What chances died with them? Did we destroy the person who could have saved any of you from harm? Could that person have helped you prosper? Each life is an opportunity and a gift. If a person is accused of something heinous, make sure that solid legitimate evidence leads you to a logical conclusion of their guilt, not intangibles like a feeling or a dream. Don't accuse a person only to fabricate the facts from insignificant things. You need to get those facts right. Hard, irrefutable evidence is needed to make sure you don't kill innocent souls. Be sure beyond any doubts. Be sure beyond any doubt. If not, you become murderers."

Some people in the crowd began to weep.

"I can't change the decisions you made leading up to today, but I can change your minds. I can change what's in your hearts. Socrates said, *I cannot teach anybody anything, I can only make them think...* I quoted that only days ago, and it has a deeper meaning now."

"Ask yourselves, is this the city upon the hill, the eyes of all people upon you, shining a light out onto the rest of your new world? Are you really giving a pristine example of how to act and how to be good people?"

A woman next to Nora murmured to herself, "He quoted Matthew 5:14... the devil couldn't do that."

Reynold said, "You call out the devil, and you see the

devil in all of us, but so are angels. So are angels. There are both devils and angels in all of us. The one we cultivate and nurture will win."

"Are you going to repent to absolve your sins? You will have to work and work until your fingers bleed. You have to atone for this vile behavior. The lives you have taken were priceless. Their lives mattered. Because as I have said, each one of them was every bit like the rest of you."

"If you think the witches you killed cursed this town, you're wrong. You cursed yourselves. And it will remain forever cursed."

"You can inspire people with a look. Heal people with words. Well, start looking, and start using words with each other. Dig deep within yourselves. Find your humanity and fix this."

"So ask yourselves; Am I a devil? Or am I an angel?"

Reynold paused, looked down at missing inspiration no longer on his chest, and was inspired to say, "You are your worst enemy, but you can become your biggest asset. It will take all of you to repair this damage. Together, you are more than the sum of your parts. A great man said, *Darkness cannot drive out darkness, only light can do that. Hate cannot drive out hate, only love can do that.* You need to make justice blind, not deaf. Listen. Listen to each other. It's the only way to hear the truth. Don't let your eyes distract you. Close your eyes and listen. Because you have the key... no, that's not entirely correct. You are the key."

He was done. Reynold turned his back to them and walked toward the bridge to get back to the main street. Somehow, he knew nobody would chase him. Nobody would shoot him in the back. They didn't dare trifle with a person who was impossible to kill and who had already walked out of their jail. Reynold wanted nothing more than to see John and Nora back at their spot in the woods and say goodbye before they went back.

Robert Calef absorbed the entire scene from the moment the Sheriff pointed the musket and fired it to the moment Reynold turned around. It lit up his brain like a lighthouse cutting through the fog and gave him a clarity of thought he hadn't had until now. He knew he was in the right place and would make a difference. He would not put this off, so he walked toward town to his horse and returned to his home in Boston.

Reverend John Higginson watched Reynold finish and was shaken to his core. Higginson thought he had been ridding their towns of witches, and now he was lost. He had doubts. Was the court doing the right thing? He had to get to the meeting that night at Samuel Sewall's to confer with the other judges, and as this was a long journey by horse, he had to get started. The Reverend strode off toward his barn. He would use that long journey to review what he had just seen and think about his next actions.

Nora and John listened to Reynold in awe. Nathaniel leaned into them and said, "Your friend quoted from John Winthrop's sermon when the first ships set aground in Plymouth. He asked the crowd a lot of questions they all answered in their hearts. This question-and-answer method of speech is how I write my sermons. He has surprised me once again. I must apologize, because I did not give him, or any of you, enough credit. He has further... blinded me to his color. I misjudged the three of you when we met. The situation seemed so hopeless, but I was selfish in involving the three of you and risk your lives. I thought I would have to live the rest of my life knowing I killed your friend. I was only thinking about how I failed the townspeople. Reynold has saved me a little for my sin of weakness. Please forgive my selfishness."

John turned to Nathaniel and said, "We... are good. We have to catch up with Reynold and find out what happened to him yesterday and how he survived. Thank you so much for all your help."

Nathaniel felt a little sad that they had to leave. His instinct was right about them. Nathaniel would never understand why they even got involved. He saw Reynold's impact on everyone in the crowd. Nathaniel looked at John and said: "I pray God look with favor upon your journey and deliver you safe back." Geoffroy De La Tour had said that phrase over three hundred years earlier, and it seemed fitting for Nathaniel to quote it now.

After John absorbed that awesome farewell, he surprised Nathaniel by reaching out and grabbing his hand, giving him a firm handshake, and just beamed at him. Nora was already trying to catch up with Reynold as he crossed the bridge back to the Town of Salem.

Nora watched as Reynold strode down the street like a Harvard professor. He knew where he was going. She caught up with him after cresting the bridge, out of sight from the crowd at Gallows Hill, and squeezed his arm to let him know she was there.

Reynold knew whose touch it was, turned around, and hugged her, sobbing into her ear. "I kept hearing you saying that thousands of people would be affected if I interfered, but then I just couldn't... take it anymore. I had to do something."

Nora was so proud of him. She remembered nothing from historical records about a black man changing the minds of everyone that was witness to the hangings. The court wasn't in session, and the judges weren't in town.

Something on this day in history must have happened though, because, after September 22nd, 1692, the hangings halted. They contributed to a lost part of history.

John jogged up and touched Reynold's shoulder, startling him. John spun Reynold around and hugged his best friend and said, "You are my hero buddy."

Reynold choked back tears and said, "Yeah, sorry we got separated guys, my bad."

At that moment that the LEDs on John and Nora's devices turned solid green.

22

RETURN TO THE SPOT

Reynold, Nora, and John walked down Main Street. They knew where they were going. It would take twelve minutes to return to their patch of woods on Israel Porter's land. Already familiar with their surroundings, nothing seemed out of the ordinary for them. They had become oblivious to the tremendous amount of smells around them and couldn't smell the animal feces anymore. The people that were weather beaten and had horrible gray teeth, awful breath, and various skin blemishes from bouts of yellow fever, smallpox, and other maladies seemed normal. The silence they noticed when they arrived wasn't as pronounced.

Houses they passed barely caught Nora's eyes. It wasn't a new experience. This wasn't history yet, so it was invisible on her radar. Most of these houses were long gone in her *now*.

Nobody from Gallows Hill followed them as the crowd was lost in their own thoughts. The victims had to be cut down and buried. The families would return after dusk, dig them up, and re-bury them in unmarked family plots. This would prevent people from defiling the bodies of the accused witches.

As they walked, Reynold told his friends about his ordeal in jail. "I woke up and was appalled by the assault on my nose. That jail cell was beyond putrid. Bugs, rats, sewage from the other prisoners in a bucket. I don't know how long I was unconscious, but when I woke up, I saw two people wondering who the heck I was, and I talked with them. One named Mary Bradbury, and the other named John Alden."

Nora said, "I will need to verify this, but I think I remember reading that both escaped from prison."

Reynold hadn't changed history, but fulfilled it. He looked at her with the best *matter-of-fact* face he could muster on short notice without practice. He began, "who has two thumbs, an IQ higher than anyone during this time-period, and the key to solve all his problems on a convenient lanyard."

Nora quickly said, "Not so fast on the self-complimentary comments!"

"Well," Reynold continued, "they were both nice, and I was nervous after getting them out of jail, so I didn't tell them my real name. But I gave John Alden a vague note to give to Isaac Newton while John hides out in England. A really vague note."

Nora hit him on the shoulder and exclaimed, "Are you insane? You wrote a note? With their pen, or yours? Wait, who has a quill and ink in jail? They haven't invented ball-point pens yet!"

Reynold didn't think about it. "Relax. I have an old fountain pen I hardly use, but I enjoy taking out occasionally for hand notes. Well, It came in handy. The ink hadn't even dried up, so we're fine buzzkill."

Nora asked, “Reynold, how did you break out of the jail?"

Reynold beamed and replied, "You didn't catch my hint a second ago? Because I had the key! It opened all the doors with no need to pre-clean the locks with WD40. They turned like the key was designed for them."

Nora stopped in the middle of the street and looked directly at Reynold. "Wait, the key your uncle gave you opened the prison doors?"

John scowled. She knew about some key he got from his uncle, and he didn't? He didn't like a girl getting in between him and his friend. He would have to break them up before she ruined animated movie Tuesdays. John said with a questioning look, "Key?"

Reynold looked at Nora and added, "Uh... yeah, and uh... I lost it."

John now stopped walking and looked at his friend and said, "So you used this key you got from your uncle in the 20th century, to get you out of jail in 1692. Brilliant."

Reynold looked a tad sheepish and said, "Well... uh... actually, Mary Bradbury pointed out I was wearing the key. I woke up dazed and in jail with red goo on my shirt. I think the red stuff is from my asthma inhaler that exploded on me. And, speaking of strange things in my pocket," Reynold reached into his pocket and took out a misshapen musket ball. "Check this out."

John looked at it and removed a perfect round musket ball from his own pocket and said, "Oh! Here is its twin. I found it while walking to Gallows Hill. It looks unused. Maybe this was the one that should have hit you when that sheriff guy shot at you... again. I thought you were a dead man. Maybe this saved your life, buddy."

Reynold looked at it in amazement. They weren't home yet, and he had one more surprise for them.

Nora wasn't impressed. "Hey guys, show and tell's over.

We have to get back to the trees behind the Jail and skedaddle!"

Both Reynold and John increased their pace to keep up with Nora.

As they were walking, the wind picked up. Clouds were forming in the sky and darkening. The approaching rainstorm would be a big one. Between the clouds, he could see a lightning flash.

They proceeded on Main street until they saw the back of the town's house on their left. Only days earlier, Nathaniel had told them the witch trials were held in that building. They found their familiar crop of trees and entered the woods, hidden from prying eyes.

Reynold shared his last bit of news with them now. "So guys," Reynold began, "I don't think I can go back with you. My Elmer was destroyed." He took it out and showed them, emphasizing the damage by looking at them through the perfect hole two inches from the top. The LED was dark.

John's eyes went wide, not realizing he was talking louder than usual. "Why did you do that?"

Reynold interrupted, "I didn't choose to be shot by a musket a few times. Elmer saved my life, aided by my dented tablet." Reynold magically produced his tablet computer.

John looked at the slight dent in Reynold's tablet, touched it for a second, thinking, "Wow!" then returned his attention to Reynold's now destroyed device. Elmer wasn't a happy device.

John thought about it. If he had materials, and his soldering gun, sure. He'd need a kiln, and stuff that won't be invented for hundreds of years. The ovens of this time can't generate enough heat to melt the metals he would need to fix this.

"Look," John started, "I got you into this mess. I think you should take my device and go back."

"Let's not get ahead of ourselves." Reynold started. "You guys may be stuck here. Until you activate it, there's still the mystery of whether the wormhole is still there and open for business."

John thought Reynold was right. They didn't know if the wormhole was still open. The remaining devices were charged, and they were together.

Nora said, "Can you salvage anything out of Reynold's thing to make ours more powerful or something?"

John thought about it. "The tool I used to seal the devices is a hex screw. The metallurgy in the here and now is only OK. I could make something small enough, but it's not just standard iron working. I'd have to heat the metal and have a precise mold. And that's just opening it up. Once there, I'd need a soldering gun or a hot metal pointy thing to melt solder without melting the metal. Uhh... rosin core solder, let's not forget that. I'd need to invent that, or buy that from someplace. They won't invent graphene until 2004. Graphite isn't discovered until 1859, one compound used to make graphene. For the ceramics, I'd need a really HOT kiln. I can't fathom doing this with sticks and stones. Reynold may be right, one of us or all of us might be stuck here. Again, we haven't verified if the wormhole is still above our heads and is waiting for us to return through it."

Nora considered their fate. "I'll stay. You guys wouldn't last a day. I peed in an outhouse, so I'm familiar with procedures. As of this moment, I'm the equivalent of a supermodel, so maybe I can pose for sculptors?" She was a curious what her compensation would be.

Reynold wasn't happy. He couldn't let his friends sacrifice themselves for him. What was their next move?

John was still examining the hole. Maybe it was only the charging circuits? Perhaps it was mostly dead? Could it be working now, and all he had to do was fix the readiness circuits? He still didn't have any equipment to help him make even an educated guess.

John took out his phone and analyzed part of Elmer by taking photos of the damage. He then zoomed in on the pictures to see what was damaged. If he had a digital multimeter to test the circuits. Maybe all it needed was wires to connect the circuits.

John scowled and examined it while Reynold and Nora watched.

Reynold considered theories about what they did when they arrived. The three bubbles merged because they were close to one another. Could there be enough atmosphere in two EM bubbles going 299,000 kilometers per second. Would he be able to go without touching the device? He had the other phone John gave him. Reynold reviewed the video. He looked up and saw the wormhole. Looked down and saw the dirt beneath his feet. This was just before the EM bubble collapsed. They were about an arm's length apart when the experiment started. Reynold had a theory that two of them might be able to use one device if they were really, really close to one another. But how close? He decided not to mention it. It was all guesswork without sophisticated computers to calculate their chances, and they would gamble with all three of their lives if the guess was wrong. Reynold didn't want his friends harmed because of a guess.

Reynold stopped the video and stared at the imprint of his knee on the ground made days earlier for inspiration. An answer was here some place.

John was reluctant to share his conclusions, but had to dive in. "Now, as precise as the hole the musket ball made, it destroyed the charging circuits and both super conductors. Nothing inside the device is usable, except the charging LED, and that's it. We have no way to fix it without a lot of things that haven't been invented yet. Sorry, but these are the facts. Not to mention, who knows if the wormhole that swallowed us and sent us here is still open, so we may have a timing problem if it collapsed. So we should activate the remaining units ASAP to make sure our ride home is available. Who knows, maybe Reynold will keep the wormhole open while he's here, and we can come back through to save him? Then again, if we return through it, will we end up back at the same moment when we arrived here over three days ago, like an endless loop? These are the questions at hand, and again, high marks for finding a naturally occurring Einstein-Rosen bridge. Good find everyone. Take Sunday off." John was trying to motivate everyone.

Nora didn't accept this state of affairs. "That's crap. We're going back together."

Reynold said, "Nora, I don't like it any more than you do. But these are the cards I've been dealt. My device was destroyed. John, I can't let you stay for me. Nora, I can't let you stay for me either. Maybe I can find Nathaniel and work for him until I get a small cut on my elbow that kills me from infection. Oh Joy."

John looked at him and said, "You're not staying. I don't think you should. You've been shot at and jailed. Your mom will be so disappointed to know you spent the night in jail."

Reynold looked at him with fear in his eyes. "That's MORE reason to not go back. My mother will blame ME for being shot at... AND JAILED! At all costs, don't tell my mom!"

John held back a chuckle, but Nora didn't even smile, not even trying to understand the inside joke. This really stank. How can men use humor to deal with emotional situations? They're not so smart.

The wind was whipping up. In a few hours, there would be a massive storm. You didn't need to be a meteorologist to see that.

John looked at Reynold and saw he would not change his mind. Nora didn't know what to think and got angry. She really didn't like this.

John was wondering if he had to say goodbye? Some tears welled up in his eyes. They had known each other for most of their lives. Was it all going to end? He hated that he had to think of losing his best friend a third time in two days.

John hugged Reynold. Was this the last moment he would spend with his friend? He desperately wanted his buddy to reminisce about these three days over the years. Remember when we went back in time? Yeah, we did that. He wanted to share copious fist-bumps, beer glasses clinking against one another with him.

Nora watched the two friends locked in an embrace. What was she going to do? She just got Reynold back and didn't want to say goodbye.

Tears welled up in her eyes. She was about to break. She didn't like showing her emotions. She felt they were a cop-out. If something terrible happened, her feelings would flow, and then would regret exposing them. Holding back emotions sucked.

Reynold and John stopped hugging, and John was a little emotional.

Reynold made a move toward Nora as if to shake her hand, but she grabbed him instead and hugged him tightly. She didn't want to let go. She was sobbing on his chest openly. Damn, this sucked. Why? She kept thinking. How did she start liking this guy so much in such a short period? Was she just a sap? Had she let her guard down? Does he know? Is he that thick that he doesn't know? She did kiss him a few days ago.

Reynold was level-headed. He had just survived being shot by musket again and had given the lecture of his life. He had to be the voice of reason. "Hey guys, you don't know if that wormhole is still open, so I think the sooner you hit those buttons, the better." Reynold honestly wasn't sure. But his educated guess was all he had to go on, and any chance was better than none. They were the first people to traverse a wormhole in history. One small step indeed.

Reynold stood near his knee divot, and Nora and John stepped back, unsure where they needed to position themselves to start the process. Out of curiosity, Reynold glanced at his watch that read **2:16pm*. He dreaded seeing the asterisk next to the time for the rest of his life. Or until the watch ran out of power. Whichever came first. It was already running on electrical *fumes*. Soon he would have no watch, no functioning tablet, and still had no internet. He would need to get used to living in pre-electronic hell.

Nora and John tapped their synchronization buttons. The two devices now communicated with one another. Now either John or Nora had to hit the start button. They held their cell phones to record the final experiment. Nora saw Reynold's puppy dog eyes and stepped two paces toward him. John followed her and asked, "Nora, what are you doing?"

She looked at John and said, "This." She kissed Reynold passionately on the lips while hitting the start button on her device at the same time. Her device synchronized with John's and generated the electromagnetic field around all three of them.

History recorded in 1642 that a single woman gave a man a long public kiss. They arrested the young woman for public indecency. She was given a stern warning by the court and released, but they forced her to marry the man she kissed in order to compensate for the offense.

Nora wasn't worried about being arrested. The kiss she gave Reynold in their personal time was a full three minutes, and although not a world record, per relativity, it spanned over three hundred years.

23

BACK AT SAMUEL SEWALL'S

Stephen Sewall and his wife arrived at his brother's house in Boston, ready for the scheduled judges' meeting. The three and a half hour journey by a horse was tedious, and all the while fearing for his family's safety.

At Cotton Mather's request, Stephen traveled with his notes and the documents he collected from the other note-takers at the oyer and terminer proceedings. The notes were written over six months and took up most of his travel bag. He still had to pack clothing for himself and his wife.

Earlier that day, the indicted witches were being hanged in Salem. Well, good. Stephen didn't like thinking the devil was alive in his town.

Cotton Mather was eager for these notes. He wanted to write many books about the trials. As one of the most prolific writers of the 1600s, he had hundreds of publishing credits.

Lieutenant governor William Stoughton arrived for the meeting. Almost all the expected attendees were there. As he walked in, they heard the first clap of thunder of the approaching storm.

The previous case of witchcraft happened in Boston in 1668. The accused was Ann *Goody* Glover. Her trial had also been presided over by Stoughton. These cases were familiar to Judge Stoughton because Ann was a servant of the Goodwin family. When they accused her of stealing laundry, an argument ensued. A doctor diagnosed that Martha Goodwin and her children became bewitched. This resulted in Goody Glover being hanged, four years before the Salem outbreak. Stoughton believed dead witches were better than living ones and was more than happy to sign the execution orders. He was the most senior and experienced judge on the court.

They called the Judges' meeting to plan their next court date, on November 1st. Its purpose was to prosecute more witches from the surrounding towns. The process was trying on the judges, and they grew weary of the additional work resulting from the number of jailed accused witches. It was impossible to complete their work without advanced planning.

Samuel Sewall's home was a lovely Boston house, two stories tall. The lower floor was large enough to have several big rooms, including a large kitchen. They used the common room for gatherings of many kinds. Mr. Sewall and his wife delighted in entertaining crowds and being the center of attention. Tonight's gathering included the most prominent men in Massachusetts.

The future of the trials seemed uncertain as more people protested their existence. They tried speeding up the process by issuing eleven orders of execution, and what would have resulted in nine executions today since Dorcas Hoar confessed yesterday, and they postponed Abigail

Faulkner's execution due to her pregnancy. John Higginson would have a report on the executions when he arrives.

Samuel was itching for more work. With the court out of session, he wanted to continue doing the Lord's work, and prevent the spread of Satan in the Massachusetts colony. His wife prepared the water for tea, and let it simmer, as the remaining guests arrived. She had even baked small cakes in the oven next to the fire, and prepared jams for the occasion, as if it were a social event.

Captain John Higginson arrived moments before the approaching storm. The clouds blocked the sun and made the room dark. He would make the long trip back to Salem tomorrow after spending the night at the Black Horse Tavern. Governor Phips strode in behind the Captain to hear the news from Salem.

After the men caught up with each other, Captain Higginson began the meeting. "The executioner hanged seven women and one man by the neck, and they were dead within an hour of climbing the gallows,"

John Hathorne interrupted, "That's excellent news! But why only eight? What happened to the ninth prisoner that should have hanged?"

Captain Higginson countered Hathorne's statement, a little aggravated. "NO! No, it's not good news. According to Sheriff Corwin, the ninth witch scheduled for execution escaped prison last night with John Alden, and a negro. I must add that the prisoners somehow slipped through stone and oak walls of the Salem prison without evidence of a single scratch. Gentlemen, I must relay what happened during the execution. The crowd I witnessed at this execution was yelling at the prisoners. Until one of the accused women spoke. Not since the hanging of George Burroughs, when he recited the Lord's Prayer upon the ladder, has the crowd become this agitated, and then completely silenced. I am in fear we are not doing the Lord's work right now. One prisoner put the townspeople in their place and begged us all to review the evidence provided."

"Why do you say that?" Phips asked.

"The crowd turned against the judgment itself. As her final statement on the gallows, Mary Etsy pronounced *If you feel you are being driven by the Lord in this work, I beg that you examine the confessing witches more. I am confident that they will be judged for their acts with a harshness befitting their crimes.* Her words were so eloquent and powerful that I recited them in my head, so as not to forget them to tell you here. I had a long ride to practice, and I assure you that is precisely what she said." John Higginson's eyes were still wide with shock. He then continued giving his report. "Then, a negro appeared, and spoke unlike any negro I've ever seen. He asked the crowd not to judge him based on his color, as he could very well be an angel instead of the devil. I saw him stare down the musket fired by Sheriff Corwin only yards away. He survived without a scratch with a crowd of hundreds watching, including myself. The day before, a guard had shot the same man in the chest and he appeared to heal instantly. This man and two prisoners passed through the walls of the Salem jail as if they weren't there. He made myself and the entire crowd question their faith in our decision to execute the prisoners. Mary Etsy made everyone question their faith in the girls who have been making most of the accusations, and the negro made me question my faith in my convictions. As of that moment on Gallows Hill, I no longer have that faith in our actions, gentlemen."

After a moment of silence between the eight men,

William Stoughton spoke first. "How do you know that man was an angel?"

"How do you know the people executed are witches?" Higginson shot back.

Increase Mather said, "Do you really think we're killing innocent people?" The President of Harvard was a powerful man, having returned from England earlier that year with a new charter for the colony and for Harvard. Harvard rewarded him with an honorary doctorate in theology.

Higginson thought about it for a moment and replied, "Yes! I no longer feel that the testimony and evidence is enough to convict these people of being witches. The Spectral evidence being produced is..."

Cotton Mather interrupted, "Spectral evidence? I thought we had warned the courts against the introduction of evidence about ghosts invading people? How can anyone prove ghosts affected these people? It is like proving the air we breathe exists. It does, but we can neither see it nor prove it."

Increase looked at the gentlemen and said, "If you are sentencing people to their deaths based on this evidence, it is not enough. It would be better that ten suspected witches should escape than one innocent person should be condemned. This *spectral evidence* could be a misdirection by the devil himself, making us his tools for evil. It should never be allowed as the only evidence."

Stoughton finally spoke. "We have been denouncing and executing witches since June. My hand is on all of their execution orders. I stand by the orders. Increase, how can you turn this around and blame us?"

"But you can not." William Phips quickly replied for Increase before the gentlemen argued. "Look, we all have blood on our hands from this conflagration, and we seem to be fanning the flames rather than putting them out. We need to consider our next actions. We can not stand by and let spectral evidence cloud these trials."

"But I've seen the girls writhe in pain, sir!" said Hathorne. "I'm telling you, someone bewitched these girls. Other than that period where Mary Warren seemed to recover, and become afflicted again."

Cotton Mather asked, "If someone has bewitched them, how can we trust that they are being true witnesses at all? Perhaps the devil is using them as his vessels to tell us lies. And what do you mean, Mary Warren became afflicted again?"

John Hathorne said, "She put a note on the church thanking them for praying for her deliverance as she was no longer ravaged by the devil. Then the girls accused her of being a witch, and she became afflicted again with the same symptoms as before."

Governor Phips became visibly annoyed. With sarcasm in his voice, he asked, "So she miraculously stopped the fits? Any guess why?"

"Well, John Proctor threatened her with beatings if she continued issuing testimony during the trials, so she suddenly got better," said Hathorne. "Then the other girls accused her of being a witch. She then accused John Proctor, whom we hanged in August." John Hathorne was now feeling painfully duped as he outlined the sequence of the events.

Phips felt hot and angry. He had been busy with matters in the Maine frontier until this moment. The Governor returned to Boston for this meeting. Now he doubted the validity of the court he set up in his absence to protect against getting the verdicts wrong. And now he believed that was exactly what happened. He calmed himself down before speaking to make sure everyone understood what was happening. "Am I the only person seeing a terrible pattern here, kind sirs? You men are the most educated in the colony, and you don't see this? John Proctor opposed the hearings, and his servant whom he could legally discipline, accused him of being a witch. She repented for her sins. Then she became bewitched again when she noticed her life was in danger because the surrounding girls accused her of being a witch because she had changed her story and contradicted them? How can bewitched witnesses be reliable as witnesses?"

Hathorne was now ashen. How had he not seen this? Was he so close to the trials he mistook the game-playing of young girls for actual suffering? Since the first execution, that of Bridget Bishop in June, the girls had played a lesser role in the trials. But the accused people were coming forward and immediately accusing others. Nobody was pleading innocence anymore except for Mary Parker. They legally used an ancient law to torture Giles Corey, who gave no plea. Had the accused seen the danger of pleading innocence that he himself did not see until now? He had been proud of his time on this court until this moment and now felt he had to think carefully about it all.

Stoughton said, "These people were bewitched. I was never duped by any children's games."

Higginson had never interrupted the distinguished man ever before, but felt the point had to be made. "Mister Stoughton. Sir, are you so sure of this? Can you be sure beyond a shadow of a doubt? Because the lives of many people have been impacted by those actions." Higginson recalled what the black man said. His words still stung, and he was embarrassed.

Phips had to be sure everyone understood what needed

to happen. This was a turning point for the trials, and he had to be concrete in his decisions. He inhaled and issued his orders. It took great effort not to scream or talk through clenched teeth. "You gentlemen have all the testimony and statements from the people. We will surely hang now if we get this wrong. The court must be disbanded. I will see to that shortly. The testimony about the use of spectral evidence must be found and we must show it wasn't the only evidence that convicted anyone we hanged. There was always other evidence. Is that understood? In no way are you to repeat this to anyone. We can let none of this information out from this moment forward. Stephen, you have the notes and testimony. We need to spend the next few hours going through them and making sure they are cohesive enough to tell the important parts of the trials, but we must remove testimony from the accusers that is solely based on this *spectral evidence*. Increase, you are right, we shouldn't have allowed this evidence to be the deciding factor in hanging people. William, I care not for your pride in your accomplishments here. You will fix this mess if you take all night."

Cotton Mather needed his voice to be heard. "But I must publish about these trials."

"And you will," said Phips, "but we must focus on only a few of the trials with more than just spectral evidence being cause for the convictions. That has been the downfall of these legal proceedings." Phips wasn't wholly educated in legal matters, but he was savvy enough to see it could destroy them if evidence was clear about the proceedings of the trial. It was his head that could roll, since his name was all over the assignments of the judges and the creation of the court.

"Gentlemen, other than Cotton's well-edited and

reviewed book about the trials, let us make sure that no evidence exists to show we have executed people based solely on spectral evidence. Put it in the fire tonight." Phips wanted to plug holes, refusing to go down with this ship. "Once Cotton's book comes out, no one will print anything further about this. Anywhere. As of this moment, the trials occurred, but the basis of the judgments must be colored differently, or we all will suffer the same consequences."

After this stern warning, all the gentlemen read through the testimony they had acquired since February of that year, and they had Stephen Sewall write replacement statements with new pages of parchment. They would throw the old pages in the fire and let the convictions stand with little documentation. If the other note-takers possessed any papers written about the spectral evidence alone, it went into the fire.

They worked for many hours, without asking questions of one another, for they were afraid to add to the problems they had created.

All the pages involving inquiries made by Nathaniel Saltonstall ended up in the fire, forever lost to the world, his involvement almost completely erased from history.

Cotton cornered his father Increase and asked, "How will we write about this?"

Increase considered his answer before giving it. He despised that the courts had used evidence that could never be proven. He could only look at Cotton and reply, "Carefully."

As they had never used their hands to write notes at the trials, Cotton and Increase Mather left Samuel Sewall's house, leaving Stoughton, Stephen, and Phips to finish the work trying to minimize the impact of the events surrounding the trials. Samuel Sewall wrote in his diary that night about the meeting, but mentioned neither Increase's nor Governor Phips's presence.

At that same moment, in a home a quarter mile away, Robert Calef sat down and wrote his thoughts for a book he would later publish with no one's consent.

The massive storm came in with force and covered Boston and Salem with a well-needed rain that prevented William Stoughton from returning home. It was a baptism of the events of that day. The healing had begun. The sky over Massachusetts wept for the souls that had been lost.

24

MARCH 31ST, 1693

Since most of John Alden's life had been spent on ships, his sea legs returned once he stepped on board his vessel. His fleet hauled cargo, not passengers. At sea, he had quality time with his crew. They didn't have to entertain pilgrims making journeys to the colonies. This trip was strictly business. So it was comforting to be back with his mates onboard. He thought about that Rey bloke who had helped him escape from jail. May as well hand that letter to that Newton fellow. It seemed the least he could do in the way of paying him back.

Since seafaring men weren't the type to do much catching up, they were quick to get to work loading, then sailing the ships, then unloading them. It was all routine. Ship's mates weren't a talkative lot, so they spoke only when it was necessary to communicate. Chatty annoying mates soon realized they stood out and fell in line with the routine. Other people's stories weren't that interesting when you've also sailed the world. "Have you been to.." "Yes mate, you were on that trip with me, remember?" etc.

Captain Alden set sail for England on September 22nd.

His ship was empty, so it didn't sit low in the water, which would have helped speed it up a knot or two. They bounced around in the Atlantic waters due to the lack of ballast, and the trip took longer because of it. He carried rum, beer, dried cod-fish, and fishing gear for the journey for him and his men. Alden didn't have time to bring many goods to England for trade, with his whole fleet sitting idly at the docks, waiting for orders he couldn't give while he was in jail.

When John Alden was brought in for questioning in May, the court made him stand on a chair as if he were to sing a song to the crowd, and they accused him of witchcraft. One judge asked one girl who had fallen down, writhing and carrying on, who was causing her pain, and she initially pointed to another man. Then someone whispered in her ear, and she corrected herself and pointed directly to Alden. She had never seen him before, yet she now pointed at him. Guards then brought him outside, and the girls circled him as if they might dance around him, but they continued pointing to him, accusing him of laying with Indian squaws and transporting arms to the French and Indians. The next thing they did was to confiscate his sword. While the girls flopped around, the Captain asked the Judge why he had not fallen as the girls did. The judge couldn't answer. He told the judge there must be a lying spirit in the girls and said, "I can assure you there is no truth in what they say about me!". Then that cumberground Nicholas Noyes had to make up more rubbish that wasn't true. The truth, John had no truck with the devil.

Merchants in the Massachusetts colony were jealous of John Alden's successes. John drove hard but fair deals as a businessman. He worked as a privateer, working to secure other ships' cargo as his own. John's ship and crew overpowered other ships and kept the larger boats, and their cargo as his spoils. But he did this at the behest of the government before Edmund Andros took power. He always had an instinct for where to trade for more goods. John began by trading goods with other parts of the East coast that weren't under Edmund Andros's rule. Alden knew how to expand his profits and keep himself safe from persecution and excessive taxes. If Massachusetts is a mess, do business in the Dutch Colony of New York. If New York had an economic downturn, he would set sail to Virginia. Virginia had a downturn, simply sail to the Caribbean. And now, having been convicted and jailed for the crime of witchcraft in Massachusetts, it was time to sail to England.

From time to time, as he sat on deck during the voyage to England, he took out the note that had been handed to him by Reynold, and turned the paper over and examined it. This strange picture of a gravestone perplexed him. It was so meticulously detailed. Did someone draw this? The stone looked so weathered and old, but it bore the date he left, Sept. 22nd, 1692 as the date the people engraved on the stone passed away. It was a drawing. Captain Alden saw George Corwin shoot Rey, and now he was looking at Rey's grave stone. How could that be? He had to contemplate this further.

When Reynold wrote the note, Captain Alden had marveled that he did not dip his pen into an inkwell, it just wrote. It didn't take more than a second to write the note on his back and hand it to him. The man hadn't blown on it, he poured nothing on it to help it dry. It dried as quickly as he wrote it. Very odd. It looked like a proper pen written note. How did he do this without a quill and a jar of ink?

John studied the image of the gravestone intensely. He enjoyed drawing, so he tried to replicate the picture. With so many days at sea, he had plenty of time to practice drawing, although the rough ocean didn't lend well to accuracy. It fascinated him that this picture was so vivid and clear. There were tufts of grass blurred in the background. Why was this stone drawn so weathered? It should still look new based on the dates on it? Captain Alden took out a piece of paper from his personal stash. With only twenty pieces of paper, he had to ration them for the long journey. John used the paper to jot down thoughts, keep the ship's inventory, or write orders. He could only spare one or two sheets to draw a copy of the fascinating picture on the back of the note before delivering it to this Isaac bloke. John needed to practice without ink first. He looked at the gravestone and practiced the motions of drawing without ink. After a lot of practice, he knew he had become proficient enough to draw on the paper. He waited for an evening when the swells of the ocean were at a minimum to draw his personal copy of the picture of the gravestone. For a first try, his drawing captured the image quite well from the paper handed to him. He compared it to the original he would hand to this Newton fellow and gave himself high marks for accuracy. The lettering surely wasn't English, but he drew it perfectly, even though he didn't understand what it meant. The partially rubbed off note didn't seem important, but he could still see a few of the letters Reynold had written, only days earlier. Washington Street? Where was that?

He put his copy of the image of the stone away. As they got closer to England, there would be more important things to do, such as keeping the sails in order, and making sure the ship stayed true on course.

On December 1st, 70 days after he embarked, the ship arrived in England. John purchased goods to bring back from England to make his trip profitable. He might as well make money while he was on the run from Massachusetts. Nobody in England was privy to his capture for witchcraft, nor his time in jail. So he could continue to do business as usual, making connections and deals with merchants.

John Alden gave the note Rey wrote as promised to Isaac Newton, who barely acknowledged him. Newton seemed confused by the note, and he put it down on his cluttered desk, piled high with hundreds of other papers and books. How could he find anything in that terrible mess? This Newton fellow asked if John had known the people's initials, and when he replied no, Newton accused him of wasting his time. Strange. Why would a person ask someone to deliver a short cryptic note to a complete stranger and say it was very important if it had no meaning to the recipient?

Once Alden concluded his businesses in England, he loaded casks of rum, beer, food, and other provisions for the crew. He filled his holds with plenty of tea, Dutch clothing, and looms, Dutch pots and pans and knives, plus jars of jams.

He set sail on January 15th, 1693, leaving England behind. John hoped that enough time had passed for the fervor to die down. He had to get back to the colonies to do more business. He couldn't lay dormant forever.

The journey home was uneventful. They had only one sailor get sick from scurvy. That was good. The calmer winter seas plus the larger ballast of the goods below made the time on this voyage fly.

The ship docked in Salem, on March 31st, 1693. When John spotted land, he raised a glass of beer to the person responsible for his freedom, then he strode onto shore. Captain Alden's gut feeling gave him confidence that the chaos he escaped had been resolved by now. He was refreshed and confident after commanding the sea. John made his first trip to the cemetery in Salem to see if he could find a gravestone such as the one he had drawn with so much detail. If the stone was not there, he would purchase a plot, and have the engraver reproduce the stone exactly as he had drawn it, and he would threaten to withhold payments for any deviations. That Rey fellow gave his life after giving John a second chance. Nobody could have survived that shot, nobody. Since the profits from this trip were bountiful, Captain Alden felt he should be equally generous to Rey.

25

27 AND A HALF MINUTES LATER

Nora's kiss startled both John and Reynold.

John's and Nora's devices generated the individual EM bubbles. Both bubbles merged with one another as they had before. Nora and Reynold were so close, one bubble stretched around both of their bodies, with John's bubble adding to the surrounding field. Reynold's theory was correct about needing to be insanely close to one another to use only two remaining devices. Thousands of miles below the strata of Reynold's mellowing mushy brain, Reynold felt a vagueness of elation for having determined that theory. His consciousness had set aside the billions of germs he had just experienced, in one of the most foul smelling places he'd ever been, and lounged in a place where it relaxed and enjoyed itself. Like entering a hot tub with tense muscles, dipping his toe in the water, he relaxed down to his core. This kiss let his brain go on a cranial vacation it had never experienced in his life. He reached a state of nirvana, or in his case, nerdvana. Nora had saved him with a kiss. He was in Heaven.

At one minute of kiss time, Reynold's brain was

exploding with information he hadn't experienced but could only form a single sentence; "Wow! This is really cool!" repeated over and over in his head like a broken record skipping on the same track. Reynold had one of the highest IQ's on the planet, and his language skills reduced to a mere five words by Nora's glorious kiss. Was he even able to think of other words? Distracted by that thought, he continued the experiment, putting his fingers into her hair lightly touching her scalp. Oh wow, the kissing seemed to get more intense. Awesome. What would happen if he gently caressed her scalp? Oh, wow. More kissing. These actions led to more kissing. He thought again, "Wow! This is really cool!"

Reynold activated his second hand, which was lounging at his side this entire time thinking to itself, "Should I be doing anything, guys? I'm just hanging here," and he reached to touch her face. "Wow! This is really COOL!" Hmm, what if I caressed the face, touching the smooth texture, and feeling the warmth against his palm? Wow! all things lead to more kissing. "Wow! This is really cool!"

At that precise moment, their combined EM bubble had achieved at the speed of 299,000.498 kilometers per second, matching the speed of the wormhole. Like a baton holding runner catching up to the next runner of an Olympic relay race, the Wormhole brought the EM bubble toward it this time rather than the wormhole racing toward the bubble days earlier. It had stayed in place from their first journey until the contents returned, which was immediate. The wormhole complied with three and a half days of wishful thinking and gave a gift to the three weary travelers. In reality, it existed in their *present* for only a fraction of a fraction of a second and collapsed the moment they returned. Nothing in the originating time, nor in 1692, was going the speed of the wormhole. Only their combined EM bubble, and the atmosphere it contained, entered it. This was their ticket home, and they had just punched it.

Reynold had become lost in Nora's kiss. Had they looked up to see the wormhole's signature glass sphere, they would have peered into the office they had left frozen in time. The wormhole was only visible as they were going light speed.

The internal temperature of the bubble was a snapshot of the atmosphere they were just in. At the moment the devices gave them their boost in speed, John was wondering if he really should watch Nora and Reynold kissing like this. It was too intimate. He could hear them breathing and smooching. In an attempt to ignore them, he made as many observations about the trip as he could. They were definitely going at light speed. He'd invest in an LCD panel that could show copious amounts of information about what was happening for version two of the devices. He hated just counting the blinking of a green LED. Occasionally, he'd glance at Nora and Reynold, still locked in an embrace, felt uncomfortable, and looked away again. John thought, "Great job, buddy. I wonder if she has any single friends? Should I ask now? Ok, I've seen enough. Get a room, you two."

As on the first trip, the surroundings seemed to rush in and out of focus, but were never entirely perceptible. Without discernible motion or vibration, the whole trip seemed rather mundane.

Without understanding what was happening, the three entered and exited the wormhole and waited for the timer to stop the experiment. Since time became dilated, that time added to the current time only. The remaining part of that fraction of a second was on the opposite side of the wormhole, waiting for *Elmer* to shut down.

As the experiment continued, the blurry swirling images resolved into their perception of walls, a floor beneath them, artificial lights in the room. The surrounding temperature of the new environment wasn't perceived by the three of them because the EM bubble was insulating them. The warmer climate wasn't noticeable. Since the EM bubble put space between their feet and the floor in the first experiment, they were able to return without being interfered with by the building's foundation. They were at the same height when they started the experiment. The drop they experienced on the first trip was due to the building not existing in 1692. The EM bubble added space to their disconnection from the floor, and then the removal of the foundation made them drop the extra 7 inches days earlier.

John was getting excited, as each of his guesses were turning into realities, and the last part of the second minute traveling came to a close. Toward the end of the trip, his LED blinked twice as fast, indicating they were approaching the final moments of this experiment. Nora and Reynold were still oblivious to her device, which she clasped in her hand.

As the EM bubble vanished, they dropped an inch. They didn't even need to brace themselves for the landing. The wormhole closed, since the negative mass of the EM bubble returned through it. The return journey completed the equation.

Nora's lips hinted that they could pause the kiss, and Reynold felt her lips change texture and intensity. So he stopped kissing quite so intensely. Reynold stood still as a statue, blissfully mesmerized, just feeling the air on his face, and thought how much warmer it felt than the environment they had left. He thought about Nora's face and how the breath through her nose tickled his face while she kissed him. It reduced him to raw feelings and was not worried about exposing them for everyone to see. Reynold kept that moment in his mind as long as possible and smiled with every molecule in his body, because it felt like it started on his toes and extended to the tips of the hair on his head.

Reynold's watch, for the first time in days, updated the time to "12:27pm" proudly removed the asterisk, never to appear again. A log entry stating "ERROR - time correction failure" was added and ignored. In many circumstances, when computers can't communicate with time-servers, they need to correct time beyond their tolerance. This was the only moment in time the error wasn't due to system error.

Later, when John and Reynold reviewed the recordings, they would calculate that the first use of Elmer sped them up to meet the wormhole and transported them to 1692 immediately. The twenty-seven minutes, thirty-one seconds of time dilation happened in 1692 over three hundred years before they started the experiment. When they returned to the present, the time dilation occurred after they emerged from the wormhole that second time. The time spent in the wormhole was instantaneous.

John looked at their surroundings in awe, as was Nora, once she opened her eyes. The air felt thinner and strange when they breathed it, but it was familiar. They were looking around and were shocked at what they thought was a dream. John said, "Nora, you ARE seeing what... I am seeing?"

Nora and John continued to look at their environment and let the moment sink in. It was there, real, and not a fantasy. This wasn't a hallucination shared between them. John saw the glee in Nora's eyes. They were standing in the office, precisely where they were before they hit the button on Elmer only twenty-eight minutes earlier. The only difference was they looked dirty and exhausted from their experiences.

Nora saw how pathetic Reynold had looked when he said goodbye three minutes earlier and her emotions bubbled to the surface. She was overwhelmed by what they had gone through, and the uncertainty of ever recapturing that moment, and the joy of returning combined with a kiss she planted on Reynold. That kiss was necessary. She didn't care about his or her horrible breath, nor his reaction. She had to kiss him. Nora had to show Reynold she wanted to be with him, in any time period. Nora had to get him home with them. Most importantly, she had to make a claim on him before another history-savvy woman tried to woo him to find another rogue wormhole.

Nora owed herself a good cry. She had banked it from earlier and cashed it in at that moment to weep tears of joy.

John had looked down and saw the back of his right hand had the beginnings of peach fuzz on it, and he cried too. Something dawned on him at that moment. He reached into his pocket and took out the fourth device with a green LED lit and said, “Hey guys, don’t be mad, but look what I just found!”

Nora ignored John and sobbed as she touched Reynold's arm to get his attention. Reynold said aloud, "Wow! This is really cool!" And at that moment, time stood still.

26

NO BUTTERFLIES!

After picking up supplies and clothing, and buying three comfortable, thick robes at the local department store, they proceeded to Reynold's house to clean up at his insistence.

John was looking around and realized that his friend had a technology obsession that required therapy. He must live at the best stereo shops. The hidden built-in speakers sounded amazing. When he walked from one room to another, sensors somewhere faded in the music and faded it out from the preceding room. It was a noticeable effect, and it worked really well. The lights also faded in and out wherever you walked, so the only place that was lit was where someone stood. He saw light switches, but never used them. There were also automatic sunroof openings that let sunlight into the rooms without the use of unnatural light sources. Those would magically shutter themselves as you walked into a different room. The place wasn't large, but the technology made it seem huge.

Reynold's wireless network speed was astounding. He had a display in his house that changed to another painted masterpiece when he looked away and looked back moments later. The texture of the glass over the virtual canvas looked like it contained thick globs of paint. This gave a three-dimensional feel to the picture, adding to the illusion that the original masterpiece was being displayed. The effect was incredible. It was a living picture frame. Without a microscope, you couldn't see the dots on the display. It amazed John that Reynold had TWO of these frames. One vertical and one horizontal digital frame. They didn't even distort the masterpieces, adding yet more realism to the illusion.

Did Reynold earn more than he did? Was it because John hadn't gotten his doctorate yet? John lived for grants, but Reynold had always worked in front of the students, compared to him being hidden in a laboratory, never seeing the sunlight. After this discovery becomes publicly known, John would ask for a significant raise.

John turned to Reynold and said, "Hey, Nathaniel mentioned that you crushed that talk in front of the crowd. He gave you kudos for quoting a guy named John Winthrop... about when you mentioned the *city upon a hill* thing."

Nora corrected him, "Uh no, it was Matthew 5:14, according to someone in the crowd."

John continued, "Also, bro - you quoted Elie Wiesel anonymously, but quoted Voltaire directly? Voltaire was born in 1694. Oops! But that Martin Luther King quote about the Darkness was impressive. You threw everything you had at them, and they took notice."

Reynold looked at them and said, "Elie Wiesel isn't born until the 20th century. Voltaire sounded generic enough and isn't known for that for a long time. *City upon a Hill* is from a John F. Kennedy speech... who's John Winthrop? Voltaire would have said it... soon enough? And anything MLK says is awesome. If I quoted any more of him, their minds would have exploded, or Nora would have shot me with a loaded musket."

They each took turns in Reynold's fancy shower, and neither Nora nor John wanted to emerge. The warm soapy luxury shower washed away the three horrible days they experienced.

Besides pulsing, and power, and simulating rainfall, and massaging the muscles, this shower also had amazing speakers. He heard sounds of nature comprising birds chirping, rainfall, and massage music with flutes and Zen bells. There was a digital panel that controlled it. He had to hit the *sync* button to make sure all jet temperatures remained the same. He took a few seconds to realize that Nora wanted a cool back shower while warm water rained down from the ceiling. There was a limit to the input he was receiving.

Reynold took the last shower, allowing his friends honorary *dibs*. During the time before his shower, Reynold's sense of smell returned, reminding him why he installed the dream shower in the first place. Eighteen minutes, forty-five seconds to go until olfactory bliss.

From the outside, Reynold's house kept its appearance from when it had been built in the mid-1800s. The inside was a reflection of Reynold's desire for a smart house rivaling the Hal-9000 computer. Besides the lights and picture frames, he removed the original wall switches and replaced them with digital touch panels. When he had guests, he made the graphics look like push button switches to ease them into twenty-second century life. The house knew when there was greater than one occupant and loaded up guest mode into the interfaces, including the shower. If a stranger walked into the house without Reynold, the house would record all motion and simulate *normal* mode to hide the technical nuances. The cameras stitched the videos together, following the potential burglar around the house to create one seamless video. If they touched any surface that wasn't deemed private, even something as little as Reynold's remote control for the TV, the system would alert the authorities automatically, and send images and videos for Reynold to review. When Reynold watched after Professor Wilson's dog, the system followed the dog room to room as it investigated, and found cheese sticks he had left out. The dog unwrapped the cheese sticks like a person. Reynold suspected the system liked the dog because he never received tattling videos of his thievery. Reynold still used an old-fashioned TV remote. He enjoyed hunting through channels for what he wanted to watch. It was part of his natural "hunter/provider" instincts, like when people still used dial-up for their internet. He would hold his microwave meal proudly and would click away until he passed out, or until he got hooked watching a random show about left-handed widgets.

His bed detected snoring, would get mad, and would automatically raise his head to prevent the offensive noise from continuing. It would also monitor his heart-rate and breathing patterns. If Reynold's snoring persisted, the bed would record it and threaten to post it on various social media accounts in the morning. Reynold would, at the bed's behest, rub vapor-rub on his chest and use a nose-strip to prevent this the next noisy night while playing the recording from the night before as a reminder of his transgression.

Reynold's memory rolled back to the last time he was in the shower. By his personal calendar was over three and a half days ago, but in this time zone, that happened only hours ago. Time didn't pass within the wormhole. The past was still in the past before they started the experiment. Reynold would never have discovered that calculation or conclusion. All of this was new territory.

Reynold emerged from his shower, relaxed and feeling a lot less offensive.

John ordered Chinese food and debated making Reynold pay for the meal, but let him off this time since he had been shot at a few times. John would slowly ease him into buying more meals and drinks. After all, he was the starving scientist, not Reynold.

They hadn't spoken yet about their experiences, nor re-watched the video they captured from their trip. Only *let's get this. We need that. Oh hey we need to get robes. Why? You'll see!*

They ate wordlessly. Once they satisfied their need to be clean first, then fed themselves, Reynold and Nora snuggled in with each other, and John was comfortable being the third wheel. John didn't mind. Who else could he geek out with about the past three days? Nora was comfortable with the silence.

Reynold finally asked, "So Nora, how did you know that by being as close as possible, the EM Field would wrap around us naturally, since John's device borrows the existing field generated by the earth?"

"I didn't," she replied. She feigned being grumpy, but was enjoying being back.

Reynold's eyes went wide. OK, find a course on relationships fast. Newton's Law of relationships: For every male action, there could be a volatile female reaction... I should write that down.

John turned to deflate the situation and said, "Yeah, that

was brilliant, a great idea! Gold Star you! Now we're all back in our time, relaxing, fed, and far less odiferous."

Nora turned to Reynold, no longer pretending to be mad, and said, "You looked so pathetic. I had to try something. So I punted and thought if we were really close, like squeezing under an umbrella, it would work. I figured the kiss could help and boost your morale. For what it's worth, not bad kissing for an amateur with stinky breath."

Reynold blushed and said, "Well, it worked, thank you so much. Thank both of you. I don't think I could have survived there without you guys."

John got a little serious, and said, "According to Nora, it looks like the history didn't change. Nora used your dented tablet to look up all the documented history from those days, and everything seemed in order. She even researched to see if anyone else other than their original author ever said parts of your sermon, and there weren't. We'd appreciate it if you listed your references next time though, buddy."

Nora looked at them and said, "It is kinda crazy. It's like you changed everything, Reynold, yet changed nothing at the same time. John Alden and Mary Bradbury both escaped from prison. That was you. Nobody from that time ever explained how they escaped. The trials never resumed, and people stopped convicting their neighbors of being witches. All prisoners were released by 1693. It took until 2001 to pardon all the accused witches. But we found something you may have messed up."

Reynold became nervous about that last part. If history didn't change, what could have happened? Reynold said, "Is this the game show *How to Keep a Physicist in Suspense*? What... happened?"

Nora and John looked at each other, and John said, "Rey,

you left your recorder on for the time we were uh... there. It was in your jacket pocket taking one picture a minute. There are some amazing shots. We saw what happened when you were shot, and when you were taken to prison. We saw you give the note to John Alden. But Nora found an episode of a TV show you need to see."

Nora asked, "Is there a way to play this video on your TV? We watched a few minutes on your tablet, and we really need to review this together. This is a TV show that aired five years before our trip."

"Uh... ok." Reynold took the tablet, did his rain-dance to make it work, and hit *play*.

The TV lit up, and audio played through the fantastic speakers. A man in a black leather jacket with a strong baritone voice said, "... and I'm the host of *Mysteries at a Museum*. Today we are in England, at Woolsthorpe Manor, and the birthplace of Sir Isaac Newton which is near London, accessible on the London to Edinburgh East Coast Main Line railway. Every object inside tells a story about Isaac Newton, and each bit of that history helps to reveal how he became the great scientist he was. Except for one item that sits alone in a clear lucite case, without a label. Elliott Bean has been the curator of the museum for over forty years."

The video changed to display an old house, similar to the style of the houses they had seen in 1692, except for the chimneys at both ends of the building.

They segued to on a gentleman wearing a kilt who spoke with a thick Scottish accent. "Today we're talking about a piece in our museum that is eight and a half inches wide by eleven inches tall. It is browning with age and contains a visible watermark. On one side, there is what looks like a faded design of some sort, impossible to discern, and on the back, there is handwriting that says, *Dear Isaac, Cheers!*

Signed, RW, JM, and NF written in ink. On the corner of the page, you see in a different type of ink, in Isaac Newton's handwriting, *Rcv. Dec. 18th, 1692.*"

"When you examine the watermark, you can see the modern logo of Harvard, with the familiar *Harvard/Veritas* on it, and four numbers underneath. When we contacted Harvard, we were informed that none of their paper had this watermark on it. The paper doesn't have the look or consistency of paper used during that century. In the late 1600s, paper was created from pulp prepared from the fibers of hemp, rattan, mulberry, bamboo, rice straw, and seaweed. The analysis of this paper shows it has a web width that is far greater than any from that time period. The web width of paper in the 1600s was significantly lower than what it could be by today's manufacturing methods. Also, the pulp of this paper is primarily from wood, with no other natural products used to produce it. This method wasn't discovered and used until the mid-19th century."

"Under examination, we can tell that the ink used in the note has a totally different chemical makeup compared to inks produced in that time period. The ink used for the markings in the corner was from late 1600s. The ink used to write the note itself is far newer. Inks of that era all have raw, natural materials in them, as they were made using plants and water. This ink examined is synthetic, showing differently shaped molecules, which was impossible for that time period."

"People thought someone from Harvard was playing a practical joke. However, research shows that this note was delivered in December 1692, directly to Isaac Newton himself. This item became misplaced until it was rediscovered in another collection of Isaac Newton's in London in the early 1800s, which is how we have documentation of the delivery. It was delivered when Newton worked for the government while fine-tuning protections for their currency. He was making their coinage less able to be snipped at the edges. People would take the snipped gold or silver for themselves, thereby devaluing the coins. Newton added a decorative edge to all their coins, preventing people from stealing precious raw materials. This decorative edge is used on coins throughout the world today. Newton also confirmed in his diary that day, *December 18th, 1692, received a strange note delivered by Captain John Alden from America.*"

"Sir Isaac Newton never publicly mentioned this letter to anyone. So it's a mystery to this day who RW, JM, or NF are. As far as we have been able to determine, he knew nobody with those initials. Also, the number in the watermark could be a date code, and if so, translates to a date over five years in the future further, adding to the mysteries of this museum piece."

Elliott's Scottish accent continued, "We here, at the museum, have been verifying its existence as early as 1836, when Harvard changed their famous Latin motto from *Veritas Christo et Ecclesiae* which means *Truth for Christ and Church,* to *Veritas* or *Truth* in Latin stated in the logo. This hasn't mattered, because according to Sir Isaac Newton's own notes, it has existed almost as long as Harvard itself."

"Now, over three hundred years later, this mystery will remain unsolved."

Reynold hit the stop button and stared. Causality just bit him in the ass.

After a minute, Nora broke the silence and said, "Hmm. So Reynold is totally fired. It's still your turn to drive me to work on Monday. Anyone want the last steamed dumpling?"

27

AUGUST 22ND 1920 EPILOG

Leonard's dad completed telling Mary's heroic story. Sam continued, "... so you may have another option for the name of your newborn son. Someone our family should finally honor. Maybe keep Douglas as," he paused for effect, "a middle name? But, give him this when he's older..." and Samuel took out an old key pendant on a leather necklace from around his neck, and handed it to his son. "Now YOU have the key. It's the key that freed Mary, and now frees you... and one day, you'll give it to your son! You are free to name your son anything that you and your wife feel is right."

Leonard was speechless as he thought about the tale he had just heard. His thoughts went back to a time when the Mayflower wasn't such a distant memory. A time when people had needed to hunt, something he couldn't even fathom. And this stranger had helped his distant ancestor. What was his purpose? Why did he do it? He had no reason to help her out. Yet, he said to her, "Come with me if you want to live," and she followed him out of jail, not knowing if they would re-capture and hang her. What choice did she have? She was sentenced to hang that morning. He saved her. He truly saved her.

Leonard held the key in his hand and admired it. This piece of history was 228 years old. To touch and hold something that had saved someone's life was strangely intimate to him. Now he had to wait for the right time to share it, and give it to his youngest son, who would pass it on to his child one day. With just the simplest of phrases, "You have the key." A sentence that has power because it expresses self-reliance. You have control. You have the key. He could give his sons the wisdom and the actual key that inspired it.

He took a moment to ponder the butterflies painted on the walls of the maternity ward, then reflected on the past again. A moment that seemed distant, but was brought to the present by his family's part in history. He silently thanked this faceless person for sparing Mary's life. It didn't change the family history, as she already had grandchildren when she emerged from jail. But her resolve, strength, and vitality come from this moment in her past. She handed the key down to her descendants. And it was an invaluable gift. Mary was seventy-seven when her life was spared and given back to her to do with as she pleased. She lived another eight years because of this man. What were those eight extra years like for her? Who else did she influence because of that moment? That one moment was still having an impact right now for Leonard.

He would discuss it with his wife, but Leonard knew with all his heart he wanted to name his son...

Ray Douglas Bradbury.

MEA CULPAS AND REFERENCES

History References

- Stacy Schiff - "The Witches" a Marvelous book. She's brilliant and is a FANTASTICALLY detail-oriented account of the Salem Witch crisis.
- Anything by Emerson "Tad" Baker, who is a brilliant researcher on Salem, MA. Buy all his books. Really. All of them. He just seems like a really cool, nice guy, and I owe him dinner and a cold adult beverage.
- Liz Covert's "Ben Franklin's world Podcast." Any history junkie should just drop this book, and start listening to this podcast weekly, seeing as you are now past the last pages of my book I'm fine with that. Hey thanks again for reading everyone! Liz's podcast kept my brain firmly planted in the 17th and 18th centuries. Before dropping this book and opening up Liz's podcast, if you are reading from an electronic device,

make sure it is adequately insured, and in a protective case. Maybe just place it down gently.

- Marilyn Roach, "The Salem Witch Trials" she synchronizes day by day the proceedings, and location of everything happening during the trials.
- Samuel Sewall, "Diary of Samuel Sewall 1674-1729." Not a page burner, but referenced to make sure I had my days coordinated.
- Charles C. Little & James Brown, "Collections of the Massachusetts Historical Society."
- Cotton Mather, "Wonders of the Invisible World,"
- Robert Calef, "More Wonders of the Invisible World" - 1700 - London - Cotton & Increase Mather were so mad when this book came out, they burned the book in Harvard yard, and published a book named "some few remarks upon a Scandalous Book" and quoted "Exodus 22:28 Thou Shalt Not Speak Evil of the Ruler of Thy People."
- John Hale, "A Modest Enquiry into the Nature of Witchcraft,"
- Samuel Adams Drake, "Nooks and Corners of the New England Coast," 1875
- Essex Antiquarian, Issues 1 through 13 - Simon Pearley MAPS of Salem MA, 1700. Thanks bro - owe ya big time.
- Henry P. Ives, "Visitor's Guide to Salem,"
- Christopher Jon Luke Dowgin's book, "Salem Secret Underground, the History of the Tunnels in the City."
- Nathaniel Hawthorne, "House of the Seven Gables."

- George Washington's Beer recipe from about 1757 was properly re-created Blue Point Brewing Company recently (See below.) and sold as "Colonial Ale".

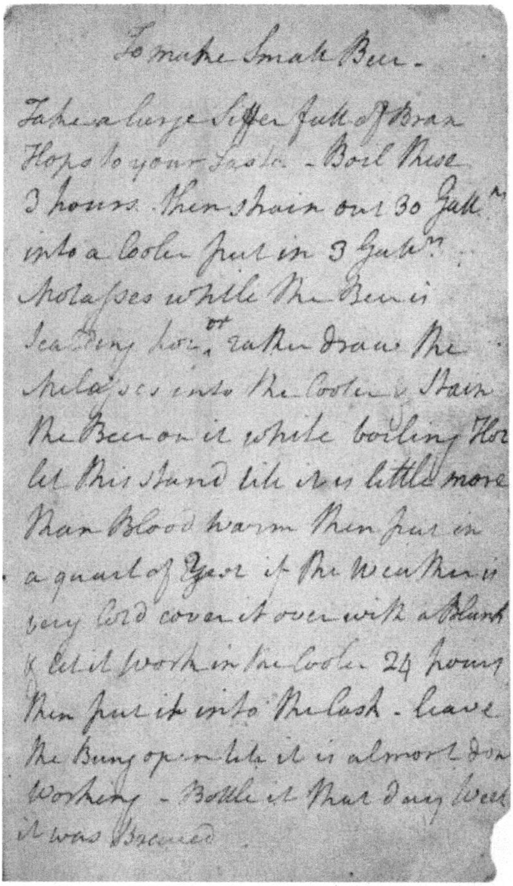
To make Small Beer.

Take a large Siffer full of Bran
Hops to your Taste. - Boil these
3 hours. Then strain out 30 Gall^{n}
into a Cooler put in 3 Gall^{n}
Molasses while the Beer is
Scalding hot or rather draw the
Molasses into the Cooler & Strain
the Beer on it while boiling Hot
let this stand till it is little more
than Blood warm Then put in
a quart of Yeast if the Weather is
very Cold cover it over with a Blank
& let it work in the Cooler 24 hours
Then put it into the Cask - leave
the Bung open till it is almost don
Working - Bottle it that day Week
it was Brewed.

- Salem Jail, visit https://www.legendsofamerica.com/ma-salemcourt/
- Stinky Past, https://allthatsinteresting.com/pre-industrial-history-gross

- Life in Taverns, https://www.gothichorrorstories.com/daily-life-in-history/daily-life-of-the-american-colonies-the-role-of-the-tavern-in-society/
- Ben Franklin's Drinkers Dictionary https://founders.archives.gov/documents/Franklin/01-02-02-0029
- Britannica https://www.britannica.com/place/United-States/The-New-England-colonies
- 17th Century New England, http://www.17thc.us/index.php?id=3
- City upon a hill, Parable of Salt and Light, Jesus's service on the mount "You are the light of the world - a city that is set on a hill cannot be hidden," https://en.m.wikipedia.org/wiki/Salt_and_light "You are the light of the world. A town built on a hill cannot be hidden. Neither do people light a lamp and put it under a bowl. Instead they put it on its stand, and it gives light to everyone in the house. In the same way, let your light shine before others, that they may see your good deeds and glorify your Father in heaven." "You are the salt of the earth. But if the salt loses its saltiness, how can it be made salty again? It is no longer good for anything, except to be thrown out and trampled underfoot."
- City upon a hill, A Model of Christian Charity - 1630 sermon, John Winthrop Arabella https://en.m.wikipedia.org/wiki/City_upon_a_Hill
- John Winthrop, Question & Answer technique to force the Puritans to think of this - https://www.winthropsociety.com/

- City upon a hill, John F. Kennedy Quote - of the above
- Matthew 10:23, "If they persecute you in one city, flee to another."
- Matthew 5:14, "You are the light of the world. A city that is set on a hill cannot be hidden."
- Geneva Bible, https://en.wikipedia.org/wiki/Geneva_Bible
- Musket balls can fall out of a rifle if not properly packed - Alex said so. He can teach some amazing Barbershop tags too.
- Let's be clear, Alex's dad served the Starbucks coffee to Nora, and she would have enjoyed it. He probably would have flirted with her too as he was a bit cheeky.
- PLEASE NOTE - the Gregorian calendar we know and love today, wasn't adopted in the British Empire/American colonies until 1752 (as Pope Gregory adopted it on February 24th 1582)- which is why it's hard to celebrate George Washington's birthday during Presidents month. The Julian calendar, adopted in 76BC was used until that moment which thought of a year as 365.25 days or 365 days 6 hours. Until that point, we had "Leap" days every four years adding up the 6 hours per year (6x4 = 24), but we needed corrective measures to make the number of days precisely 365.2425 or 365 days 5 hours 49 minutes 12 seconds a reduction of 10 minutes 48 seconds. This way the "Vernal Equinox" (Springtime.) (or as I call him, Vern) falls precisely on the correct date. This new calendar calculation was used in

1600 and in the year 2000 to keep the calendar in sync. Now in 1582 we can figure out the precise measurement of the rotation of the Earth around the Sun to digital precision without a single computer, satellite, nor second-hand watch, but we can't read a thermometer in the 21st century saying the earth is warming. Things that make you go "hmm". Here's a link to the "leap-seconds" https://en.wikipedia.org/wiki/Leap_second we add.

- Cumberground Noun. (plural cumbergrounds) (obsolete) Any utterly worthless object or person; something that is just in the way.

Science References

- Kip Thorne - "The Science of Interstellar" - in the making of that movie, they perceived the wormhole as a glass sphere - now, I don't want to toot my own horn, but when I envisioned this in my concept for the book, I thought of it as a nebulous glass sort of unshaped, so not bad for a music major with a minor in Computer Science.
- Calculation for Time-Dilation where c= Speed of light in a vacuum (you know the c squared in Einstein's formula.) Visit https://keisan.casio.com/has10/SpecExec.cgi?id=system/2006/1224059993 to calculate time dilation if you're traveling any time soon and want to make sure your fruit cup isn't returned due to tardiness!

$$\textit{Time dilation}$$

$$T = \frac{T_0}{\sqrt{1-\frac{v^2}{c^2}}}, \quad c = 299792.458 km/s$$

- Moon's Magnetotail - https://www.nasa.gov/topics/moonmars/features/magnetotail_080416.html
- Moon Phases - note the wrong calendar - Should be Julian Calendar - http://soundofheart.org/galacticfreepress/moon/phases/calendar?month=9&year=1692 (Full moon on 9/25/1692) Mea culpa - Waxing Gibbous moon - boom http://soundofheart.org/galacticfreepress/moon/phases/calendar?month=4&year=2016 2016 - way better moon cycle... SORRY MAN.
- Susan Jocelyn Bell Burnell is an astrophysicist from Northern Ireland who, as a postgraduate student, co-discovered the first radio pulsars in 1967. She should have won the Nobel Prize for this, however I would now like to give her the Nobel Prize for discovering my wormhole. Congrats Dr. Burnell! Your thesis was approved by Dr. Reynold Woodbury, and Dr. John Milners! When she told Dr. John Milners about the wormhole she discovered, he called his best friend Dr. Reynold Woodbury immediately. To be fair, she only waited 10 minutes while he was on the phone. Read more about it here - https://en.wikipedia.org/wiki/Jocelyn_Bell_Burnell

Mea culpa (s) (of which there are a few...)

- "You can know the name of a bird in all the languages of the world, but when you're finished, you'll know absolutely nothing whatever about the bird... So let's look at the bird and see what it's doing — that's what counts. I learned very early the difference between knowing the name of something and knowing something." Richard Feynman, the story about not knowing the names of things is also his, but seeing as I used it creatively and you learned about him a little more, I get credit for learning you more stuffs. Go me.

- So in calculating time dilation, hitting the maximum calculable speed limit of 299,792.457999 km/s for 120 seconds before the formula gets wonky, is about 10,000,000 seconds which calculates to just over 115 days of dilation, but you know, these scientists are assuming they hit the 299,792.458 km/s wall which the formula calculates to "infinity", so for all intent's and purposes, they think years of time-dilation due to the formula hitting that "infinity" wall. Look, give me a break, on Star Trek they shout "beam me down" and something captures and encapsulates your whole body into a computer, transmits you to another place, then restores the encapsulation into an environment that always has plenty of breathable nitrogen/oxygen environment with all your atoms of your body in the same order they were in when you left, and coincidentally gravity is kinda perfect always. That was science fiction - so they were worried about arriving years into the future because they hit the infinity wall with time-dilation is pretty dang plausible. I mean the trees are really really mature around them, the office they were in is gone, and they did that without propulsion - what would you think? Don't get me started on doing the Kessel run in 12 parsecs - that means someone found a shortcut - the ship didn't go any faster. (Although, the movie "Solo" tried to describe this...) For example, if I shout "hey it only took you 8 miles to get to my office instead of 26!" you may have found a wormhole. What do I know? You would probably still get stuck in traffic, anyway.

- While standing in Israel Porters wooded area, they may not have been able to see across the street from the jail to where Giles Corey was being crushed to death, but hey, maybe it was behind the jail. Perhaps it was a lovely clear day? You don't know!
- I transferred John Alden from Boston to Salem's jail - I signed the order. For this I don't ask forgiveness as I needed him to deliver the note to Newton. But he was incarcerated in Boston's jail where he actually "somehow" escaped (he probably bribed someone to let him out!) There were a few court hearings in early 1693 that he didn't show up because he was "on the lam" someplace.
- Mary Bradbury - DID escape from jail, and the order to execute her was signed on September 9th, 1692. We just don't know how this could have happened. Bettina Bradbury - if you could ring me up for a conversation, that'd be awesome. Let me know if you have Reynold's key, and or a really neat family story about how she escaped!
- I know of no reference that John Higginson attended the hangings on September 22nd

however he lived in Salem, and also attended the meeting at Samuel Sewall's in Boston - so he jumped on his trusted horse, and rode out there which took about 3 to 4 hours. It's been done. So there. Don't hate...

- I'm not sure what motivated Robert Calef but I really like that he took on "The system" and tried to speak out for what's right and wanted to give him a push in the right direction. Go Bob Go!
- I have no clue what Samuel Sewall's house looked like in 1692, however it may be listed on Zillow if anyone is interested in looking that up for me.
- There are no records of Governor Phips attending the meeting at Samuel Sewall's on September 22nd, but ya know - he must have had a hand in hiding the original information, and 2 weeks later started the process of ending the court of oyer and terminer.
- There were no records of a Privy for men & women at Thomas Beadle's tavern, but it had to be there. Look I wanted my travelers to have a halfway decent meal, and a place to go potty. I'm not a monster, and believe in proper treatment of protagonists. I'm officially forming "People for the ethical treatment of protagonists" - feel free to venmo funds for this.
- Thomas Beadle's tavern may have had a Kitchen. Look, they ate near that enormous glorious fireplace and I'm sticking to this 'cause wow - what a neat way to include it in the story, no?
- There is also no evidence of a tunnel leading to the docks in Salem - this was an idea I had since

they are virtually parallel to a dock that was possibly washed away in 1690s. Derby may have originally had the name Darbie after the 'Darbie Fort Side Ferry Landing. Foot's point may have washed away in 1690 and were re-built to the significant docks on that spot today. Landfill may have added to modern landscape as well.

- I was going to have my travelers stay at the tavern known as "The Sign of the Black Horse" but as I couldn't find evidence of this tavern's existence until 1693, nor its exact location, I called ahead, and transferred them to Thomas Beadle's tavern taking advantage of my extensive points I have with a major hotel chain. I'm LIVING THE LIFE. In 20 or 30 years, of going to that chain, I'll have enough points to stay one night for free.
- Life in prisons was terrible. The Judges inspected the prisons around October 1692 and were appalled at what they saw.
- I'm unsure of the price of a beer during that period so I extrapolated that it's the same price as it was in Shakespeare's time 100 year before this story happened. Sorry. Here's my reference to what things cost - https://abagond.wordpress.com/2007/05/02/money-in-shakespeares-time/ and http://elizabethan.org/compendium/home.html so it's a half of a penny, billed directly to the court of Oyer et terminer. Monetary standards are hard to nail down, since England wasn't thrilled that the New England colony was making their own laws, so they DID make Pine-Tree shillings, and kept the date "1652" even

though they were minted well into the 1680's, this way if England put the kabash on this behavior, they can clearly say "look we haven't minted these since 1652." Eventually they were using something like promissory notes for their money, which were fairly worthless as they were basically "IOU's" for money the colony didn't have.

- I did kidnap my cover artist, Robert and made him watch "Big Trouble in Little China". He paid for the movie, I'm proud of that moment. He also will deny that it ever happened, so please don't press him for details. Feel free to ask him if he ever watched the DVD of that movie I bought him for his birthday.
- So you know (not a Mea culpa) taking money for guiding someone in the Law (i.e. BEING A LAWYER) was against the law at this time.
- Mary Parker is the 8th times great grandmother of George W. Bush.
- There were so many people named Samuel, Elizabeth, Abigail, Nathaniel, and other names would make people loopy.

Easter Eggs (look some of you are probably pretty smart and found 'em)

So as a nerd, I did hide things in this book. Since it's better to educate you about them than hide them here are the examples I remember.

- Dunne Electronics, Inc. The person responsible for the cover Art for this book, is named Robert

Dunne (Easter egg 1) however DEI is Caltech talk for "Dabney Eats It!" These initials are written on the moon, and various places that Caltech people have traveled. A double thanks to JoAnn for giving me the proper response of FEIF or "Fleming Eats it Faster!", and as my grades, nor my choices of majors (Music & Computer Science.) led me to Caltech, as their chorus wasn't world known, nor did I think an engineering college had a sufficient music department. Watch the movie, "Real Genius" to get a plethora of awesome REAL Caltech references.

- Elmer is the name of the puppet I perform with, who is named after the test dummy lovingly called Elmer from the book "Contact" written by Carl Sagan.
- As a double "Easter Egg" I reference the speech J.K. Rowling made to graduates at Harvard in 2008, and I also reference Douglas Adams, a Hitchhiker's Guide to the Galaxy, RADIO show at the same time. To quote her speech, "You see? If all you remember in years to come is the 'gay wizard' joke, I've come out ahead of Baroness Mary Warnock." I'm Sorry. Reynold and John remember nothing from their graduation. My bad. But I listened to the speech and thought it enchanting.
- "everything will be fine!" Doc Brown, Back to the Future.
- "I'm going to have to science the shi..." "The Martian," - Andy Weir, a really nice guy.

- I'm also a huge fan of William Goldman's "The Princess Bride" and hid a reference to this work, and as I decided to be coy about it, I will let the reader writhe in frustration trying to figure out where I put that juicy tidbit. Hint, Nora's 325 year kiss, longest in literary history period. I did that. That was me. Nothing but net.
- Ray Bradbury wrote a short story named "A Sound of Thunder" which detailed the Butterfly Effect. This book disproves the Butterfly effect using Ray Bradbury. Also, it's in the past - it happened already - how do you change that if it's already happened, and if you DO go into the past to change anything, it ALREADY happened before you went back in time!
- If any of the Bradbury family reads this book, this is not how your dad was named. I may have made the whole thing up. Ray's dad was a linesman, his younger brother Samuel did pass away before he was born. One fascinating tidbit, I found out while researching for this book; Mary Bradbury was accused during the countries first witch hunt, and 7 generations later, June 8th, 1959 Ray Bradbury was investigated for being a communist, under another ridiculous witch hunt during McCarthyism. The circle is oddly complete.
- Feel free to ask yourself who created the original inscription on the tombstone. Go on... who? Art. That's who. It was created... by art...

The page in Robert Calef's book "More Wonders..." with Mary Etsy's final plea as sent to the court, published London, 1700.

WHAT HAPPENED IN 1692?

A perfect storm of issues, combined with religious views of the time.

- People believed in the Devil and believed in Puritanism and believed that witches could exist and were agents of the Devil. Being a witch was as bad as being a murderer. (S. Schiff)
- George Burroughs is not the town's favorite Reverend, and the village stops paying him. His wife passes away and he can't afford to pay for her funeral expenses and is placed in jail. In court, George defends himself by stating that had the town paid him, he would have the money for funeral expenses. So he is paid and released and Samuel Parris becomes the next Reverend.
- Samuel Parris is hired as the town reverend. The town isn't thrilled with him nor his sermons. His contract requires wood delivery (S. Schiff) and they stop paying him by the fall of 1691 endangering his family. His sermons became

laced with fire and brimstone as he became angrier (guess) and angrier at not being paid and also thought the devil's influence was high.

- Abigail Williams and Betty Parris are documented as patients 0 and 1. Reverend Parris sought out many doctors, and eventually one Doctor diagnosed the girls as being bewitched. Both girls had seizures and wrapped themselves around chairs. My guess is Abigail Williams had a condition that caused seizures and Elizabeth immitated her to get out of chores like her sister. Abigail disappears from testimony midway through the trials. doesn't survive beyond 1697 and the site of her her grave is unknown. Her sister, Elizabeth (Betty) Parris lives until 1760 having had a long succession of grandchildren and great-grandchildren. Betty never publicly apologizes for her behavior during the trials. Abigail continued having seizures after the trials ended (Marilyn Roach). This made her unpopular and quite embarrassing to everyone involved.
- Mary Warren suffered from similar symptoms of the first afflicted girls. My guess is they're not doing chores, so I ain't either! Girls around the parsonage (Salem Village, now named Danvers) are catching on to this since they don't want to do their chores. Each may have had their own personal motivation for imitating the Parris daughters.
- Mary Warren retracts her testimony in April 1692 after some severe beatings at the hands of John

Proctor, who is eventually accused of witchcraft and hanged in August 1692.

- There was a great mystery surrounding the deaths of the two wives of George Burroughs and was accused of witchcraft and extradited from Maine. This was weeks of travel without roads. A child bewitched was more horrific to the townspeople than the strange deaths of his two wives. Accuse him of witchcraft, and they travel weeks to get him. George Burroughs was a physically powerful and intimidating man, known to be able to hold an enormous musket normally meant for two people to operate.
- The girls in town played "Monkey See-Monkey Do" during most of their expert testimony. So they would see someone testify and imitate them according to Mary Etsy's trial accounts. The girls all doing this at the same time was taken seriously by the judges. Why didn't the accused witches bewitch the judges?
- The judges were successful men, who suffered staggering losses during that period - they knew it wasn't their bad decisions, so they were prepared to face the devil now that they were revealed. (Emerson "Tad" Baker)
- Giles Corey's pressed to death (deemed a suicide by the court) for not entering a plea of Guilty/Not Guilty, and Mary Etsy's appeal to the crowd prior to her hanging helped stop the entire process. Everyone seemed to come to their senses at that moment in time on September 22nd, 1692. Per Samuel Sewall's diary, the judges' meeting took

place on that same date and could have included reviewing events recounted from gallows hill.

- By October 3rd 1692, the legal process to find the witches was dismantled.
- By 1693, all suspected witches were released from custody.
- It took until October 31, 2001 to pardon the remaining witches accused, including Bridget Bishop, Susannah Martin, Alice Parker, Wilmot Redd and Margaret Scott.

CLOSING THOUGHTS

The guy circled in the back of the photo is Albert Einstein, taken April 1st, 1934 for his retirement dinner. The couple circled a few rows ahead of him are my grandparents. Fate is such a fantastic thing. After writing over 60% of this book, and studying two years of studying Richard Feynman lectures and Salem history while figuring out how to write this story, I find this photo in my parent's house. Seeing my grandparents, four rows from Albert Einstein at a dinner in his honor was one of those moments. I even found a reference to Richard Feynman pop up on a CD I own called *Back Tuva Future* with the bonus track where he's playing bongo's and singing in a weird accent about his favorite drink, orange juice. (If you're curious, search *Richard Feynman* and *orange juice* on YouTube.)

The world is much smaller than we realize. All of our solutions are close. We just have to trust that we can achieve them faster together than we can achieve them separately.

ACKNOWLEDGEMENTS

I'd like to thank everyone who's helped me out with this project. My lovely amazing wife for being patient with me while I sat in a corner wearing down the keys of my laptop. Cheryl, my editor who heard "isn't THIS so cool" 1000s of times and kept encouraging me. My bestest buddy Christine for reading the first draft of a supremely flawed manuscript and saw through the millions of issues appreciating the juicy bits that had potential. My brother for bravely reading a flawed second draft, and giving me story pointers. The young Ryan for helping me with the reaction of the *younger* crowd representing the pre-teen world. And my friend Joanne who bravely read my book and redlining all but two pages, and making me feel super proud of those two pages. #LearnEnglishThenWriteABookDangIt

Made in United States
Orlando, FL
21 October 2025

71138949R00164